SCOUTING FOR COUCHES

C.A. Smirnova

ISBN: 9798684708923

Library of Congress Control Number: 2018675309
Printed in the United States of America

CONTENTS

FOREWORD

It isn't easy to transform your mindset into one that you despise. That's what I had to do though, in order to write Scouting for Couches. I cloaked myself in the contemptible for days at a time, and forced myself to think like my main character, Victor. I felt troubled on a daily basis, but stuck with it.

This was my first book, and I found it immensely challenging and upsetting. During the course of writing it, I lost my career, money and home. I hope my efforts have been worth it.

Please enjoy.

Catarina Alexandria Smirnova

FLIGHT 865 TO DUBAI

"Feet, what do I need you for when I
have wings to fly?" – Frida Kahlo

Magda Schmidt double-checked passenger details in the first-class cabin of Emirati Airways flight 865 from Macau to Dubai. As usual, prohibitive pricing meant the list was short. Very short. In fact, there had only been one occupant during the entire trip from Australia to Macau. An elderly Asian gentleman named Mr Chung, who had been Magda's ideal traveller. He'd slept most of the time. That had made it possible for supervision from a sole attendant. Extended naps on crew seats were the welcome result. Jet engines had hummed lullabies as earth and ocean passed underneath.

Mr Chung had disembarked, but two people had boarded. One was a short and podgy Qatari, dressed in his traditional white thobe and red checked headdress. Title and family name confirmed he was royalty. A minor prince though, otherwise he would have been on a private jet surrounded by bodyguards instead of slumming it in first class sans entourage.

The sheikh, laying his eyes upon towering Magda, revealed a toothy grin as broad as a piano's keys. Similar colour pattern too. Angry tobacco and sandalwood fumes chanted protests inside her nostrils, demanding recognition. His vision focused several centimetres below her face, seediness simmered in sockets. The smile oozed saccharin. She seethed and clenched teeth, before wishing him a warm welcome onto the plane.

Her blonde hair and green eyes often got unwanted attention and awkward advances from male passengers. That was especially true for men of exceptional wealth. No matter how many chances she gave, their entitled mindsets seemed hardwired to believe money and status equals women for purchase. Tempting sums had been offered. A fast-track to paying off her apartment in Munich. One night on back versus twenty-five years on feet. What price was dignity worth though? She could never settle on a comfortable amount.

The seats were mini suites enclosed by chest height partitions and sliding doors. Once the Sheikh was in his, she approached her colleague Davide. He was a wiry man from Quebec with preened brown hair always held firm with wax or gel. The tongue suffered no such restriction.

With a smile and rub of his forearm, she asked, "Davide, would you be ok seeing to the royal chap? And I'll take care of the other guy if that's ok?"

Placing his palm on her hand and stroking, he peeked along the aisle. "Ok dear, I get you. Seems a bit keen, doesn't he? And that's sober. He's already ordered a large whisky. In a teacup, of course," he smirked.

"Thanks, Davide, you're a gem," she said pinching his cheek.

"But you need to do something for me first," he teased.

"Of course. What?"

He gestured downwards with his eyes. "Mine's hotter than yours. Admit it."

Tutting, she checked nobody was near before saying, "Best butt in Dubai. Happy now?"

"It's all in the squats, you see. Now, I'd better take his highness the whisky," he said.

"Careful with your measures. We can't put a sheikh in restraints," she said noting the large cup of spirit.

Upon hearing her words, he rolled his eyes. "Aucun probleme, mademoiselle," he said lifting his nose in mock arrogance. "He will be princely putty in my palm." Davide put emphasis on each 'p', so the words popped like potato bullets from his pale elfish features. He strode down the aisle with tray and humour.

The other person to board had been a Westerner. Mr Victor

Fyric. Around the 1.82 cm mark; without her heels they would have been the same height. Borderline obese, cheeks stubbled raspberries above a thick double-chin, and hair soggy; she didn't find him attractive. His shirt shone though. Dark blue, the elegant material was rich and embroidered with ornate golden-orange flame pattern running along it's lower half. It was traditional clothing. Like Hawaiian, but without loudspeakers. And that wasn't the only notable thing about him.

He had a black eye. It wasn't swollen, but the bruising looked fresh. There was also a large square plaster across the first two knuckles of his left hand. Soaked through with blood. Curious.

After giving him time to settle, she went to see if he needed anything. He was in the window suite nearest to the galley, while the Qatari was on the other side of the cabin, nestled in the far corner. Two rows of central suites made fine obstacles.

Approaching closer, she could see he was looking out of the window, sliding his hands along the chair's white leather. It had a broad range of reclination—even into a bed if so desired—but was positioned upright. In fact, he was perched right on the edge. The soaked strands of his long brown fringe were tiny tree branches dangling in a glistening lake of forehead. Perspiration was scrapping with powdery deodorant. The latter swinging a little harder.

"Mr Fyric?" she half-whispered. Hoping it was the correct pronunciation, she again said, "Mr Fyric?"

Preoccupied, he stared with intense interest at the apron of Macau Airport. Then focus switched to his watch. It was a stunning Deitling. Pink-tinged gold encircling jet black steel, glimmering as it reflected honey hues from the Macanese sun. It must have cost the same as her annual salary, at least.

"Mr Fyric?" she repeated with raised tone.

Snapping out of his trance, he spoke with agitation. "Yes? Sorry. Sincere apologies. When will we be taking off? Is it soon?"

"I'll go and check, but I think it'll probably be about twenty minutes. I'm Magdalena, I'll be looking after you for this flight. May I get you something while we wait? Something to drink, maybe?"

The offer sharpened his attention. "Absolutely. What have you got?" he asked, itching his right forearm, and yet again looking at his watch.

"Perhaps some champagne?" she suggested.

He sucked air through gritted teeth. "Eh, I think I need something stronger." He glanced at his watch again. "Please just give me the best whisky you've got".

"Of course, Mr Fyric. We have a 21-year-old single malt. I'll get you one right away."

"Thank you, Magdalena."

"My pleasure. Would you also like a cold towel? It's so sticky outside, isn't it?"

"That would be fantastic. Thank you".

Poking from between the sliding doors, he called out, "Oh, and make it a large one. The whisky, I mean. Not the towel." His mouth smiled, the eyes not so much.

The plane took off twenty-three minutes after she'd served him his first drink. In total, he'd managed to gulp two treble whiskies and three flutes of champagne before they soared into the clouds above Macau. During take-off, she sat in the jump seat next to the emergency exit, with the harness straps loosened so they didn't dig into her chest. What was the deal with that Fyric guy? Was he afraid of flying? But then if that were the case, would he really be so impatient to get in the air?

* * *

Once they reached cruising altitude and the seatbelt lights pinged invisible, she stepped into the restroom for a quick chest check. The cotton uniform blouse was clinging against her breasts. Tucked in at the waist, it had ridden round and coiled at the back. She adjusted her skirt and pulled her top straight, making sure the material was loose but tidy. A strong exhale of frustration gusted from between her cherry-red lips. Despite a custom-fitted minimizer bra and a top one size bigger than she needed—tailored to fit her size ten waist—she was unhappy with the concealment. Mint green eyes sighed in the mirror's reflection.

The chime of the flight attendant call button interrupted. She stepped into the galley and Davide was there preparing a meal for his passenger. He had a fresh teacup on the counter and was opening a vintage Bordeaux.

"It's your one, buddy," he said while driving the corkscrew and motioning in the direction of Fyric's suite.

Arriving beside it, she could see the seat was now reclined, and he was making use of the footrest. His cheeks were still flushed, but the fringe was swept to the side showing a dry brow.

With calm clarity, he asked, "Could I possibly have another drink?"

"Of course," replied Magda. "Another whisky?"

"That would be great. Another large one, please. And, also"—his voice turned hesitant—"I hope you won't think me rude..."

Oh no, she thought. Was he going to make flirty chit-chat? Already? Or give some sleazy compliment on her appearance. Damn alcohol.

"Would you happen to have your makeup bag with you?"

"My makeup bag?" she said, tilting her head to the side.

"Yes, this thing," he said, pointing to the purple badge covering his eye. "I don't really want to go through immigration and customs looking like a street thug."

"Oh, of course, yes. Yes, I have it with me. I'd be happy to lend you it."

"Ah"—he cleared his throat—"now that's the thing. As you can see, I'm not exactly an expert at dolling myself up. I don't suppose you could help me?"

It wasn't a rude request. Unusual, but not impolite. And anyway, he was a passenger in first class. She only had him to look after on this long flight. If he were in economy, the service would have been a simple chicken or beef scenario, but Emirati Airways did emphasize keeping first and business customers happy. That was key to profits. What the hell, she saw nothing wrong with it.

"Yes, of course. But can I suggest you move over to one of the two central seats for now? I can sit in the one next to it." She stepped into the neighbouring suite and clicked a button. The dividing wall receded like a car window. "See? I'll be back in a few minutes."

Sitting beside him, she leaned over the minimised partition. But not too close. That after-nap grotty taste still lingered on her tongue.

She'd brought a concealer stick, a tube of liquid foundation, a sponge, and a compact mirror, and laid them on the desk area beneath the TV screen. "Shall we begin?" she asked.

"Sure, just one moment." He took a big gulp of whisky then set it into the arm rest. "Ok, make me beautiful. And please take your time. There's obviously no rush."

"Of course, don't worry," she said. "Your skin is a little rosier than mine, but this is good stuff. I think you'll see quite a difference when I'm finished."

"You're very kind."

"You're welcome. May I ask what happened? You look like you've been in an accident?" she asked as she made gentle dabs around the tender skin. Adonis he wasn't, but his steel blue eyes were pleasing.

"Yes, that's right. Car accident. Damn drivers in Macau are maniacs. I was, eh, stupidly, sitting in the back of a taxi without my seatbelt on, when we got rear ended. I smacked my face off the headrest. Sorry, can you stop for a second?" He took another mouthful. "Apologies, please keep going. I do appreciate this."

"Oh, no problem," she said, continuing with the makeover. "I'm glad you weren't more seriously injured. So, do you have business in Dubai? Or is it just a holiday?"

"Well, neither and both really. I'm a writer, you see. I like to travel around while I do it. I'm supposed to only be transiting when we land. My next flight is to Muscat. I thought I had business there, but"—his focus wandered— "I didn't realise the plane was going via Dubai, when I booked the ticket. The city has a lot of skyscrapers, doesn't it? Nice views I should imagine."

How odd. You book a ticket costing several thousand dollars, and you don't check the details of it first? And he was talking as if he might get off in Dubai on a whim? Who does that? Was there something cryptic in the way he spoke, or was she imagining it? All that mattered was his respectful attitude, so she decided it was best not to burden herself with questions.

"Oh yes, there are plenty of those. Especially along Sheikh Zayed Road. A lot of them are 5-star hotels. There's even a hotel in the Burj Khalifa. That's the tallest building in the world, but I'm sure you knew that. May I ask where you got your shirt? I love the pattern."

"Thanks. I bought it in Indonesia. They call it a batik. The designs have meaning and vary from region to region. Pretty funky, isn't it? To be honest though, it's not as expensive as it looks. Was only fifty dollars."

"Interesting. Well, it was worth the price." She sat back to inspect her work from different angles. "There, I think it's done now," she said, putting the sponge back on the desk. "Would you like to see?"

"Is the Pope a catheter?" he replied.

"Sorry, I don't understand?"

"It's ok, never mind. Yes, let's get it over with then." He drained the whisky, leaving a few paper-thin ice cubes.

She flipped open her compact makeup mirror. He sighed as he took hold of it to examine the results. She got the feeling he didn't like his own face much, injury or not.

His neck moved back, emphasising his double chin. "Wow," he said. "Holy crap. That is a fantastic job. Thank you very much". He angled the mirror around, holding it close, then far away. He chuckled, "Maybe he's born with it?"—he paused and turned to her— "Maybe it's Magdalena?"

She gave a half-genuine giggle. He was complimentary in a laid-back way. Also, the whole time she'd been leaning, he hadn't stared at her chest, gazed, or made creepy comments.

The interaction had been asexual. It was refreshing.

"While we're patching me up"—he raised his left hand and nodded at it— "perhaps you've got something to give my cut a clean with? And a fresh plaster? The stickiness seems to be wearing off. It's not staying on my hand now."

"Sure. I'll go and get some things from one of the first aid kits."

"Please, call me Victor. And…" he held the glass, tilting it side to side, causing what was left of the watery ice to slosh together.

"One more?" she smiled. This guy was drinking like there was no tomorrow. Did he also think they had spare livers in the first aid kit?

"Thanks. You're a star."

When she returned to the cabin, he was back sitting in the window side suite. Taking the glass from the tray, he thanked her and slurped. Then laid his hand flat on the arm rest, peeling off the adhesive bandage.

Magda saw the wound and exclaimed, "Oh, what a nasty gash!"

"She certainly was," he mumbled, before taking another swig.

"Sorry? I didn't catch what you said."

"It certainly is."

Was he teasing, or was the liquor starting to muddle his words?

"How did it happen?" She took a disinfectant swab and wiped. He didn't register any discomfort, despite the depth of injury. Alcohol is traditional anaesthetic, she supposed.

"After hitting my head, I felt dazed. I opened the car door and stumbled onto a broken bottle. Not my luckiest day, right?"

Indeed. She didn't realise glass shards could cut so precisely in a straight line. It looked like a knife had done it. And wouldn't it be his palm cut, and not his backhand?

Stop overanalysing, she told herself. You're cabin crew not FBI. Drying the wound with a cotton ball, she placed the large square plaster over it, pressing around the edges. "There, that should keep for a while, as long as you don't get it wet. Here, have a few spare ones, in case you need to change it again."

"You are a dream," he flattered.

"Thanks, Mr—"

"Victor," he chided with smile and finger wag.

"Of course, sorry. Victor". She'd been examining the Deitling on his wrist while she gave him first aid. It was beautiful. "May I ask where you bought that watch? It's gorgeous. I have a small collection myself. Nothing as fancy as yours though."

"Oh yeah," he said, gazing at its face. "One of the best things from my travels. I found it in Kuala Lumpur. Nice isn't it?" He took it off, handing it to her. "Try it on if you like".

She laid it across her palm, admiring the craftsmanship. "It must have cost a fortune."

"Hmm no. It was a bargain, actually."

He was being modest. Placing it on her wrist, she could see it was too chunky to suit a woman. Stunning though. On the strap beside the clasp there were two large red spots. They looked like old blood stains.

"Unfortunately, it was a casualty of the accident too. Some of my blood spattered onto the strap. I'll try and have it cleaned as soon as possible".

She handed it back to him. It was blood, just fresh. "Oh no. Well, it could have been worse. You were lucky the face wasn't smashed in".

He snorted whisky and spat the liquid back towards the glass, causing it to spill over his fingers and onto the thick grey carpet. He coughed some liquor for the first couple of seconds, then followed into loud laughter. Sherried vapours filled the air.

"What? What did I say?" She was chuckling too, but not sure what at.

"Oh nothing. Just being silly. And of course, this"—the glass of saliva infused liquor and ice glistened in his grasp— "making me laugh at childish things. Please ignore me." He took a deep breath, calmed, then again succumbed to a minor bout, before regaining composure. The shrill tone of hysterics seemed unjustified by the quiet observation which had sparked it.

Weird. What was so funny? It occurred Victor had eaten nothing except the bowl of nuts served to him with his first single malt. That had been back on the ground. She didn't want him puking in the toilet. "Erm, Victor? As I'm sure you know, meals in first class are on demand. You can have anything to eat, at any time". She took the leather-bound menu out of the suite's document compartment. "Perhaps you'd like to order something?"

He gave it straight back. "Is fillet steak on the menu?"

"Yes, we—"

"Give me two fillet steaks, plenty of veg, pepper sauce, salad, and a small amount of mashed potato. Just put it all on one plate. That ok?"

She found him abrupt, but not rude. "Of course, and something to drink?" As if she had to ask.

"Hmm. Whisky doesn't go with steak, does it. Just give me the best red wine you've got. Trusting in your judgement, of course. I'll take one glass now, and then another one with the steak. Thank you so much."

By the time she brought the meal, he was staring into his laptop. The wine glass sat empty, smudged by finger and lip. His intense stare was broken as he realized she was waiting to place a tray onto the same surface. Smiling, he pressed the shutdown sequence. Before it went blank, her eyes caught a glimpse of what he'd written on the screen. It looked like the opening line to a new novel.

The rest of the flight was uneventful. A few simple alcohol requests from Victor. He wrote on his laptop, drank, and visited the toilet. That guy could really put it away. A couple of hours before landing, he fell asleep.

Her and Davide had gossiped about each other's passengers in the galley. The sheikh hadn't been so bad. Apart from dozing, he was mostly eating, drinking, and tinkering on his phone. He had offered his own hospitality too, developing a rapport with Davide.

"He likes his hummus spread on both sides of the pitta," whispered Davide. "He told me French-Canadian boys are so charming. He's got a yacht in the marina. Asked me to go for the weekend. I'll have to get some new deck shoes."

"Oh Davide, what am I going to do with you?"

"And Monsieur Fyric? I'm sure he was delighted, with a foxy chick like you serving him. Have you finished administering medical aid, Florence Tightingale?" Face contorting in theatrical lust, he made an hourglass shape in the air with his hands. "You're just too hot, that's your problem".

He was so cute. "I'm glad to say he's more interested in liquor than ladies."

The plane landed at Dubai International Airport. She couldn't wait to get back to her apartment. Two precious days off awaited. Priority was a long sleep. Then she was looking forward to gym, pool, sunbathing, and playing with her iguana Theodore. The job of EA crew was a good one, but long-haul flights were draining.

As the doors opened, mobile stairs led to an exclusive first-class transfer bus. Warm desert wind washed into the cabin. Before the Qatari sheikh descended, a 1000-dirham tip and business card were gifted to Davide, along with a smile of invitation.

It was different between Magda and Victor Fyric. He collected his suitcase from the locker and stopped beside her before descending the stairs. There was no offer or request given.

"Thanks, Magdalena, I won't forget you. How's my eye? Still ok?" he croaked. His face was bleary.

"Thank you so much. Your eyes look fine. I hope you have a nice onward trip to Muscat." The co-pilot and a few of her fellow other crew were milling around. She gestured to the stairs. "Your bus is waiting. Take care."

His breath was flammable. He hiccupped, "I'm still flying. No need for feet, at least, right? Thanks again for all your help. Goodbye."

Clutching onto the thick steel handrail, he ambled to the luxury coach. She wondered if he really would ditch his flight to Oman. He'd been an unusual passenger; with an aura somewhere between charming and unnerving. Perhaps it was because he was eccentric and had an obvious alcohol problem.

In any case, she'd be keeping an eye out for his books. Unsuccessful writers didn't travel first class on Emirati and wear a giant Deitling. Crime or thriller might be his genre. She thought back to when she'd been serving steak and caught a sneak peek at his laptop screen. There had only been one sentence on the page. It sounded like a great opener to whatever novel he was starting. It went like this:

One murder does not a serial killer make.

SCOUTING FOR COUCHES

"The best way to find yourself is to lose yourself in the service of others." – Gandhi

Hello, I'm Victor.

It's nice to meet you. Thanks for taking an interest in my story.

Before I begin, I'd like to introduce the social networking organisation known as Scouting for Couches. And if you don't mind, I'll abbreviate it to SC for ease of reading.

Keeping it brief, SC is a blend between homestay and socialising platform. You can build profiles, post photos, and have people stay either by inviting them or accepting requests. This can be for any length of time, but two to three nights is the average. Even if accommodation isn't being looked for, you can hangout for a drink, meal or join parties and activities. There's an email-style member messaging service, special interest groups and forums to ask questions. Following interaction—online or in person—members can post references to each other's profiles. You have to label these as either positive or negative.

The focus of SC though, is always on finding places to stay as you travel. People who provide the accommodation are the hosts and the ones who make use of it are the guests or scouts. You can search for hosts in cities across the world.

SC is free of charge. That's the key point for guests who use it. You can pay money to verify your profile via credit card, to make it seem more trustworthy, but it's by no means necessary if you want to use the site.

As someone with a spare room in a beautiful Parisian apartment, I concluded SC was preferable over for-profit hosting. People are grateful for gratis. They also have reasonable expectations. If you far exceed those, contended travellers will leave gush-fest references about how amazing you are. These snowball along with opportunities to host more guests.

In contrast, renting out a room, if even five bucks a night is paid, will induce the customer mindset. They'll view you as a hostel superintendent rather than a new friend. Any flaws in your service or home will be highlighted and criticised both in person and online. I needed neither stress nor money.

SC is primarily for young people travelling on a shoestring. Aka penniless bastards. I did host a handful of people with good jobs, including three doctors, but these were individuals trying it once or twice for the experience, rather than to make their budgets stretch.

Regardless of occupation or social status, the emphasis is supposed to be on cultural exchange, meeting new people, friendship, deconstructing harmful stereotypes, practicing altruism, teaching and learning new things, and developing a network of contacts across the globe. All the good stuff.

That's the dream. The reality is a sizeable percentage of SC hosts are middle-aged males inviting attractive young women to stay at their homes. Yep. Ditto for the gay members. Aside from say, fifteen to twenty percent of well-meaning hosts—usually the female ones—sex is the true driving force behind SC.

Fuckseekers & Freeloaders would be a more pertinent name.

If you want to check their website, then enter 'Scouting for Couches travel' into your favourite search engine and scroll three or four results. You can join within a few minutes and become one of their—claimed—15 million members.

That's what I did. I was drawn by opportunity and variety. If you host on SC, you'll meet different races, skin tones, eye and hair colours, hairstyles, accents, heights, and body shapes. I can't think of another platform via which a man based in one country would have so many nationalities of women coming to stay over.

I've only ever hosted in Paris though. That city has millions of foreign visitors every year, hence the steady flow of SC guests. If you're a man reading this and the idea of SC is starting to appeal, bear in mind visitors are dependent on location. Baghdad will differ from Bangkok.

So, yes, opportunity knocks at the door and men can't resist trying to add to their sexual CV. Some charge at it like a bull, unable to control their urges, while others employ the more subtle, slow-building approach, evaluating when the best time to pounce is. It varies, but they are all, be under no illusions, taking advantage of opportunities to indulge themselves in carnal pleasure. Frequently without success.

And that's the basics of Scouting for Couches.

I hosted a lot. In providing service, I found and lost myself at the same time.

HAZARDS AND RISKS

"I prefer to be alive, so I'm cautious
about taking risks." – Werner Herzog

Hazards and risks are often confused. I thought then it might be proper to define each term before we continue. Apologies in advance for my continued repetition of the words hazard and risk in this section, but it is necessary for clarity.

A hazard is anything that can cause harm or damage to people, animals, the environment, or property. Think of it simply as any dangerous thing. Our earth has countless hazards. Some examples are venomous snakes; high voltage electricity; single malt whisky; nuclear weapons; hurricanes; roulette tables; stuffed-crust pepperoni pizza and mega tsunamis.

A risk is the likelihood something bad will happen in relation to a hazard, should you interact with it. Let's take the example of a loaded handgun. The danger posed is obvious. But what if we remove the ammunition and lock it in a steel gun cabinet? The level of risk reduces.

Conversely, if we chamber a bullet, release the safety catch, and hold the weapon with our finger resting on the trigger, what then? The risk increases. As interaction with the hazard goes up, the risk of something bad happening rises in turn.

What about a violent criminal? He or she is a walking, talking hazard. But if that person is locked away in a maximum-security prison cell and guarded with competence, then the risk to the average person on the street is near zero. The prisoner cannot interact with the public; therefore, they are not at risk of harm.

However, what if you were sat next to him or her on the subway? Tinkering with your phone in blissful ignorance as someone plots your demise in silence. The situation has completely changed. Protective barriers are not present, and the criminal can engage with you. The risk has now escalated.

Now imagine you're sleeping on his or her couch. Lying in the dark. In a foreign city. Alone.

And that is a possible situation, within the world of SC. Not every murderer is in prison. Some are, of course, but then many aren't. This could be because they haven't been caught, but a lot are free because they haven't committed murder. Yet.

The same can be said of rapists. They might be elusive, or not been given the opportunity. Urges may not have been activated. Human sensibilities are fickle though, and there's always a risk of malice being teased awake by testosterone. You may not realise how capricious your host is. Until it's too late.

As you read this book, please bear in mind what's been discussed above. Remember I was an active host in the most popular tourist city in the world. I know what I'm talking about.

If you're considering using a service like Scouting for Couches, ask yourself: What, or who, are the hazards? What are the risks? And are they worth taking?

PODGORICA

"Either give me more wine or leave me alone." – Rumi

I'm now in the grungy capital city of Podgorica in Montenegro. I had thought about Dubrovnik in Croatia, not too far from here, but the reported tourist congestion put me off. Who wants to go where everyone else is? I'm enjoying being in a location most people would struggle to find on a map.

And it's fitting my story be written across a few countries, making use of western passport power and surplus funds. This is a tale which wouldn't be possible without those who adore globetrotting. But I don't include myself in that statement. When it comes to travel, I can take or leave it. Entertainment, tasty food, a few bottles of alcohol, and it doesn't matter where I am. Don't get me wrong, I adore exploration, but one doesn't have to travel to discover.

The rain is hammering outside as I write this. Two bottles of Montenegrin merlot and 10mg of diazepam are intensifying the weather's calming effect. Belly's warm; the world's soft and fuzzy. I like to divide the 5mg diazepam pills into quarters and chew a piece with every glassful, swirling them together in my mouth. A murky cocktail of comfort.

Apart from the weather, it's unremarkable here. I went for a walk around the city earlier in the morning, enjoying the cool drizzle, having an obligatory look at what few tourist sights (or is it sites?) there are in Montenegro's capital. There was a very nice-looking Orthodox Church called Sigourney Ham something, something. I've forgotten the name and can't be bothered searching for it. I don't recommend this place as a fun destination.

They have good wine though, and this hotel's room service food is decent, served until eleven at night, so I'll be happy for the next few days at least. However, if a holiday for you means more than being stupefied with alcohol and wanking in your hotel room, then perhaps chase photo opportunities in Dubrovnik.

Looking like bed for the entire day tomorrow, sleeping off this indulgence, then maybe I'll start researching a destination with female opportunities. The girls are gorgeous here, but attractive young European women don't look twice at flabby, middle-aged men with red-wine stained lips. They feel no sense of obligation to give you their undivided attention, or pretence at caring what you think or say, as you aren't providing them with free accommodation and food.

I miss you, Scouting for Couches.

PARIS I - THE START

"Sometimes one pays most for the things
one gets for nothing." – Einstein

I'd like to take you back to how my involvement with SC began.

I was working in the oil and gas industry in what is known as a rotational job. What's that, you say? Well, it involves two employees filling one role. These job-sharing partners are known as back-to-backs.

The system functions like this: One person works a continuous shift of twenty-eight days—although lengths vary—while the other has equal time off. Then at the end of that period, the one working flies home and his partner arrives as replacement. The process is repeated throughout the period of employment.

So why do companies bother? The guiding principle is men and women don't cope well with dangerous or difficult environments over extended periods of time, unless they have large breaks. This system is used in isolated areas such as deserts and barren tundra or places which pose considerable risk to the security of personnel. West Africa, for example.

That's where I did my rotations. In harsh, high-security conditions. Not an easy task for anyone. The company I worked for had operations in camps across four countries. They were all rough. But it wasn't the grim surroundings or scalding temperatures I found most challenging. It was having to be in close quarters with intolerable people.

However, it also meant collecting a healthy dollar salary with all flights and expenses paid. I kept it in multiple offshore accounts, saving a fortune in taxes. With no dependents or major commitments, I had the means to rent an impressive two-bedroom apartment in central Paris. My disposable income was such I decided to keep it year-round; despite only being there half the time.

As already mentioned, my comfortable financial situation was borne of suffering. The days in the camps were long and tedious. Civilian workers like me were caged in most of the time, surrounded by heavily armed guards. These places looked like maximum-security prisons, although there wasn't any rape (that I'm aware of). Days were spent sitting around in port-acabin offices staring at computer screens, trying not to have a tenth espresso, and engaging in idle chit-chat.

With some colossal pricks. I was stuck in an office with them for twelve hours a day sometimes; no alcohol available to numb the irritation. There was a Canadian dickpipe who used to sit and run his mouth for hours. I would nod and grunt with feigned interest; thinking of ways to persuade the manager to fire him.

Anyway, through that worthless piece of shit, I was introduced to the SC website. He was over thirty-five, and, despite his large salary, used SC to get free accommodation on his travels. He suggested I might do the same. I thanked him and said I'd investigate it, thinking under no circumstances would I ever emulate the behaviour of such a loathsome sack of putrid vomit.

Camp boredom got the better of me, however. It seemed like a waste of time, but I then had a surplus of it to kill. I opened a profile on the site and added a few photos. A female co-worker even agreed to write a reference for me. I didn't think it would make any difference though.

My lack of enthusiasm stemmed from a sincere belief nobody sane, never mind young women, would ask to stay in the home of a male stranger met via the internet. It seemed crazy at the time.

❋ ❋ ❋

Imagine my surprise when two ladies requested a night. I couldn't believe it. And this was only a week after I'd created and verified my profile. Ukrainian, with one middle-aged and the other in twenties; they wanted to try something new, for one night, to see what it was like. Unbelievable. Was getting female scouts going to be so easy?

The younger one was above average looking, at least by my low standards. Even the one my age would have sufficed. After accepting their 'couch request' I had been anticipating taking them for a nice dinner, having a few glasses of wine, regaling them with my many stories from around the world, and who knows where the night would lead?

It wasn't what I had expected. They showed up late at around 11:15pm—even though I'd invited them for dinner at 8pm— and wanted to go straight to bed. It became clear within a few minutes I was being used as a free hotel. However, I was starting to see the bigger picture in SC and wanted to make a good impression. Their positive references as women were valuable to a newbie. Not all chicks are the same.

Through friendly but persistent chat, I persuaded them to have a glass of wine on my balcony. They were both smokers so puffed as they partook. People say it's a filthy habit. Possibly? It's not the kind of filth that appeals.

After some dull chat about Paris, baguettes, the Louvre, and so on, during which the younger one put continual emphasis on the fact her boyfriend existed—as if that ever deters horny guys anyway—they went off to bed. Boring cows.

The next day they left for a hotel, having saved at least one hundred euros courtesy of my free apartment. I almost deactivated my SC account that same morning—you can't delete—but decided to stick with it for a little longer. You wouldn't be reading this book otherwise.

One kind gesture they showed was posting a positive reference on my profile. It gave a further boost of legitimacy to Victor Fyric, a host in Paris. Effort well spent.

And it paid off the very next day. I was sent another couch

request by two much more interesting guests. Two teenage girls from Japan. Holy Christmas.

I decided to meet them at a well-known city centre spot. The place I'd chosen was the lobby of the Biarritz Grand Hotel. 5 stars of Parisian swank.

It was easy for anyone to find or get directions to. Also, being one of the most decadent hotels in Paris, it would start off their trip with something more than they had been expecting. Amidst the super deluxe, I would treat them to a coffee or an alcoholic drink (or two). It was the pinnacle of European civilised living. And they wouldn't have to pay a penny.

There's a cost for everything though.

JAKARTA

Now *this* is living. I mean, I'm still running out the clock in an ongoing state of depression and anxiety, but *this* is the place to do it. Steinbeck had the right idea about where to do his writing. He didn't have the opportunity though. And that's one of the keys to how our lives play out. Sorry, John, so many of our wishes go unfulfilled.

But here I am. In a furnished room where nobody knows me. And I don't care to know them. This is the executive lounge of a 5-star hotel in the heart of Indonesia's capital, Jakarta. The décor is chic, comfortable and spacious. It's also quiet, so I can keep my earplug use to a minimum. I don't want to look like a weirdo.

My supply of soothing pills is running low. As of this morning I have only twelve diazepam and a miserable six alprazolam. Getting a script in Jakarta is a pain. Against my natural instincts, I'm having to employ that revolting habit promoted by health experts known as moderation. Horrible. This is the big problem with international travel. Access to pleasures ease and restrict in different measures. You can't have everything you want, all the time. It's fucking annoying.

I am encouraged though when I see what's outside. The streets of squalor are more uplifting than Champs-Elysees glamour. Because I'm looking down; not up.

To help me with my narco-fasting, I'm taking advantage of

the free cocktails offered every evening. Yesterday, I eased my frayed nerves with nine caipirinhas. That's a Brazilian drink made with cachaca spirit, lime, demerara sugar and crushed ice. They're a zingy brain ointment.

The only irritation last night was I swear they were pouring them weaker towards the end of the complementary session. It's bad enough I'm forced to moderate myself. Do others have to add to the misery? I topped up with half a litre of Turkish anise spirit from Istanbul duty free. And no, I did not touch one single pill all night. I swore moderation and stayed strong.

I'm on the same cocktails again tonight. I tend to find something I like, then stick with it. Aside from the free alcohol, I like being waited on by the lounges' young ladies. They're wearing snug fitting lime-green and black patterned traditional Indonesian style blouses known as batik, and tight pencil skirts.

Standing at the bar area about fifteen feet away; they're all sweet smiles. Saccharine is closer. I sense concern over my excessive drinking. No chance of me keeling over though; not with the measures they dole. Anyway, they're both around 5'5 —in heels—early twenties and attractive. One is skinny but has a pretty face, with high cheekbones and pale skin. The other is also cute, but dark skinned and plump, with big round brown eyes. Both are my type.

Of course, I will not be having either of these wenches. I might if I strove, as Indonesian women are notorious for their lust towards Caucasian men. Even more so in the case of older guys like me. Javanese daddy issues abound. This island seems the world's best kept secret for middle-aged, overweight leches.

But I'm staying another month in this hotel and need to keep my nose clean. Let the booze flow as I continue to pen my story. The round table in the middle of this circular leather sofa booth is gleaming. I can smell the synthetic vanilla of the wood polish. It could fit at least 8 more fatties, but I've got it all to myself. Moccasins slipped off discreetly; I'm rubbing the bare soles of my feet across the red carpeting. Rich fibres are sending mild tickling sensations through my toes.

As I write this paragraph, the chunkier waitress has come over. She's asking me dull questions. I'm telling her about being a writer, travelling the world and staying in 5-star hotels. She's feigning interest. Why do we bother with these empty gestures?

I do so wish we could know each other better though. On this table. Right now.

Another caipirinha will have to suffice.

PARIS II - KON'NICHIWA

"One life, one encounter." – Japanese idiom.

It was a winter's night in Paris. No frost or snow, but the wind battering between buildings enforced strict clothing requirements. A duck-down ski jacket and woollen hat were my urban survival gear for the time spent entering and leaving the taxi to the Biarritz Grand Hotel.

Walking up the marbled steps, I said a good evening to the doorman. His gold-braided crimson uniform was both grandiose and belittling. Masking pity with a smile, I went inside to find my little scouts.

What a beautiful hotel it was. Polished brass, chandeliers and cello. The sort of place that makes most question their own worth: Do I belong here? Isn't this place for rich people? Is common folks' money even accepted?

I stopped caring about answers a long time ago. Those grey or black-suited bozos standing around the peripheries; hands behind backs, scanning, scouring, simpering; they had no authority over a man whose wallet was obese from 50 and 100-euro notes.

And then I caught sight of my guests, admiring a gigantic oil painting on the far wall. With backpacks and boots more suited to the Siberian tundra; I was endeared to them straight away. It was amusing to see an oasis of luxury invaded by backpackers.

Anyway, the girls were tired, and declined my offer of a drink. Shame, as I bet the Biarritz had a fantastic cognac collection. It hadn't been a long journey for them though. Interrailing round Europe during their Winter break from university; they had only taken the bus from Geneva.

The two intrepid travellers were Kimiko and Ayako. Both nineteen, according to their profiles. Kimiko was fairly tall at around 5'8. I'm 5'11, so any girl in that height range gets me a bit nervous. I don't want to meet eyes if she puts on heels. She was also a bit model-like. High cheekbones, perfect teeth, shiny hair, and seemed reluctant to talk with me. Can be a tough interaction. These tall statuesque girls are challenging work. They expect a lot from life. And they often get it.

Now as for Ayako, she was much more like the kind of female that made me comfortable. Shortish, about 5'3, average size breasts with a slightly oversized bottom, and thick geeky fringe reaching to her eyebrows. She had a genuine smile made of teeth that should have been put in braces several years before. The ensemble was topped with a pair of black thick-rimmed glasses. No doubt had much lower standards about who she would fuck than her lithe companion. She was affectionate and gave me a long and tight hug when I made the gesture to her. Kimiko gave a faint, token gesture of the same.

We took a taxi. Anyone who's done that in Paris knows even a short journey is double digit euros. They both made a polite—but disingenuous—reach for their purses when we arrived. I dismissed any possibility of contribution, of course. This was generous hosting at its finest. What woman is impressed by a stingy guy?

The SC website isn't short of negative reviews of those over-committed to frugality. That wasn't me.

I wanted this encounter to be memorable. And it was.

PARIS III - LA MAISON DE VICTOR

"Now, at last I can live like a human." – Nero

Before I continue, let me take a moment to describe my former home in Paris. The accommodation was guests' priority, not me. Bearing that in mind, I think it's necessary to give you a clear picture of the place I was offering. This was all free to visitors. Kind of.

I think the pretentious would describe the building I lived in as Neo-Classicist. But I'm not sure. All I know is it was spacious and clean, and located in a safe area near to the city centre.

An ideal place to be the ideal host.

There were only four apartments in the building. It was a tall but narrow construction of stone, hidden in a dimly lit alley. The ground floor was lived in by the landlady, Madame Fontaine. She was one of those people who wastes away with age, as opposed to gourmands like me who seem to go up at least one trouser size every decade. A chain-smoker: I don't recall having seen her spindly digits without a cigarette hanging between them.

It wasn't clear if she spoke English. At the least, she showed no desire. Our interactions were in French. The first time we had anything even close to a proper conversation, was around three weeks after my lease had started. I had knocked on her door to discuss boiler problems.

"Monsieur Fyric," she rasped. "Come in." She meandered over to a grubby armchair and eased herself into it. "What do you want?"

"It's about the hot—" I started to explain.

"Can you please come in, and close the door? I don't want a draught."

"Sorry, of course". I closed the door, to stop the warm spring air entering. Nothing resembling fresh oxygen was to be permitted.

"As I was saying, it's—"

"Can you pour me a cognac?" Zipping her woollen housecoat fully to her neck, she motioned with her head to the oak cabinet in the corner. "Will this freezing weather never end?"

I'd checked the temperature less than an hour earlier. It was 21C. Sunglasses had been a necessity while I was outside sipping my morning coffee in jeans and a polo shirt.

"Sure, of course, madame." What am I? Your personal bartender? I opened the cabinet's wooden doors and looked at her alcohol collection. Impressive. She had more bottles than some actual bars I'd been to.

"Which kind do you want?" I said, turning to look at her.

She lit a cigarette and took a long drag before replying through the exhalation of the smoke. "Reamy. But not the XO. The other one. And pour a large glass." Eye contact wasn't given, never mind hospitality.

I handed over the tumbler of booze and sat across from her on the shabby three-seater sofa. All the furniture matched. In griminess. Perching on the edge, I was keen to minimize contact between my expensive clothes and the reek of ingrained tobacco emanating from underneath my backside.

The walls were queasy yellow. Years of nicotine waft rather than it being her favourite colour. I was nestled in an ashtray.

Taking a mouthful of the spirit, followed by another, she gave a small gasp of relief. "Better. I hate this weather. I have this awful cough that won't go away," she grumbled. And as if to illustrate, she let loose with a phlegmatic wheezing bout, then returned the cigarette to her lips and puffed for the next minute, saying nothing.

I looked at it smouldering, pinched between her liver-spotted fingers. The glow dimming as it retreated into the filter; almost burnt out.

"Old age, Monsieur Fyric. Old age." She took yet another gulp. Ditto with puff. "Your health fades and you are helpless to prevent it," she said, reaching for the packet and lighting up. "So, what is the problem in your apartment?"

"Well, as I was saying, it's the hot water. It's only lukewarm at best. It's been like that for about a week now."

"Strange. I had the boiler serviced not long ago. Not long ago at all, in fact." Did that mean pre or post Nazi occupation?

"Well, I—"

"Are you operating it as I showed you?" She tapped towards the ashtray. A few flakes made it. The rest joined their ancestors between carpet fibres.

"Yes, absolutely, I—"

"Because the plumbers in this city are expensive. I am not made of money." If only tradesman accepted payment in tar eh?

"Yes, the prices are scandalous, aren't they? But I can shop around for a cheap plumber if you like?"

"I will get some quotes. Leave it with me."

"It's really no trouble. I have a lot of free time when I'm not working."

Gaunt skin stretched like crinkled baking paper as she formed a thin smile. Yikes, veins within veins. "I will find an acceptable price. It may take a while though."

"Yes, of course. Please take your time." Fuck it, I'd pay a plumber myself.

She began coughing again, and once it had settled, comforted with another long inhalation of smoke. "Anything else?"

"No, that's all I can think of".

She took another drag, tapping again. More spent tobacco spread across the coffee table and fluttered to the floor. The smile re-emerged, this time full of mottled teeth, as she nodded at the now empty glass. "Well?"

Perhaps she wasn't so awful? I'd see if I could sample the more expensive stuff.

"Sure, I'm fond—"

"Thank you. Make it another large one. This cough is terrible. And I will enquire about the boiler as soon as possible. Don't forget to close the door behind you too."

Old bag. I made myself a promise to buy her four hundred cigarettes every Christmas.

So, yes, Madame Fontaine. The only thing I liked about her was the lack of fuss about visitors I was inviting from SC to stay over.

Though there were no windows looking into the landing areas, and the narrow, dark alley which led to the communal door didn't make it a place for easy snooping on. In any case, she spent most time indoors.

There was no lift, only a smallish stone staircase with a cast iron railing. The space to manoeuvre was minimal. Barely enough space for two people to pass. This wasn't a problem when inviting guests in. Although it did end up an issue on departure.

Sightings of the other residents were rare. On the second floor, above my landlady, was another senior citizen. Even more frail than Fontaine. To be fair, on the rare occasions we bumped into each other, he was congenial. He may well be dead by now, as he had a terrible cough when I last saw him. I hope he's having a restful time, in any case.

On the third floor, the one underneath mine, was a couple in their late fifties who led a quiet life. That is my favourite kind of neighbour. I did have the woman at my door around 3 am one morning though. She was peeved and complaining about my television being too loud. I was shitfaced and had been playing video games with the balcony doors wide open. I hadn't noticed the volume. I apologized several times and promised it would never happen again. The incident taught me that despite not seeing my neighbours, they could still hear me.

Moving on to my apartment; I'll start from the outside. The original front doors were solid, but I hadn't felt they were enough. There was no security system at the communal door, and I was leaving my apartment empty for four weeks (or more) at a time. I didn't want to come back to find all my stuff stolen, so I invested in a fifteen-hundred-euro front door. Reinforced steel with several locking mechanisms, and opening outwards from the door frame, it would have been next to impossible to smash off its hinges. The French army would have struggled to budge it. Judging from their history though, not the benchmark for military strength and organisation.

I also paid around a thousand euros for an anti-burglar solid steel shutter, which could be secured across the balcony doors at night before going to bed. It was overkill, being on the fourth floor. I liked the idea of locked and bolted. I could be sealed inside my impenetrable lair, isolated from the world outside. As could my guests.

The apartment was two-bedroom. There was a large—at least by Parisian standards—central living room, and all doors opened into it. The spare bedroom had sat empty until I joined SC. Once I'd decided to become a host, I had it redecorated and got DYKEA's finest to deliver and assemble a brand-new double bed in there. By the time I'd finished, it matched most 4-star hotel rooms in Paris. A bargain for guests, at zero euros per night.

Everything was bought from DYKEA, a furniture company founded by Swedish lesbians. And not because I think their products have brilliant style or quality. I'm simply no different from many people when it comes to shopping. I want to go into a single store where it's all under one roof. Life's too short, and all that cliched shit.

The bathroom sat between the guest and master bedrooms. It had an open-plan shower with a longish, sunken floor. There was a shelf for toiletries halfway between the head and button panel, and another one on the far wall opposite it, with more bathroom essentials. It had a clouded glass side screen, which spanned from neck to calf level, to ensure the modesty of persons washing. A flimsy bolt lock prevented unwanted intrusions. Isn't it odd how the smallest token can make us feel safer?

And safety was something obsessed about in my industry. So much the case it even influenced my furnishings. I'd grown comfortable with green. Signs of that colour denote a safe place or action. For example, emergency exits. Ever see a yellow one? Don't think so. Hence my décor.

Oh, and teal. I had a fair amount of teal as well. I love teal. There's no complexity there. I just think it's a beautiful colour.

Accommodation at work was functional and austere. I resolved my time off would be spent in a different environment. I replaced the two old couches left by the previous tenant with expensive beige leather ones and tied the room together with a beautiful Turkish rug patterned in blue, white and green. The apartment was transformed into a delightful refuge.

I wasn't satisfied with only that though. As well as your ass, what you lay your eyes on is also important for soothing the soul, so I decided to seek tranquillity in art. Making visits to artists' studios around Paris; I spent thousands on paintings. I didn't care about the style or the name of the artist. I bought art which spoke. I also took a trip to Montmartre to see if there was anyone suitable to draw my portrait.

✣ ✣ ✣

That day stays fresh in memory. It was spring when I found myself at the square of Place du Tertre, the centre of Parisian street artistry. A picture in itself, I recall tree branches coated in dark green badges; glistening from golden rays which filtered through onto the streets below. A caressing breeze encouraged rustle and sway; above cobbles worn smooth from centuries of footfall.

The throngs of strolling sightseers were crammed. Chattering, eyes smiling behind sunglasses, they huddled and peered at portraits being crafted with panache. Nods and whispers of admiration pervaded as customers perused displays of art for sale; the untalented masses were awash with awe. I alternated mosey with nosey and enquired about prices; watched works in progress. I saw impressive pieces but wasn't impressed. The artists were working to please; for a paycheck. When I looked at the subjects and compared to their depictions on canvas; I concluded unvarnished truth wasn't lucrative.

Enticing vapours of buttery pastry and pungent coffee wafted from restaurants and creperies lining the square. Their circular tables and stools congesting tiny pavements; with patrons who sipped, smoked, and partook of overpriced delicacies. Waiters hustled back and forth with loaded trays.

As I was manoeuvring my way past one of the quieter eateries, a voice in English hissed, "Hey mister, you want the best portrait? I can do it for you."

Turning, I was met by a young man with spectacles, wispy beard and shaven head. He was sitting at a table beside the doorway of a brasserie named Le Coq (The Cockerel, in English). His skinny legs crossed; the foot nearest to me was dangling over the kerb, revealing grubby beige sock inside scuffed brown leather. The green corduroy trousers were frayed and filthy. A shabby black sweater hung from his bony torso. If he was aiming for the starving artist of Paris look, he'd nailed it.

I didn't see any easels or paintbrushes. I replied in English, asking, "You're an artist, are you?"

"No,"—he took a puff of the near microscopic roll-up pinched between his grubby fingernails— "I am a genius."

Inflated ego. I was licking my lips. "I see. And if that's the case, why don't you have any stuff?"

He tapped on the wall of Le Coq with his thumb, and said, "It's in there. I don't paint out here. Too many distractions." His accent was thick, but he formed words with confidence.

"So, you paint in there because it's quiet and you can focus on your art?"

"Yes, mister. I cannot be expected to produce my masterpieces in such an environment," he said looking around the bustling street with a pout of contempt.

This was fucking great. "That makes sense. I rather stupidly thought you might not have a licence to work here."

Breaking into a restrained smile, his bulbous Adam's apple bobbed before he chuckled, "I think you are not a tourist, yes?"

I smiled back. "Why not just get a licence?"

"The waiting list is ten fucking years. And you must jump through hoops to get on it. It's undignified." He was almost sounding sincere.

Tourists were jostling past, bombarding with nudges, so I stepped onto the pavement and sat on the seat across from him, resting my elbows on the table. I switched to French. "And were you also bullshitting about your talent?"

"Ah, very good, you speak Francais. And no, monsieur. I may have to bend the rules a little to make a living, but my talent is from God. My passion is from God. Everything I have is a gift from God."

I hoped that didn't include the trousers. "Then you're truly blessed. What's your name?"

"Jacques, monsieur. And yours?"

"I'm Victor. And what does a genius charge for a portrait drawn in colour, Jacques?"

"250"

"250? That's more than double the highest price from over there. What makes you worth that?" I'd brought 500 cash with me and had no qualms about paying for quality. I wanted to see if he could justify himself.

He looked at the street, scanning with disdain. "Monsieur, there is something you must understand. There are those that dabble in art; that pay lip service, and perhaps what they can do is pleasing to many. But that is not art. That is playing at art. Merely dancing around the periphery. There—"

"And you're the only person in this whole place, with hundreds of artists, who takes art seriously?"

Gesturing at the square with his eyes, he said, "Maybe some know deep down, but they have sold out. A way to pay the bills. That is a parody of art. As I was saying, there are those that play at art, and those that breathe it"—he took in a deep breath—

"live it"—he raised two clenched fists in the air— "and die in it!" he said, slapping the table.

I nodded at his skeletal physique. "Do those same people eat it?"

Tilting his head to the side, he grunted. "Where others are prepared to haggle, I stick to what my talent is worth."

"I think most people will choose the lowest price."

"I think most people are stupid." We agreed.

I loved his pretentiousness. It was platinum entertainment. He'd already got the job. But if, after placing himself on a pedestal, he disappointed me, I was going to report both him and the café owner to the police.

"Ok, I'll give you your 250, on one condition."

"And what is that, monsieur?"

"Don't sugar-coat my portrait. I want to see who I really am."

"Of course, I don't sugar-coat. I am an artist, not a chocolatier."

"I'm serious. I want the truth."

"Ah, the truth. But what is the truth, monsieur? It is elusive. My truth may not be your truth."

"Do you want to continue the Jean Paul Sartre impression, or eat a solid meal?" I dangled a bunch of 50-euro notes. He was a clever man, but his clothing and bodyweight betrayed his situation.

Staring at the money, he swallowed, cleared his throat, and said, "Ok, no sugar."

Inside Le Coq, we occupied a discreet corner booth and I sipped anise spirit with ice as he sat in silence behind his easel. No words were uttered or offered, except to the waiter when I needed a top up. Once finished, he invited me to take in his creation.

Skinny little motherfucker. I hated him. His work was so brilliant I struggled to look.

I still had a full head of brown hair, but that was the only remnant of youth. Grey was growing among my chestnut stubble and choking it, like facial weeds. Did I really have that many wrinkles? Were my cheeks so stricken by rosacea? Was my nose really mottled with broken blood vessels?

What disturbed me most was my eyes. The sadness in them. He'd captured it without mercy. They told the story of my childhood. So many tears shed in desperation; pleading against the unwarranted neglect and abuse shovelled onto a defenceless little boy.

Sorrow hundredfold, and none of it deserved. Like when my father, drunk of course, told me at age 13, I had been the result of him using baby oil as a lubricant, which had caused the condom to disintegrate during coitus. I'd spewed into my mother without his consent. Unintended and unwanted. Everybody owes their existence to a johnson. In my case it was three.

Anyway, I thanked Jacques for his efforts and paid him the agreed amount. That evening, after staring at my portrait over a couple of bottles of wine, I burned it.

In addition to re-traumatising myself with decorative attempts; I like a clean environment. The work camps of Africa were lacking. Mud and sand coated floors in clump and grain. Gaia would fart waves of creepy crawlies. Locusts, flies, cockroaches, frogs, ants, and geckos all had seasons. Thankfully, rat sightings were uncommon. I was told venomous snakes killed and ate them.

My off shifts in Paris had to counterbalance misery. A spic and span haven was the solution. I had a cleaning agency send someone once a week to make sure the place was without spot. The cleaner in question was a tubby old Albanian woman called Dilara, who spoke no English. She did an excellent job, and didn't steal anything, so, I used to give 12-packs of cheap lager or bottles of paint-stripper liquor, which slapped a fractional smile onto her crinkled mask of misery.

All these efforts resulted in a home fit for humans. My own little palace. It wasn't as grandiose as those of the Roman Emperors, but then none of them had a 42-inch HD television to play video games on.

PARIS IV - EMPIRE OF THE FUN

"Whenever a thing is done for the first time, it releases a little demon." – Emily Dickinson

To be honest, I don't register excitement like normal people. Positive emotions I experience tend be fleeting. My personality is cloaked in apathy.

I can fake it; I'll never make it. If you happened to bump into me, you'd see a pleasant and optimistic man. What is it they say about books and covers? People never learn.

Anyhow, I was as close to excited as my character was capable. I had my first proper guests. Two young and sweet-smelling teenage Japanese girls were staying with me for three nights, and I was going to be the best host in Paris. At the least, I would get an extra reference to further boost my profile's positive image on the SC website. As a bonus, Ayako might be persuaded into adult activity at some point too. I didn't hold much hope for a genital summit with Kimiko, but you never can tell.

Their English was decent. They were both studying language and literature at the same university. I noted the contrast between how the girls communicated with me and each other. Reserved and bashful versus chattery and confident. I wondered what they were saying about me.

After introducing them to my home, and letting them know the casual house rules, we sat on the sofas—or couches, whatever—and chatted over hot chocolate. Mine was fortified, of course.

It seemed like once their bed was within easy reach, they were able to dig deep for making a good first impression. I appreciated the gesture. There was no coaxing involved, like with the Ukrainian users. The Japanese are known for their politeness.

They also committed the Rape of Nanjing, but nobody's perfect.

Anyway, we talked about Paris and its wonders. Reclining on the comfortable seating with two girls was pleasant. And they were attentive, which was refreshing. I was the centre of the conversation. Normally, fat middle-aged guys need something like fame, fortune, or prestige to command the focus of attractive young women. I had a spare room. Their interest didn't even seem feigned, although it's hard to tell. People can be so deceptive.

I was discovering things about myself. Like how I had potential acting talent. I adopted a responsible, mature persona, emphasizing my concern for their safety and wellbeing in gay Paree. It was a charade I would invoke throughout the years of my hosting career. I didn't want to be their father, just the uncle. The super cool one who has lots of time for his nieces.

The hot drinks were finished, and they started to yawn.

"Ah, Victor, may we take a shower before sleeping?" asked Ayako.

Sure, let's all strip off and hop in together shall we? "Sure, do you guys need towels?"

"If you have, that's very kind," she replied.

"Thank you," chimed the delicate voice of Kimiko.

"Ok, let me just check there are some in the bathroom already." I was in an out within a few minutes. I said, "Remember there's a bunch of shower gel and shampoo on the shelf under the shower unit. Help yourself. I bought it for guests, so don't be shy."

"Ah, thank you. So kind of you," chirped Ayako.

"Thank you," said Kimiko. She was a sexy parrot.

"Just one thing, girls, if you don't mind. Can I politely ask that you don't touch the stuff on the other shelf in the shower? I prefer to keep those toiletries for personal use."

With a yes and a nod, off they went into the guest room. I turned on my games console, poured a glass of rich red and started playing.

Ayako was first in the bathroom. 20 minutes later she appeared in pink-striped pyjamas; wishing me good night with a precious smile and bow. At least, I assumed so, as I had bid her a gamer's good night. This involves issuing pleasantry sideways from the mouth while engrossed in gameplay. When you're trying for the sixth time in a row to defeat a near-impossible end of level boss, you can't divert attention. Banter is a burden. It's the same as when driving a car, as far as I'm concerned. You can't get distracted. Playing games is a serious business.

Kimiko was next. I succeeded in getting past the difficult fight was able to pause when I heard the bathroom door open, in anticipation of saying a proper goodnight.

Something seemed awkward though. I was struck by the flush in her cheeks. The eyes averting.

"Good night, Kimiko."

"Ah, hi," she said with a sheepish smile. Japanese 'hi' not English.

"Was the shower ok? Hope the water was hot enough?"

"Yes, nice. Goodnight." She gave a quick bow—more like a nod —and hurried into the guest room; her white plastic slippers scuffing as she scuttled. Odd.

I decided it was time to go to bed myself. Having made sure all non-essential electrical devices were switched off, I made my way into the bathroom. They'd been tidy. The mirror was steamed and floor still wet, but apart from that it was like they hadn't been in. I had a quick peek in the laundry basket. Perhaps she had her period and had got blood on her towel? Or she'd shit-stained it from drying her ass crack? Teenagers got embarrassed over these trivialities. Nope. Damp but spotless.

Then I noticed. Oh, crap. The toiletries on my personal shelf, at the far end of the shower area, facing directly across from the unit, had been moved around. The rearrangement was minor but clear. I knew because of having placed everything in a specific way. A few minutes before the girls took their showers.

The original layout had been with a deodorant stick nestled between bottles of shampoo and shower gel on one side and a Ganel Antioch eau de toilette spray on the other. Now it sat further forward, near the shelf's edge. Oh dear.

This was a stubby roll-on with a bulbous head. The type which had a screw-on cover top and a large plastic rollerball underneath, for applying the container's liquid to your underarms. It was tapered at the neck, extending out again for the main part of the container. The whole bottle was black, except for some of the front label design and information on the back. You'd normally find it in the supermarket for a few euros.

Except this one had cost me three hundred. It wasn't for personal hygiene, although it performed that function. The smell was generic, but it didn't matter. The truth was the whole container was a shell to mask what was inside: a tiny hidden camera.

It was an ultramodern one, in fact. I'd ordered it online from a company in China which catered to cash-rich voyeurs. It had to be manually activated when you wanted to record anything, which is why I had gone into the bathroom before the ladies began washing. The micro-sized lens was hidden in the large lettering of the front label, near the top of the stick. Honestly, it was a deviant's delight.

Despite this if someone were to scrutinise the container; chances are they would figure it out. That's why I'd placed it tucked at the back, with only the necessary part facing the shower area. The polite request for nobody to touch my personal shelf was an extra safeguard. Which hadn't worked. Why couldn't people show a bit more respect?

My plan had been to take the deodorant into my room once the girls had gone to bed and connect it to my laptop to enjoy some night-time viewing. Now there was a growing fear Kimiko had discovered the camera. Her and Ayako could be sitting huddled in bed, whispering about it.

If that were true, then best-case scenario would be them feeling too awkward or scared to confront surrogate uncle Victor. They would make their excuses the next day and leave. Knowing human nature, that was probable.

What was also likely though, was this being reported to the SC safety team. One email sent and I could be banned from the site. And even if they didn't report me; a damning reference on my profile would deter female guests. Which would make membership a waste of time.

Worst-case scenario was they would report me to the police, but the deodorant stick was still in my possession. There would be no evidence to find. Except the last thing I needed was authorities snooping around, asking me questions about my residence status. I had a tax-free lifestyle to protect. I didn't want a test of my deceptive skills. If you pass, you don't win any prize. But if you fail, you're fucked. The worry was snowballing.

I took a deep breath and remembered my strong tendencies toward paranoia and anxiety. Nothing was fucked. Yet. Whatever happened must have been caught on film. I'd look at the recording. I made certain my bedroom door was locked, closed the curtains, opened my laptop, and inserted the headphones, keeping the volume low. Next, I unscrewed the top part of the stick, taking out the rollerball and its adjoining chamber of liquid. That revealed the false compartment underneath, holding the main part of the camera and its memory card. You could either detach it and insert it separately or plug the whole device straight into your computer via USB port. I did the latter for speed, and transferred the file onto my desktop, moving it into a password-protected folder. After that, I erased the memory card, screwed the deodorant stick all back together again and placed it in the drawer of my bedside table.

Now, I'm one to savour the female form, but in this case, I had to remain focused on any detection. Ayako's chubby bottom and little boobs were not top priority, although I still took it all in. Not bad. Her entire bathroom routine passed without incident.

Then Kimiko's slender naked body came into view. It was a

pleasure to look at. Her skin was pale caramel. Think of milk with a drop of coffee spread throughout it. She was bony around the hips, ribs, and collar bone, but not so much as to be unattractive. I guessed the dark-nippled breasts to be a pert A cup. She had a thick layer of jet-black pubic hair covering her vagina, but it had been trimmed into a neat triangle.

The rear was a little disappointing. Her bum cheeks were a tad elongated and devoid of the roundness I favoured. They also wore a cluster of pimples. Nevertheless, she was a good-looking woman with her clothes off.

After having done a general body wash, she started to clean her pubis. She was facing the camera's direction, soaping the hair, when she took the shower head from its resting holder and started rinsing her privates; with it pressed against her bush. She turned from the camera. The slim hips were gyrating back and forth; her buttock muscles contracting and relaxing. Was she stimulating herself with the hot water spray? Upon her shifting face forward, my question was answered. Her free hand was rubbing in a circular motion around her clitoris as the water washed over it. That hairy banjo was being strummed. Naughty little Kimiko.

Her eyes began to gaze towards the camera. Gaze concentrated to stare. I felt like she was looking at me. Oh shit. Replacing the shower, she stepped closer. But the deodorant stick remained. Instead, she carried one of my shower gels—a cylindrical one—under the cascading water. It was glistening over svelte chest and abdomen. She started to rub pussy with the bottle's tip. Holy crap.

The thickness prevented it being eased up. That wasn't the tool for the job. And believe me, a few attempts were made. As she stepped in front of the lens again, I could only see her chin, neck, and upper chest while she rummaged. It wasn't easy to tell what was going on. Then I saw a giant palm, and it went black.

Shit. That was it then. She must have discovered it. My heart started to pound. I felt sick.

Except, what was going on? Vision appeared again for a millisecond, then back to black. Repeatedly. It was like one of those blooper videos when a cameraman (or woman) gets hit by a soccer ball or butted by a goat. The camera tumbles about and it's a blur. All I was seeing was black interspersed with flashes of white and tan. I wasn't sure what was happening. After three minutes of this, the camera view returned, this time unobstructed. Kimiko had placed it back on the shelf, and, with the shower stretched, she was aiming the spray at the lens, hosing it.

What the…? Was she cleaning it? Kimiko then spread her labia apart with two fingers, rinsed, switched off the shower and stepped out. The last thing I saw was my own upper body as I took hold of the deodorant.

Then I realised what had happened. With its top shaped like a swollen glans; she'd used it to masturbate. The picture had turned black every time it was rammed up her front passage. Wow. A mixture of water, vaginal juices and carnal desire had stopped her discovering the device.

She had instead fucked herself silly with it. That explained the rosy cheeks. She must have been exhausted from the vigorous wanking. There could well have been post-masturbatory shame going on too; hence her awkwardness. If so, it was well-deserved. Cheeky young lady.

My neck and shoulders unclenched. I laughed. Nausea subsided and heartbeat dimmed.

I watched the entire video again. Sans pants.

✳ ✳ ✳

The following morning, I served a breakfast of eggs, bacon, sausages, toast, and waffles, along with orange juice and herbal teas. The girls sat together on the central couch, still in pyjamas.

As they enjoyed the spread, I asked, "Do you mind if I open the balcony doors, ladies? Feels a bit stuffy in here."

Ayako replied, "Ah, sure, no problem. Fresh air is good."

"No problem," said Kimiko with a demure smile.

A pleasant coolness pervaded once the doors were unlocked and wedged. Not chilly but refreshing. I sat on the adjacent couch and buttered toast. Ayako nibbled on a waffle. Kimiko was sucking a sausage. It was all good.

After less than five minutes, they started to shiver, rub their arms, and say what I imagined was 'It's freezing' in Japanese. Ok, hint taken.

As I closed the balcony, Ayako said, "Sorry. So cold."

"It's fine, really. I hate to see you shiver," I replied with an empathetic smile. Fucking women.

As they chattered, poring over maps and sightseeing info on phones, discussing a possible itinerary; I had a quick shower. After dressing, I took the special roll-on deodorant from my bedside drawer.

I stood behind the unoccupied couch, grasping the gadget with front label covered. But also making sure Kimiko could recognize the toiletry. I gave pretence at multitasking my morning grooming regime while advising the girls on what would be nice to visit.

"So, girls, where were you thinking you'd like to go today?" Little point in asking. I knew the answers.

"Definitely Eiffel Tower, Louvre, Arc de Triomphe," said Ayako as she took another peck at her waffle. "Do you recommend other places?"

I unscrewed the top, to reveal the roller-ball underneath. Time for a tangent.

"Hmm do you guys like history?" I asked.

"Sure," chirped Ayako.

Kimiko's eyes had gravitated to what was in my hand. The supple skin over her high cheekbones lifted; the mouth forming a wry smile. "Yes, I like."

I shook the liquid in the container. "Then we definitely should go"—I pulled my t-shirt out at the bottom and gave a quick coating to each armpit— "Sorry, excuse me. We should go to the Army Museum. They have a special exhibition about musketeers. Have you heard of them?"

"No, what's that?" asked Ayako.

Kimiko was enjoying her cup of peppermint tea. Sipping through smirks.

"You've never heard of the Three Musketeers?"

No, they hadn't. But I was happy to explain. Musketeers had been elite soldiers. They were famous for, amongst other things, their swordsmanship. I took a fencing stance and gesticulated with the deodorant; pointing the rotund head towards the girls as if it were a sword, saying "En garde, mesdemoiselles!"

I made sure the head pointed right at Kimiko's eyes.

They both giggled, expressing an interest in going to the Army Museum. I didn't care either way. Ayako zombified back into her phone screen, but Kimiko continued to chuckle. Cheeks growing pink, her beautiful white teeth nibbled on the tea cup's edge.

She was having a private joke. Except it wasn't exclusive.

"What? What's so funny, young lady?" I asked with a smile, screwing the top back onto the deodorant.

"Oh, nothing. You are funny," she said before placing a slender, manicured hand over her delicate mouth to stifle the laughter.

Yep, I could rest easy. She was smug about her errant behaviour but had no idea I'd been audience to it.

I decided to keep the deodorant camera locked in my bedside cabinet, using it only when prudent. If any guest seemed perceptive or untrusting, then I wouldn't take the risk. Unless they were super-hot, of course.

If I took care, I would be able to see my female scouts in the nude and discover things most would never. The thought of that gave pleasure. We don't see the real person clothed. Different labels, styles, types, and colours of fabric, sure, but not who they are. I would set myself the goal of trying to know at least one hundred women in their entirety. And why not? It was victimless. There was no embarrassment and payment for their Parisian adventures didn't cost a penny. If that's not a win-win then what is?

Ayako and Kimiko had a shared SC profile and they left me a

glowing reference a few days after leaving. The pampering had worked its magic. According to them, I was an amazing, caring, generous and funny host. Indeed, the best ever they said. What sweet girls.

And what a load of bullshit they had written about me. Pure fiction. I laughed while reading it.

I had discovered something profound which would go on to change my life more than I could have ever imagined.

A little demon had been released.

HOSPITAL

"Evil is easy, and has infinite forms." – Blaise Pascal

I'm still in Jakarta. My daily regimen—if you can call it that—is tending towards slothful. I dip in the pool a few times per week, but most energy is directed towards trying to tell this story. I don't leave my room except to eat breakfast or get cocktails in the executive lounge. I'm in a cage of convenience.

It's more comfortable to stay within luxury hotel boundaries than swelter in crammed, sticky streets of exhaust fart extravaganza. Ten minutes out there and I'm drenched. Can't God afford a dehumidifier? If he's so perfect, why doesn't earth have one? Or air conditioning?

Thank—well, not God but someone else—this hotel is equipped for climate. The air is clothing me like clean, thin cotton pyjamas. I'm propped on bundled duck down pillows. Unlike the universe, they're bending to my will. Moulding in delightful co-operation as I catch whiffs of fabric conditioner from their crisp folds and flaps.

Even better, I've found a company in this city delivering rare single malt. Although taking the outrageous tax into account, you don't pay through the nose. That would be easy. Imagine the price is a pineapple and must be wrenched from your sphincter by a trio of enraged stallions.

And that's what I'm enjoying now. Not traumatised anus but whisky. A variety of Scotch liquid gold called BardBelg. It's from Islay—a tiny Scottish island—which means the liquor has a unique aroma and taste. Raising the glass to my nose, I smell salt, seaweed, and iodine.

You know what that combination resembles though? Disinfectant. Which is something nobody should be keen to drink. But here I am, halfway through the litre in less than 2 hours.

That pungent bouquet is leading me to my childhood. No, dragging. It's not somewhere I revisit with pleasure. Who wants to be where they're weak, naive, and timid?

But I say to myself, you're a man now, Victor. It's the past. Long faded intangible. The invisible can't cause harm. Except we all know that's not the case. Assassin's blades aren't seen. They still plunge deep.

Memories are monstrous, aren't they? Stabbing, singeing, pinching, and pummelling; we're all slaves to what's gone before. There's no greater turmoil than facing what wallows in the murk of times deceased. I'd rather wrestle a Komodo dragon now than go back to hospital when I was 11 years old.

Yet as the whisky's potent fumes slither, I feel compelled. Let me wipe my eyes, neck this spirit and refill. Then we'll begin.

* * *

The rail gave a metallic buzz as nurse Warren whisked the light green curtain, cloaking us from the ward. A brown plastic basin sat on a small trolley. Beside it, a chunky cloth folded, frayed and oatmeal coloured. Harsh soapy scent was filling the cubicle. Medicinal, it smelled like when my mum cleaned the bathroom. Or when dad had too much of his favourite drink.

Nurse Warren unfolded and dipped the flannel, squeezing so excess water returned to its origin in sploshes and drips. The acidic odour grew stronger. I could hear voices from across the corridor. Sounded like Timmy's mum and dad were visiting.

"So, let's get you undressed, shall we?" she said in a soothing voice, putting down the soaked cloth. I clutched the mattress, biting my lower lip.

"Erm, nurse Warren," I stuttered. Shifting on the bed, I felt tiny ripples of vibration as sickly bed springs struggled, wailing for treatment.

"Call me Lysa," she said, walking round the trolley and patting my thigh through the grey woollen blanket. A smile revealed yellow-tinged teeth; wrinkles bunched around her eyes, their blue shade penetrating.

"Nurse Ly—"

"Just Lysa." Mouth spreading further; the outstretched lips seemed to quiver. They were pink and shiny. Face freckled; brown dots concentrated on the bridge of her crooked nose and spread both ways in cheek direction. The one-piece uniform had no crinkles and was two shades whiter than the sheets and pillows I lay on. She had bumps on her chest—like all girls—but not big for a grown up.

"Lysa. I'm...shy."

She stepped closer. "Shy? There's no need to be shy"—she grasped the covers and yanked them to the bed's bottom, revealing my scrawny body clad in blue and red superhero-themed pyjamas— "ok?"

With throat dry and forehead hot, I repeated in hesitant protest, "But I am."

Perching on the bed, her slim hip pressed against the top of my bare foot as the smiling continued; she rubbed my lower leg through faded cotton. Tutting and with a roll of eyes, chuckling snorted through her nose as she said, "You mean you're shy about"—she gestured to my crotch area— "showing something?" Her yellow hair was drawn tight and held in place with a white clip at the back. It looked like a dried-out dandelion.

"Yea, I am." I could smell perfume battling with the basin vapours. Strong flowers.

She slid her hand to my exposed foot. It lingered there, rubbing my toes. Her palm was rubbery and hard like cheese left too long outside the fridge.

"Oh. There's really no need to feel that way"—leaning forward she ruffled my shock of soft brown hair— "Really. Believe me, ok? I've washed lots of boys' cocks." Her breath smelled like poo. I didn't know the word cock, but I guessed it meant willy.

"But I—"

"And I'm sure there's nothing to see anyway," she sniggered, standing over me—seemed 8 feet tall—as speckled fingers clamped onto the waist of my trousers and underpants, tugging them down. The cast on my left ankle got in the way so they lay bunched there. Then came my top. I was left shivering on the bed, but not from cold.

You might wonder why I was even in hospital, getting this compulsory wipe. It wasn't sickness or disease. The evening before, I'd taken a tumble on the stairs and got a broken ankle and cheek bone, plus sprained wrist, cuts, and bruises.

My dad had called an ambulance, then sat the entire ride talking to the paramedics. Explaining the accident. He kept hiccupping into his closed fist. Didn't look at me the whole way. My mum had been at Church.

Now they were both coming to visit. I hoped they wouldn't spend the whole time arguing. It made me scream inside.

Anyway, nurse Warren finished. Turned over on my front, she had given my bare bottom a pat and said, "All done, little Victor." I didn't like the way she said *little*. Dressed again; I was thankful of the covering but knew it could be stripped at any time. I was unhappy about showing my willy—especially to girls—even if they were old ones like nurse Warren.

"See?"—she patted my head and replaced the covers— "That wasn't so bad now, was it?"

My cheeks pulsed with heat. She'd not only seen but given commentary. I had lots of time to develop though, according to her. What was there to say? Without meeting her gaze, I said a quiet "Thank you."

"Now you're nice and clean for your parents coming, aren't you?" There was a clock on the bedside table. The cracked plastic screen filmed in dust said I had five minutes.

"Yes, Lysa."

"Ok, be a good boy until they arrive." She drew the curtain to its original place and clacked away over the linoleum. I could now see the ward. Bare white walls, frosted windows set in beige wooden frames—the paint from which was cracked and flaking—and long lights on the ceiling shining too bright.

The beds on either side were empty. Across from me was Timmy. He was 12 but didn't have any hair. I mean none. He looked like a little old man. But I never said because I didn't want to be rude. His parents had left, and he was sat in bed, reading a small, thick comic book. It was rested on his knees and he was browsing the pages with matchstick arms.

"Timmy," I called with a raised voice, not being too loud for fear of nurse Warren's scolding.

His pale face broke into a wide but frail smile. "How's it going?"

I felt bad after my bed bath, but I wanted to be positive. "I'm good, thanks. What are you reading?"

"Oh, my mum brought me a bunch of these. They're great. This one's called *Super Tank Commander*." He lifted it to show me the cover. I sat forward and peered. A giant American tank was fighting off lots of smaller German ones. Looked cool. His hands and forearms trembled as he held it.

"Thanks, Timmy. Hope you're enjoying it."

"Yea it's great. You want to read one of my other ones?" he asked, nodding at the pile by his bedside.

"Can I?" He was so kind. I'd only known him for a day and a night, but we were already friends.

"Yea, of course. I have loads."—he turned to the comics and started to read their spines— "What do you like? I've got *Secret Submarine Captain, The One-Man Army, Swordfighter Soldier, Escape from the Evil Prison, The Great*—"

"The escape one sounds good!"

"Ok, cool. I'll bring it over to you."

That wasn't a clever idea. The nurses usually helped Timmy walk or took him round in a wheelchair. And I couldn't get up either because of my ankle.

"Timmy don't do that. Let's wait for nurse Warren."

His face screwed in disgust and he said, "Eww, not stinky Lysa. She's only nice to the older boys."

I looked left and right along the ward corridor before making sure it was safe to join in his giggling.

"Then how will I get it?"

"I'll throw it to you. Get ready to catch." Thumbing through the pile, he slid the one I'd chosen. "Ok, you ready?"

I stretched far forward. I could feel pain in my ankle but didn't care. That comic was going to be awesome. With my fingers outstretched, I waited to catch. "Ok, ready."

He threw. The pages flapped. Then flopped. Landing beside my mum's brown ankle boots. Next to those were the white stockings and shiny black shoes of nurse Warren. It was visiting time.

My mum lifted it, inspecting the cover. Timmy gave both ladies a cheesy smile. Full cheddar. You could have served it with wine and crackers.

Handing it to nurse Warren, she said with a stern voice, "I'd rather my son didn't read about war for fun. But"—her tone softened as she approached Timmy— "May I give you one of my ones, young man? It's like a comic, but the hero is Jesus." She pulled a handful of thin magazines from her bag, placing one on Timmy's blanket-covered lap. It was the same kind she stored in piles around our house. There were two kinds, called *Wake up!* and *Beacon* and they had new pictures and words on the front every week. Dad didn't read them. He'd once thrown a thick bundle into the back garden during an argument with mum.

She opened it and flicked the pages, pointing and chirping. Timmy nodded and kept quiet, as polite boys do. Mum rubbed his arm, but not like nurse Warren. Her hand was only there for a second.

When turned from him, kind expression melted blank. She sat on the blue and white metal chair nurse Warren had placed at my bedside. Magazines still in hand; they all had the same cover. *Wake Up!* was written at the top, then a gravestone, below which was the question: What happens when we die?

Opening her bag, she slotted them before revealing a large red book. Its front had a beautiful garden filled with smiling people. Tables were covered in lots of different fruit, the colours like a rainbow. Everything was bright and perfect. It said: Live in Paradise on Earth!

"I thought we could read it together. To cheer you up," she said placing it in my hands. The stuff Timmy's mum had brought was more fun.

I glanced across and saw he was holding his Tank comic with a cheeky grin. I waved, which caused her to shift and look. She saw him staring into the gravestone magazine with fascinated face. I had a silent chuckle.

"I hope you like it," she called through a broad smile.

"Thank you, Mrs...Victor's mum!" he replied.

"Oh, you're welcome. If you have any questions, I can answer them tomorrow."

She drew the chair closer. Her pale face was serious again. Unhooking horn-shaped duffel coat buttons, she pursed lips before muttering, "Poor boy. I was told his leukaemia is terminal. He hasn't got long."

"Hasn't got long?" I didn't understand.

Leaning closer, she hunched so broad coat-wrapped shoulders obscured our mouths from Timmy. Puffy cheeks rose, forming into milky lumps, and skin around her oak brown eyes folded into chubby crinkles as she hissed in a whisper, "Until he dies."

I copied my mum's volume. "Dies? But I don't want him to die."

"We don't always get what we want. Oh, that reminds me—she released a strong huff—your father won't be coming. He had something important to do."

I didn't care. I was upset over Timmy. "Why does Timmy have to die? Can't God save him?"

Smiling like I'd asked a stupid question; she hung her coat on the chair. Air wafted. Mum never wore perfume, but I could smell mint. She often sucked boiled sweets. Dad said that's why she was so fat.

"God *will* save him. Don't worry."

"How?"

"God will remember him."

"Remember?"

"Yes, when the time comes, God will bring back all the dead"— she tapped on the red book's front cover— "to live here. Won't that be nice?"

"But won't he go to heaven?"

"No, he won't. He'll go to Sh'eol."

I only knew heaven and hell so was alarmed when told he wouldn't go to the first one. "Is that bad?"

"No, it's not bad. Everyone goes to Sh'eol. Even bad people. It's a place where you sleep until Jesus wakes you. Then you live on earth again."

"But we're already on earth."

She chortled, "Yes but you'll be brought back onto a perfect earth. There won't be any wicked people. It'll be called paradise. Just like this book says."

"Bu—"

"Listen, you don't have to worry about anything, except pleasing God with righteous works. Then paradise is guaranteed for you."

"What does 'righteous' mean?"

"It means good in the eyes of God. Like what I just did for that dying boy. Giving him spiritual food to digest instead of that"— she tutted and rolled her eyes— "violent rubbish his parents gave him."

Mum sat and read the book to me. After four pages, my focus strolled. I took occasional peeks across the ward. Timmy was reading about soldiers and battles. Smiling despite sickness. I wondered if *Escape from the Evil Prison* was as good as it sounded.

* * *

Bottle's almost finished. Never saw Timmy again, but mum heard through gossip he'd died a few weeks later. Poor kid. On the day I left the hospital, he offered me that comic as a farewell gift. My mum wouldn't let me accept it.

KUALA LUMPUR

"Never fear quarrels but seek hazardous
adventures." – Alexandre Dumas

I'm now in the Malaysian capital of Kuala Lumpur; staying on the edge of Chow Kit district. Impressions have been good. KL is spotless and orderly compared to Jakarta's filthy ruckus. People seem friendly and the standard of English is decent.

The timing of my visit hasn't been great though. Forest fires in Indonesian Borneo and Sumatra are causing haze across Malaysia. My eyes aren't coping. The air is neither smoky nor clear. It means constant squinting at essentials while outdoors: signage, shop windows and women's asses.

I was going to unwind with a swim this afternoon, but a note was slipped under my door saying the pool's closed for maintenance. I'm glad of the excuse to continue lounging and take a well-deserved rest.

Because this trip has been quite draining. I arrived early in the morning four nights ago, and, after a lengthy sleep, went on a dating app, from which I persuaded a Chinese-Malaysian to come to my room. She was plain-looking, and chunky round the mid-section, but did all the things I asked. Wish she hadn't stayed over though. Snoring, burping, and farting are supposed to be the man's department, aren't they? I can't get the women I want.

She gave me a lift the next morning. The shrill, non-stop nattering was goading me to smash face against steering wheel and scream for the shutting of dim sum hole. I don't do well first thing in the day. I restrained myself; she was driving the car and we would have crashed.

The night after was rewarding. Food options in this hotel are pathetic, so I opted for dinner at the Bitz-Falton in high-end shopping district, Bukit Bintang. It wasn't the fanciest Bitz, but their fare was tasty. I ordered a small feast complemented with Chianti.

I noticed they had a cigar lounge tucked in the corner. I'm not a smoker, but Cuban aroma can be pleasant. Once my meal was finished and I'd paid the bill, I went in to see the choices available.

The place had a gentleman's club feel. A strong odour of stale tobacco circled mahogany and burgundy leather furniture. Reminded me of Madame Fontaine's place back in Paris, except the armchairs and couches were expensive. As was the smell. It spoke of stacked money sacrificed to decadence.

The humidor was disappointing though. They only had large cigars. The type that would have jutted from between Castro's lips. Each one represented at least 90 minutes of committed smoking rather than the casual puff I'd expected.

I was turning to exit when a voice called to me. I saw a group of gents sitting in a circle. The focus was on one man—the oldest looking—who was reclining by himself on a three-seater couch.

"I'll give you a cigar, my friend," he said through smoke whirls. "Would you like to sit?"

He muttered something in Malay to the sharp-suited chunk of beef on his right, and an extra armchair was brought. All the chaps budged and adjusted to make room.

The leather was smooth and firm against my back, the chair sturdy. Felt nice. Not as comfortable his sofa, but good enough.

Peering through the smog and spotting a waiter, he snapped his fingers twice. "Would you like some coffee or tea?"

We've got a little finger snapper here. And there was no alcohol on the table either. I suspected this gathering was drier than Gandhi's sandals. "No thanks, I'm fine," I said with a smile. I'd have a chat for 15 minutes and make my excuses.

There was a wooden cigar box on the table. From it he took

a thick robusto extra around five or six inches long. It was the length of my erect penis, so we'll say six. Snipped, pre-brazen with a windproof lighter, and placed on a saucer; it was ready to smoke.

The small paper label said Royo de Montevideo Delicisio Especial. They were in the humidor at 120 dollars a pop. I drew smoke and let it seep, getting a taste. Damn, it was strong.

"Thank you so much. These things are expensive. I really appreciate it." These big shots wallow in false modesty while craving adulation and I'm happy to comply through empty words.

"My pleasure." He tapped ash into the overloaded ashtray. The short-sleeved peach shirt he was wearing didn't have a single crease or blemish. Quite a contrast with his skin. "Where are you from?"

Did it matter? I was there for him to have a whimsical conversation in English. "New Zealand."

"Oh, New Zealand. Nice." He took another lingering suck. "And what are you doing in Kuala Lumpur?"

Nice. I should have said South Waziristan instead. "Just a holiday. I'm travelling round a few places in Asia. Malaysia's the nicest so far though." People like hearing their country is the best.

A slim-built fellow with a large moustache chimed in, "We have a good country because of our government." This was followed by chuckles and beaming smiles from the huddle.

Except the grey-haired leader. He shrugged, palms up and reclined before saying, "Maybe, but we have shit police."

More laughter. The slender chap with the dirty sanchez took a pat from the guy next to him. Light-hearted ball breaking.

It turned out this frail-looking man was the Minister of Interior and entourage. The skinny guy was Kuala Lumpur's deputy police chief. The rest were low-level lackeys, bodyguards, and aides.

Mr VIP had been hitting the upscale boutiques hard. The floor was littered with thick paper shopping bags. I noticed, amongst many, Artier and Carmani; brands which surprised me with their quality. How did Vietnamese child slaves make such good stuff?

"Artier", I said, nodding at the bag with its brand. "Nice. What did you get?"

"Oh, some sunglasses for my wife"—he acknowledged the abundance— "actually, most of it is for her. I just got myself one or two unimportant things," he replied with dubious sincerity.

"She's lucky to have such a generous husband," I flattered. Did he spoil his mistresses too?

The ashtrays were heaped with crumpled stubs. They'd turned half a Cuban tobacco harvest to cinder. This was confirmed by the minister as he extinguished his half-smoked cigar. "I've already smoked five of these," he said sounding unsettled. "I may have to go and throw up."

Five? Shit. He must have been smoking non-stop for hours. Nobody in his detail had warned it unwise.

When he announced it was time to leave, the whole group stirred into action. The wad of ringgit for the bill was hefty. Must have been a couple of thousand in dollars. I'm sure he had card too, but that doesn't communicate the same message.

He stood and had a dizzy turn. A burly looking suit steadied him. I rose in feigned concern. Waving me into my chair, he said sleep was the solution. I said a good evening and watched him drift with the two thickest companions shadowing; their hands placed on his forearms and shoulders; in preparation should he keel over. I guessed this wasn't the first time he had smoked to the verge of unconsciousness.

Once they had disappeared, I moved to the full-sized sofa and stretched. The supple leather was comforting; albeit warmed by the conducted heat from another man's buttocks. I continued to suck on the Royo, appreciating the price. My mouth would be desiccated shit the next day, but it seemed a waste to stub it.

He hadn't even asked my name. Big fish, eh? No genuine interest in small fry.

I reached for the drinks menu. Now they were gone, it was time for a nightcap. I'd already had a few though, and combined with thick tobacco smoke, it was hard to read while reclining.

As I pushed into sitting position, my left heel struck something under the couch. The corner of an object was peeking between my moccasins. What I lifted was a presentation box bound in brown leather. The symbol in elegant gold print was one I recognised: Deitling. One of the most prestigious watch manufacturers in the world.

The entourage, having their minister's wellbeing as priority, had been distracted by his complaints of not feeling well. Scooping the dozens of bags; they had scurried off tending him. The box must have slipped unnoticed. Its colour matched the rug and furniture so it would have been well camouflaged, especially in a room obscured with billows of burning tobacco.

And now it was in my hands. I'd always admired Deitling watches and found myself opening the case. It was love at first sight. That old guy had chosen a beautiful example of craftsmanship. The piece had a large-sized black circular face, with three smaller dials carved inside. The whole watch part was set in red gold, joined to a luxurious brown strap. Finest leather, of course. Knowing how expensive the brand was, I estimated its price at minimum 30,000 dollars.

Even in a rush, how could someone not notice this being missing? It had only been twenty minutes since the group left, but I was expecting one of the stocky, no-necked bodyguards to reappear. Someone was going to be searching. But if I left straight away, could I keep my souvenir?

Stubbing my cigar, gladly, I decided it was best to forgo the cognac. If I met the old boy's cronies on the way, I'd say I was returning it. No harm done.

As the escalator was bringing me to lobby level, I encountered a dramatic scene unfolding. The VIP was still in the hotel. He wasn't focused on his shopping bags though. Laid flat in the middle of the floor; he appeared unconscious. Two paramedics were administering medical treatment. He had an oxygen mask on and was being eased onto a stretcher.

As often happens in these situations, morbid curiosity had drawn a crowd which was being kept at a distance by the minister's bodyguards and a uniformed policeman. A couple of unempathetic individuals were filming with their phones. Reaching the ground floor, I saw through the multiple glass doors of the entrance an ambulance and police car were parked outside. There was another cop standing next to the vehicles, trying to stop people entering.

All the politician's fancy-branded purchases were piled beside the concierge's desk in the centre of the reception area. A couple of them got kicked over by stumbling guests staring at the ongoing medical emergency. Clothes and accessories spilled; scattered across the carpet. Amidst the chaos, anything could have been stolen from that pile of goodies. By anyone.

I peered through the encircling crowd, examining his wrinkled face. It was bloodless grey. This was familiar.

The Reaper's reek pervaded. Had he been hovering in the lounge? Scraping skeletal mitts, waiting for the hour glass's last grain to flutter. Sharpening scythe in silence.

Corpses don't need watches. Only a coffin or urn. I made a solemn resolution to forever wear my new timepiece as a mark of respect to the old geezer on the stretcher. RIP to the VIP.

As I was making my exit, a coach pulled into the arrival area, and out of it started to disembark dozens of Asian tourists. Shouting and chattering in Mandarin, this small percentage of the People's Republic swamped the solitary cop. Looking back at the stampede in the foyer, I couldn't help but smile at those ignorant fuckers.

* * *

The next day passed without incident. Wine kept me company. I browsed porn and scanned for reports on the Bitz but found nothing. Checking Deitling's website, I saw my watch. The price tag was just shy of 34,000 dollars. The evening had been a bonanza.

The hijinks didn't end there though. Earlier on today, I decided to get rid of the presentation box. My paranoiac tendencies were flaming, and I wanted as little connected to me and the Bitz as possible. I didn't want to leave the packaging in my hotel room for the housekeeping staff to find. You never know. Being cautious is one of the keys to keeping your freedom. And punishment for stealing from the rich and powerful is never light.

I'd take a walk and dump the box discreetly. The official dealer's papers too. I had no intention of re-selling it anyway.

I decided to wear the watch on my walk, but with the face on my wrist's underside and only strap visible to others. It was an attention-grabbing piece. I wrapped the box in a supermarket carrier bag, and off I went.

Strolling for around twenty minutes, I searched for a quiet spot with a dumpster or public bin. I kept having to unstick the polo shirt from my chest. Haze and humidity made it feel like God had boiled an enormous kettle over Kuala Lumpur.

I turned into a side street flanked by tall buildings. There was a winding slabbed footpath, at the start of which was a courtyard which might have been intended as a place for office workers to enjoy fresh air while being sheltered from the sun's relentless burn.

It had fallen into disrepair though. Bushes were growing unchecked, engulfing two pigeon-soiled benches. Crumpled cans of beer, shattered green glass and cigarette butts littered the mossy concrete.

In the centre of this grimy situation was a shoeless man in ragged clothes, lying flat on his face. Arms at sides and forehead pressing unsupported into the ground; it looked a mighty uncomfortable way to nap. Like he'd faceplanted and not bothered to get up. I did for a moment wonder if he was dead, but then these down and outs are a hardy bunch; he was shit-faced or high. Also, I think even a corpse would have adjusted itself into a less awkward resting position.

There was a dumpster not far up the path. Perfect. I slid back the top, held my breath against the stench and threw the bag in.

Returning, I saw the guy who had been sleeping like a badly stored cadaver was now sitting. Bleary-eyed, his gaze began to sharpen as I approached. His instinct was to hold a hand to beg and make an eating food gesture; to assure me he, of course, wouldn't spend it on alcohol or drugs.

What the hell, I'd buy the poor bastard a few beers, or huffs, or whatever his poison was. I took a fifty ringgit note—that's around 13 USD—and offered it. However, not viewing him as a hazard, I had kept my bi-fold wallet out while doing so, with the two flaps extended, showing off the thick wad of fifty and one hundred-ringgit notes held inside. I also had a bunch of hundred-dollar bills too.

"There you go. Don't drink it all in one place," I said, extending the cash.

This wretch saw two hands hovering in front of him. One with fifty ringgit, and the other holding more money than he'd ever seen. His addled mind made what must have seemed the right decision. He snatched, taking half a fistful of the notes. At least a dozen more spilled onto the ground as he wrenched for more.

My reaction was to drop what I'd been offering as charity and give him a solid backhand across his nose. I'm not a tough guy, but I spent years boxing and weight training in my youth. My belly belies capability. As this ungrateful toad was about to discover.

He recoiled upon being struck. Holding both hands across his nose, he dropped the money and twisted into a foetal position, moaning in pain. There was blood gushing from between his fingers. I'd got him good. The force had been compounded by the watch's weight on my wrist.

I checked for anyone passing by. The place was deserted. I did a soccer penalty-style kick into his lower torso, causing him to wail and further compact. After I'd taken a moment for breath, I stooped to gather the scattered currency. Once it was in my pocket, I decided I wasn't finished with my would-be robber.

"You fucking miserable cunt! I took pity on you! You try to rob me?" I screamed into the side of his head as he clutched his guts and groaned. It was unlikely he understood the words. The message must have been clear though.

I had a powerful desire to pound his face, but it was bloodied, and I didn't want that on my clothes. Instead, I circled and began laying into his back with heavy kicks and stomps, putting all my weight into each blow. When I lose my temper, I sometimes overindulge.

"You fucking"—I stamped on the side of his bony rib cage and he let out a yelp— "cunt!"

With every battering knock, he made high-pitched squeals not worthy of a man.

"You fucking rat! You motherfucker! I'm gonna kick your fucking skull in!" I was panting. What great exercise!

My fury was interrupted by a shriek. Looking on the path, I saw a tiny, bespectacled old woman. She was grimy and dressed in a drab maroon one-piece and flip-flops. I judged her to be a street food hawker who was up a couple of steps socially from the wino cowering under my shoe.

"Hey you! What you doing? You crazy? You leave him! You leave him!" she shouted.

"Wait!" I said, presenting palm while I guzzled oxygen. My face and hair were soaked in sweat. Kicking shit out of people was exhausting.

"What you doing? Why you kick him?" she scolded.

I wanted her to understand the situation. I took more deep breaths. She continued to berate.

My heart already hammering from adrenaline and exertion, I stormed forward, intending to scream he was a thief and deserving of punishment. That wasn't what happened though. Impetuousness and tantrum held firm in their grip. As I reached within a few steps, my strides lengthened. I swiped hard and my knuckles connected with cheek. There was a smack of colliding bone and skin.

I had perpetrated an amateur flying fist attack on a midget

pensioner. I bet that was the last thing she expected. And yes, I know what you're thinking. But you had to be there. It was hilarious. You know when the laughter is so strong you worry about pissing yourself? That's me, recalling the way her glasses flew off in such a comedic fashion.

Anyway, she crumpled, writhing on the filthy slabs. "Fucking shut it, you old bitch!" I screamed. "Mind your own business next time! You fucking busybody!"

My throat is still sore. I made a swift departure from the scene, but I'm not concerned about being caught for my outburst. I didn't kill either of them, so the Malaysian police won't waste their time. Does anybody, on the misfortunes of street people? They'll say it was an intoxicated dispute that got out of hand. And why should I feel bad? I had kindness spat back in my face.

Something that does bother me though, is blood spattered on the Deitling when I backhanded the guy. There are stains on the strap. But I'll keep them there. They can serve as a reminder to be grateful, or at least feign so. Lest someone smash your fucking face in.

So anyway, you might wonder why I'm here in this new country, where so much entertainment's taken place? The answer is I came to process a 1-year business visa for Indonesia. With the help of a dodgy agency in Jakarta—for a bargain 600-dollar fee—I'm going to try basing myself in Bali while I write. A lot of tourists, admittedly, but the place also has ease of access to scripts, booze, and women.

I would have liked to stay a little longer in KL. However, my beautiful new watch is telling me it's time to leave. Less pretty are the blood stains around the buckle, but they're saying the same thing: Seek your hazardous adventures elsewhere.

PARIS V – CRAVING

"We always long for the forbidden things, and
desire what is denied us." – Francois Rabelais

How do you react when you see physical human beauty? Do you
feel envy? Lust? Inadequacy? Admiration? When I was a teen, it
caused a mixture of primitive urges. A part of me wanted to fall
at the feet of pretty girls and worship. I also wondered how their
delicate voices would sound squealing. I was a lad of contrast.

I'm in middle age now, so I often feel sad upon seeing a gorgeous woman in the street. But why would an attractive female
create sorrow in a heterosexual male? Shouldn't it be the opposite? No. For a guy like me, 999 times from 1000 she's unattain-
able. It's depressing. A vessel of pleasure that floats by unused;
makes me feel so unhappy. I'd rather it didn't exist.

The most enticing and intimate secrets could be inches from
my face, but they may as well be in another galaxy. For example,
stewardesses and their pencil skirt-clad bottoms as they wiggle
through the aisle, the tight clothing teasing heaven. I want to
partake. I want to eat. But I'm left to starve. It's inhuman. Life is
hellish.

But I take comfort in the fact everything beautiful will wither
and die. The exquisite is shackled to repulsiveness. Supple-
cheeked vitality is wrinkled frailty; a flash of time separates
them. All God's flawless handiwork includes expiry dates. Even
the Sun's fearsome inferno is doomed to become smoky submis-
sion. These truths calm me when faced with beauty's disturbing
radiance.

Pausing my melancholy; following on from Ayako and

Kimiko's visit I had been getting a growing number of couch requests on SC.

Quick explanation: If you're using their website, you can choose from a drop-down list of categories to search within. A guest who's looking for somewhere to stay can click on hosts then enter their desired destination. All those hosting in that location will become visible in a list. Advanced filters include things like if a host allows pets, smoking or last-minute requests.

My profile was always near the top of search results in Paris. And I had added photo albums of my swanky apartment, nearby attractions and smiling former guests. A lot of hosts only offered a couch or—which was a little on the nose—a shared bed. I had a well-furnished private room for my scouts.

I would say on average I was getting eight to ten requests a week. Around twenty during the summer. Whenever a SC notification told me a female had requested to visit—I would usually be able to tell from the name—a little spark of excitement fizzed. I read their message then went straight to the photos. These were pleasant times. Potential mischief was tantalising. I was always hopeful of 1 beauty in 1000 knocking at my door.

In the early days I wasn't picky. I wanted my profile to gain legitimacy through positive references. I said yes to almost every girl.

They were drawn from a broad range of nationalities. In fact, I can recall guests from 38 countries over the whole three years I hosted. The only continent not ticked was Africa and that's a pity. I mean, there's something about black booties. And I don't mean the kind you lace or zip.

Perpetual visitor flow meant the hidden camera was getting lots of use. It was a real pleasure to view so many naked bodies. I saw the full spectrum of female anatomy.

But it's obvious a ravenous appetite isn't satiated by looking at pictures of food on a menu. Not unless the dishes are served soon after. In my case, I was enjoying a visual smorgasbord of womankind, but my stomach was starting to rumble. It wasn't enough to take in the view. It started to make me sad. I was pining for more. I wanted to enjoy succulent flesh. I was longing for the forbidden things.

My achieving the necessary coitus in this situation was complicated. Firstly, the guests were young and dynamic; brimming with youth's energy and the ludicrous expectation of being destined for remarkable things in life. And that, of course, included the assumption their bed partners would be vigorous and attractive. Their male equivalents.

Problem was my man boobs and double chin tended to exclude me from their sexual aspirations. It's not like I'm an ogre, and I did have some success with women in my youth, but I'm not a guy that gets lusted over. Oh, and I was always 10 to 20 years older than them too. Age is only a number? Croc of shit.

Added to these shortcomings, was the annoyance that women can compartmentalise their sexual activity into specific situations. What I mean is most female guests had the stubborn mindset SC is not a dating site and therefore should never be used as such, on principle. And, of course, they are right SC isn't intended as a forum for singles to mingle. But then, by their logic, bars are only places for consuming alcoholic beverages. Right? They have no official romantic designation. The same goes for sports clubs, churches, university classes and even bus stops. None of them are intended as venues to find intimate companionship, but what if you bump into someone nice there? Ignore them because you didn't meet on a dating site?

* * *

I had a lot of conversations on this topic. I recall one which took place with three scouts during a balmy August weekend. It was six months into my SC hosting experiment.

"So, what happened, exactly?" I asked Josefina.

"Well"—she took another mouthful of chardonnay— "It was really weird. The guy was super nice on the first night and I thought this is a cool guy, you know? Then on the second night we went to a bar and were talking a lot. He started to get a little flirty and I was uncomfortable, but I tried to ignore it. And then he suddenly kissed me and—"

"He kissed you?" snapped Burcu. She was leaning forward in her chair. Contempt glimmering in her hazel eyes.

"Yea, on the lips. Shitty, right?" The lisping Mexican accent was soft on my ears.

Burcu's serrated Turkish one not so much. "It's more than shitty. It's criminal," she said drawing in a breath through flared nostrils. Her pineapple juice was untouched, glass sweating with condensation.

"Exactly. Criminal behaviour," agreed Josefina's compatriot who was sat to my left. Imelda was leaning an arm on the top railing of my balcony. The flesh spreading as flat iron pressed a crease in the flab. Atypical for an SC guest; she had even less room to manoeuvre in the rattan armchairs than me. And no wonder. I like big asses, but hers had more crack than 1980s Harlem.

We were talking about Josefina's experience with an amorous Italian SC host. Her and Imelda were best friends staying in the guest room. This was their second night in Casa de Victor. It had been nice. They liked wine and chatting. Josefina's wide nose and crooked teeth meant she wasn't good-looking in a conventional sense, but that was compensated by human warmth. And big tits.

Burcu—a bleached-blonde Turk from the Black Sea region—had arrived only a few hours earlier, but I'd already noticed a change in dynamic. Her father was mayor of a city called Zonguldak. The centre of the earth it seemed. I found her assertiveness intimidating. The smile struggled to conceal smugness. Something simmered under the polite façade. It had tainted Imelda's vibe.

We'd not long returned from an evening walk along the Champs-Elysée's. The heat wasn't Saharan but then I was no Tuareg. I felt drained. Sweating was healthy though, right?

Chilled, fruity wine gave a cooling internal massage. A lukewarm wind caressed my moistened brow.

The balconies were on the building's side opposite to the alleyway and main entrance. Gaps between rooftops gave glimpses of a street nearby. I glanced through the railings and saw Madame Fontaine's scrawny figure hobbling; no doubt for a cigarette run. She had a jacket on.

"He kissed you?", I said with fake surprise. "I'm so sorry, Josefina. Then what happened?"

"Oh thanks. You're so"—she slurped from her wine yet again—"kind. Well, I was shocked. And I said I'm not interested. And he said don't you like me? And he was really insisting and saying he liked me. And all my stuff was at his place and—"

"I would have slapped him and called the police," said Burcu with the certainty of someone who hadn't faced the dilemma. She was seething with confidence. Her father, who art in Turkey, was close friends with the Turkish president. That made him a corrupt, fascist henchman, but her idolisation of him was fascinating. As were the delusions of self-importance.

You know, it wasn't only sexual motives which propelled my SC misadventures. I had the chance to observe and learn about people who wouldn't otherwise have crossed my path. And as provider of free accommodation, I was given a licence to speak. Within the normal boundaries of decency, of course.

Conscious of nuance; I decided to explore the moral conundrums of SC and dating.

"You're a tough woman, Burcu." In hypothetical situations. "Josefina, how did it end?"

"Well I lied and said he was nice, but I had a boyfriend. I was able to get my stuff and leave," said Josefina, before draining her crystal tumbler of chardonnay.

I grasped the half-empty bottle on the table and nodded at her glass. "Little refill?"

"Why not?" she said smiling, before tying her deep brown hair into a bun. Didn't blame her. It was getting soggy round the temples.

I turned to Imelda, who was also running low. "Some more?"

She outstretched her arm, saying a faint "Gracias." I sensed her lowered eyes were something to do with silent vibes of judgement from teetotal Burcu. I wished I hadn't accepted the bitch last-minute to sleep on one of my couches.

"So, Josefina, may I ask a question? Purely hypothetical and with all respect"—I raised my hands in a gesture of defence— "about that situation?" You can't say anything these days without emphatic disclaimers.

"Yea, of course. No problemo," she said revealing malformed teeth.

You know when you're aware of someone hovering to interject? And hope they'll be polite enough to show restraint? Cause it'll disrupt the flow? Burcu's face was heaving with dialogue. But the tongue was held. Probably saving it for Erdogan's ball sack.

"And I know the guy was a complete jerk, and so, so wrong for doing what he did." Wrong, wrong, wrong! Rwandan Genocide? Step aside. Nagasaki? Make way for Grabakissi.

"But what if he been respectful and you'd liked him? I mean a lot. Would it have been any different?" I could see Burcu's mouth contorting; principles of the fascist-driven life desperate to spill forth.

"Hmm...Ok, being honest if he was an amazing guy and I felt a connection—" Josefina replied looking into her chilled wine cup.

"That's sounds reasonable," I said with an empathetic smile.

"And hot, and way younger cause he was 39. Then yes, maybe." I was 41. Fuck sake. "More wine anyb—"

"I disagree," said Burcu. "Scouting for Couches is not a dating site. It's simple." She sipped from the pineapple juice. The motion of gripping and drawing the glass revealed taut muscular definition in her arm and shoulder. Mouthy cunt had no fat.

"Pretty simple, yes," I replied with a sage nod. Because it's against the principle? Against the rules? Wonder if your daddy takes the same view on political perks?

Imelda—whose plump bosom had been centre stage in her SC profile selfie—piped up, "If these guys want a date, then they can use Kindler. Are they stupid?"

I gave Imelda's statement my strongest sentiments of agreement. Insincerely, of course. Dating apps like Kindler are shit. They're based on whether you like photographs. Personality doesn't come into it; except a token space to write a few short lines about yourself. The notion plain-looking men can open a dating application on their phone and connect with a female who excites them sexually is poppycock.

Women who think like Burcu or Imelda are showing ignorance of men's role within the sexual arena. This is because young girls can have sex any time. They can match with a lot of guys on dating apps. Or go to a bar or nightclub where they're offered free drinks by fawning suitors. They don't need SC as a sexual avenue and assume the same applies to everyone. Spoiled bitches. Millionaires lecturing paupers, except the currency is sexual. They really did irk me with their lack of empathy.

Suffice to say, I was against the odds in my ongoing mission to unlock the bountiful treasures of SC. How could I feast? Or at least nibble. I mulled the problem over many nights, often while watching recordings of guests showering. It was torture to be denied such delights.

The first thing I thought of was body massage but offering that seemed too brazen. I didn't think anyone would accept it and I feared negative references or being reported to the SC safety team, who would ban my account.

Perhaps there was something else? An activity resulting in physical contact but more innocent. I scoured the internet for types of alternative therapy. Acupuncture? Nah, it was sticking pins in people and not the kind of prick I wanted to administer. Alexander technique? Not so great. It was wishy-washy crap with minimal touching.

Reflexology, however? Hmm. Until that point, I had no idea what it meant. I watched a couple of videos and discovered it was foot and calf massage, and it didn't look complicated to learn.

I loved feet, and calves were nice too. My gentle hands had potential.

BALI

"The only paradise is paradise lost." – Marcel Proust

"Victor"—she fumbled and pulled at my fingers, trying to pry them from her windpipe— "please. Please. Sorry," she wheezed.

A foot shorter than me; she was teetering on dainty tip toes, struggling to keep balance as I raised my outstretched arm higher.

Words spluttered again. "Please. Please." Eyes bulging, welled with fluid; her tan skin had passed blush and was turning burgundy.

It's been four weeks since I flew from KL to Bali. And everything had been going well until three nights ago. Then this happened.

The girl's name was Putri. And—as you can deduce—she'd pissed me off.

We'd met at a popular restaurant and bar on the boulevard of Sanur Beach in south eastern Bali. A cosy place with bleached-blue wooden tables and chairs on thick sand. Stubby scented candles and giant cardboard menus under thatched shade. Vegan friendly, but it wasn't only for woke dickpipes. They did beautiful barbecued meat and seafood. My mouth is watering as I think about it. God how can anyone live on vegetables alone?

Anyway, Putri was one of a growing class of young Indonesian women who flee to Bali seeking western-like freedoms—relaxed attitudes around dating often being a priority—but find heaven hellish expensive. And what's a girl to do?

Privately educated with impeccable English; she had never asked me for a penny. My bank balance was dented all the same.

Meals, wine, cocktails, trips, taxis, and gifts mounted.

I wasn't casting stones though. The pulse of paternal hatred had been so intense she'd flown to this place with a mere few hundred bucks as security. I understood despising those who spawned you generates irresistible urges. Except—unlike her—I'd not had the courage to leave home at 19 years old.

Our two weeks together had been pleasant. Barely a cross word spoken. Bed shared without snoring complaints. She seemed happy to do the things I liked. A beautiful young woman treating me like a boyfriend. Something inside niggled the affection wasn't true, but then that's no different from my whole existence. Entitled but said thank you a lot. Shallow—with eyes wandering to younger men—but never criticised my weight.

So then why was her throat being constricted? Because of the previous night's near calamity.

Small slim girls shouldn't try to outdrink big fat men. I'd cracked open a bottle of Swedish vodka and she'd wanted to keep pace. I was also nagged into giving her two diazepam pills —which a Balinese doctor had prescribed in abundance—for mixing with several large vodka and cokes: with her boasting of high tolerance.

The villa I was renting suffered minor damage from her stumbles and tumbles, but that wasn't the issue. Money could pay for breakages. But not dead bodies.

When she passed out on the bed, I was relieved. Until convulsing started. Lying on her back; the puke started to sputter like a volcano. Yellow semi-digested chicken and bright green pak choi sprayed. She clutched the blankets and her feet flailed; too shitfaced to help herself.

I fucking flew. Trained in first aid; I dragged her, stood behind, and dislodged the vomit. Our bare feet were splattered in chunks of rancid goo. Bitter foulness attacked. Stench worse than shit. She took a series of hoarse gasps before heaving signalled a rush to the bathroom.

And there we stayed until her organism was deplete of liquid. Two hours of vigil. Holding her brown locks in a bunch as she retched; I reassured, patted, and consoled.

Confident sleep wouldn't mean dying, I helped her to bed. Then I cleaned lump ridden froth from the floor with disinfectant and sprayed pricey perfume—which I had bought her—everywhere.

Lying awake under the air conditioner's comforting flow; I sipped on vodka while contemplating fallacies about Bali. It was no peaceful retreat. Tourists I'd expected, but not immeasurable hordes of grubby hippies and lager-swilling louts. Crooks too. And not only the cops. Bali has an atrocious level of ATM card skimming. As for the traffic? Scooters, cars, trucks, and buses, form a monstrous dragon, contorting its swollen belly, limbs, and tail through roads large and small. And if it feels like a few hours' nap then you have no choice but to sit and endure the grate of its smoky snore. Why did people like the island so much?

I decided then I would research other places to stay in Indonesia.

※ ※ ※

The next morning, I awoke to tittering. Eyes blurry, I rolled over to see Putri sat in bed, scrolling through social media videos. She looked fucking chipper for someone who'd almost died the night before.

"Hey, how'd you sleep?" she asked while continuing to swipe and tap.

As a child, did you ever experience major dramas in your home of an evening—quite often alcohol related—then the next day it's as if nothing happened? My dad was keen on living that way. I wondered if Putri's had been too.

I reached for my standard mug of bedside water. Taking a mouthful, I watched. Her face looked normal. I had expected sweaty and gaunt. The fingers prodded and played without shakiness. She didn't even look tired. Shit, was I as resilient at

19? Had it been so long I'd forgotten?

"So, are you feeling ok?" I asked, despite the answer seeming clear. I wanted some thanks for saving her life. Or even an apology for broken glasses and ornaments, and spew soiling the shiny white tiles.

Still staring at her phone, she replied in mild valley girl speak, "Not really"—she gave a chuckle— "I'm super hungover from last night."

We had different definitions. For me, that meant being soaked in salty angst, curled in a frail quivering ball, praying to the Unknown God for mercy.

"You remember last night, right?" I wasn't going to let her ignore this.

"Yeah, I was pretty drunk. Sorry if I kept you up." Her hair was hanging too close to the screen, obscuring it. The silky strands shone with vitality. She tucked them behind her ear. They would have been drenched in puke and toilet water if not for me.

I was grinding my teeth, tapping them together. Fingers shaking, agitated; I could feel my pulse quickening. Her lack of gratitude was upsetting.

"You don't remember choking on your own sick? If I hadn't known first aid you could have died."

"I remember puking. I don't think my life was in danger. You're exaggerating," she said with a rub of my shoulder. Her skin was warm and soft. But not enough to appease. I wanted an admission of wrongdoing.

I removed her hand. "You could have fucked my whole trip. My life."

Have you ever stayed in an Indonesian prison cell? No? Neither have I, but the reviews are dire.

She sighed. The swiping stopped. At least towards the screen.

Huffing, she turned with tone growing agitated. "Yeah, I remember we drank, and you gave me two pills that made me fucking wasted. No wonder I threw up." She was resentful? After I'd saved her life?

Breathing deeply, and feeling my temperature rising, I got out of bed and put on some jeans and a plain white vest. She flapped the covers back and bundled into light floral green beach pants and a grey t-shirt. Why do we find it uncomfortable to argue naked with a sex partner?

"You insisted on those. Begged even," I challenged.

She started gathering clothes and throwing them in her small suitcase. Muted fury. The actions swift, face scowling. I waited for a reply, trying to remain calm. Nothing.

Silence is silver. It conducts current. I could feel voltage being circulated along its invisible threads.

"So, you're angry at me because I saved your life?" Neck stiffening, heart thumping and body pulsating; my system was flooding with adrenaline.

With her back to me, she said, "Yea, right. I was just drunk. And you gave me those shitty pills and the vodka. Nobody forced you."

"For Christ's sake, Putri. You know how this place works. What do you think happens when the Balinese police turn up and—"

Tone devoid of ease, she spun from her hurried packing and snapped, "What? Ok, I got wasted. I'm sorry, ok? Jesus, fucking Christ. You get drunk every day, Victor."

Raising my voice a notch, I asked again, "What do—"

"What? You are not my father. Stop lecturing me." Her soft cherubic face was distorted with temper. The baby browns telling a seething tale.

"No, I'm not. But you're happy for me to take care of you all the same," I replied, my voice trembling.

She slammed her suitcase shut and zipped it. The forceful closing caused waft from the floor. Disinfectant with a hint of vomit.

Slipping on flip-flops, she pulled the case onto its wheels and glared. "I never forced you to pay for everything. Now I'd like to leave. Please let me past."

I was leaning into the doorway between the bedroom and living room. My ample frame blocking the exit.

I stepped aside and gestured to the front door. "Go on then."

As she wheeled past, I grabbed her throat. Not full throttle—so to speak—but exerting enough power to cause instant alarm.

"Now, I want you to listen."

She was struggling, trying to pull away.

I tightened my grip, causing her to squeal. "I said LISTEN!"

The jostling continued, but our eyes were fixed. Mine said rage. Hers screamed panic.

"What do you think happens when the police come here? And there's a fucking dead girl on the bed? Eh?"

"Victor. Can't breathe. Please," she croaked. Squirming, the muscles of her neck tensed. It felt like a fillet of firm meat.

"And the dead little bitch isn't old enough to drink? And has my fucking pills in her blood?"

"I'm sorry. So sorry," she gasped. This had become a rhetorical conversation.

"You'd be asleep. You wouldn't feel a thing. And I'd be the one in hell."

Hands clasped around my wrist, she made frantic nods accompanied by a whistling croak. An attempt at screaming perhaps.

"It would be your fault. And yet I would be the monster. I WOULD BE THE MONSTER!"

That was when burgundy bulged. Then I let go. Collapsing, she gasped for air. Coughing and rubbing at her throat; she wore a mask painted with shock and terror.

A spoiled, clueless brat. Messed up but not malicious. A hedonist and rebel; I couldn't hate someone so like myself. Despite the fact she'd almost caused me disaster.

As she recovered, I wheeled her suitcase to beside the door and took deep breaths. The animal that had been bouncing in my ribcage began to tire; grey fog was clearing.

She walked towards me; sniffling, wiping tears. Unable to meet eyes, she squeaked, "I'm sorry. You're right."

Which translated as: I'm fucking terrified, please let me go.

Blowing deep exhalation, I opened the door. "Have you got everything? Your phone? Purse?"

She nodded. "Yes, thank you." Warm air was bustling in, contrasting with coolness inside. Bright rays bathed her petit form, the skin and hair shimmering dull gold. Such a tiny girl. Defenceless.

"Ok. I..." Why is it so hard to be honest? "I..."

She took hold of the suitcase handle. It rattled when her fingers wrapped. "Can I please go now?"

I reached into my jeans for a wad of rupiah. The red notes told me at least a month's salary for locals. "That'll pay for your taxi. You'll get one round the corner."

"Thank you." She left with hurried strides.

Closing the door, I felt hollow. My toxicity ruins. There's no way to tear out the Y chromosome.

About four hours later I got a text message. I'd deleted the number, but I knew it was her.

It said: Have you seen yourself? There was a picture of us taken at Bali Zoo. She'd edited it to highlight my belly. With a laughter emoji next to it.

* * *

So, that was the Putri incident. She's off with somebody else now, I guess. But her words echo in my skull: Have you seen yourself? Have you *seen* yourself? I pretend not to.

And I'm still at the same villa, sitting here on the terrace under a parasol as I punch my thoughts on keys.

You should see this place. Lined with brilliant navy-blue tiles, the pool's surface is glistening, dynamic, fed by three small fountains which babble in harmony. Birds warble a contented concert from the eaves of coconut palms. The gardens are a manicured masterpiece painted in green, yellow, and orange; its canvas tilting and adapting with ease as the wind sings an orchid-scented serenade. Everything's vibrant and alive. There's even a tiny frog staring at me from among the lush, loved grass. Cheeky little rascal.

As I sit here alone, with the mellow Balinese breeze billowing through my hair, I must accept the crushing reality. The terrifying truth.

There is no paradise for people like me.

PARIS VI - SOLE SEARCHING

"I should like to lie at your feet and
die in your arms." – Voltaire

So yes, I had decided to turn my hand—or hands in this case—
to reflexology. I'd gained several degrees and diplomas over the
years, so informal learning via internet was no challenge. Easy
peasy tootsie squeezy.

Delving, I found repeated claims proper caressing of feet can
result in genital stimulation. The abundance of nerves there
was phenomenal, and they could send pleasure all over the
body. Sounded promising.

Manipulation of mind would have to precede flesh though.
Verbal before physical. I didn't feel comfortable offering a foot
massage to young scouts directly. That was too ham-fisted and
awkward. I felt at ease with suggestive deception. And anyway,
to manoeuvre a situation so people would ask me for the things
I wanted—rather than making blatant offers—was a great deal
more entertaining and challenging.

I was sure budget-minded SC guests staying with me would
have aching feet and legs from all the walking they were doing.
If mentioned in the correct way—after the false establishment
of trust—some would ask for my expertise. And I could enjoy
handling bodies, even if it wasn't private parts.

Now, I have to say, it can be a painful art—even a torturous one
—steering a conversation to insert a titbit of information which
will result in the activity you're dying inside for. In this case, I

would be slipping into the conversation my time in India and the reflexology course I had studied.

And lies would be partial truths. This is the easiest way to mislead. Falsehood sprinkled with facts. That allows enough credible details recalled from memory to convince people what you're saying is true.

For example, I had been to Kerala; a region of India well-known for massage. And while there I had chatted with a retired therapist in a beach bar about treatments and courses. I hadn't had one single minute's training though.

The solution was a few hours of free instructional video clips and considerable embellishment. I was transformed into a trained reflexologist from a reputable school in western India. I'm not a duck but I still went quack.

Anyway, the first massage interaction which took place was a lot easier than expected. I had two girls staying with me during late autumn: towards the end of my first SC year. May was from Xian in China and Loviise an obscure village in Estonia. They were 21 and 23, respectively.

It was supposed to have only been Loviise, but early in the evening of her second night I'd got a last-minute couch request. This was from May, saying the SC host she was staying with was talking dirty. Some old French horndog who wanted a taste of tight oriental clam. She hadn't been physically harassed but found his verbal aggressiveness and crudity upsetting.

I expressed concern and accepted her at once. There must have been a good dozen of those emergency cases over the three years I hosted. The irony still makes me chuckle. Victor Elijah Fyric the saviour of women in distress.

* * *

"Hey, how you feeling? You ok?" I asked as she had stood limp-shouldered at my door, her sheepish smile failing to convince.

She hugged me tight; not saying a word. The top of her shiny black bob pressed into my middle-aged tits. I cradled and re-assured while having a discreet nose of lovely shampoo scent. May was a damsel, clinging to her white knight.

I said a silent thank you to the stupid prick from whom she'd ricocheted. You can get away with a lot when people are vul-nerable. And—at least in my experience—girls seem desperate to believe soft when they're recovering from a barrage of harsh. Never fear though; my empathetic uncle mask was on. Fixed in place with a thin elastic band.

Once her stuff was in the guest room, we sat on the couches—Loviise and May together and me on the other—and had a group outrage.

"I'm so glad you're ok," said Loviise, giving May another hug. To be honest, it's difficult for me to write about Loviise. The double vowel looks odd, doesn't it?

"What a horrible piece of shit that guy is!" I said, settling us into a cosy echo chamber.

"It was so disappointing. His profile Scouting for Couches seemed so, so good," May said, sipping from a glass of water. She had a shaky hold of English, but her pronunciation was decent.

Yea, his profile was good. I'd had a nosy when May mentioned the username. Guy had 62 positive guest references. All from beautiful young women, of course.

"Well you're safe now," said Loviise smiling across at me. "Vic-tor is a proper gentleman. A *real* couch host."

I smiled. She was such a sweety. And that Estonian ass looked delectable in grey yoga pants. The peach-like curves driving me crazy. I'd been in discreet admiration since her return from sightseeing. "Thanks, Loviise. And you're a real friend."

"What I don't understand how he got more than 60 references and all positive?" mused May with insufficient grammar.

I knew the answer. I'd let May deliver. "Yea, that's weird. Isn't it? You'd think he'd have acted like that before maybe?"

"I think definitely," said Loviise leaning on the couch's arm. Golden-tanned feet pressed and rubbed their pink soles against the leather. One big toe was protruding over the edge in all its clear-glossed glory. God, I wanted to suck it. The fucking furniture was having more fun than me.

"Well, it's unacceptable behaviour May. You should definitely report him to Scouting for Couches safety team," I said. Christ, if there were medals for insincerity...

"It's awkward," she mumbled into water.

I tutted in empathy. "I know, I get it. Maybe just count it as a valuable lesson then?"

Shame is mightier than missiles. Used for millennia across countless cultures to terrorise and subdue myriads of the female gender. What difference did one more instance make?

"Yea, he's got a lot of good references and you don't have any yet. But I'd say at least leave him a negative, right?" said Loviise.

I sighed. "Yea, you should. I can even leave him one too if you like. Obviously not as a guest, but in his personal column?" The personal references could be left by any SC member, without need for a stay having been arranged through the website or app. I'd given an empty offer; there was zero advantage to involvement in another guy's business.

"I want to forget it and enjoy here. I'm in Paris! I think you and Loviise are so cool," she said smiling.

I wondered how many girls had fled his house with the same attitude. 62 positives. God alone knew the unwritten negatives.

❋ ❋ ❋

It was evening, and everyone was hungry. As the good host I ordered a delivery of steak frites, side salads and garlic bread. It was still mild enough for eating al fresco, so I suggested dinner on the balcony. I'd been planted on the couch playing PSBOX all day, so the fresh air would do me good.

Opening the balcony and preparing the table; pleasantness of cool air seeped through the fibres of my long-sleeved shirt. Once they were seated—on either side with me in the middle chair—I placed fluffy DYKEA blankets over both the girls' shoulders and wrapped them at the front, leaving their arms free. I couldn't bear to see ladies shiver with cold. Cause it was fucking annoying.

I also popped the cork on an 80-euro bottle of Chateauneuf-du-Pape. It goes great with steak, but I used to drink it with most meals when I lived in Paris. Strong in alcohol but gentle on the palate; it speeds the soothing of ragged nerves. And tended to make my quips and anecdotes more amusing. I'm not a humorous person, but being a host fostered that delusion. Scouts like May and Loviise were my captive, grateful audience.

"So how was the food, guys?" I asked, reclining in my armchair as far as my oversized love handles would allow.

"Oh, so good. Thank you," said May. Her pale unblemished cheeks creasing into dimples; beautiful white teeth revealing. There's a myth all Chinese people have slanty eyes. All I saw were big oval ones on May, the irises a rich mochaccino. She was a mild-mannered, adorable doll. No wonder the old guy had wanted to fuck her.

"Thanks, Victor, that was amazing," concurred Loviise, wrapping the blanket tighter and swirling her wine with tanned fingers.

I lurched forward in my seat, glass in hand. "Wait! I've just had a fantastic idea!"—raising my index finger as a signal to wait, I tipped the large measure of red down my throat— "Ah!"

They shared a look then stared with anticipation. After a few seconds of polite waiting, Loviise asked, "Ok, so what's the fantastic idea?"

"Eh?" I replied.

"Fantastic idea. You said fantastic idea. What is it?" asked May. The charming contours of smile were forming again.

I rested my index finger on the empty wine glass' rim. "To drink that," I said in mock confusion.

They both giggled. It's flattering to crack stupid jokes and have pretty girls laugh at them.

The sky's dark blanket was peppered with shimmering pinholes. A candle I'd lit was releasing vanilla and cinnamon teases as its flame stuttered between flickers and proud stance. Potent blackberry and plum coursed over tongues. Chattering released vapours of dark chocolate mingled with liquorice.

A second bottle was opened. Loviise had an impressive thirst. She was keeping pace, which takes some doing for a woman. May wasn't a drinker and had been taking polite sips through-out the meal. I made a note to quaff her leftovers. I've wasted a lot of things in my life—youth, health, money—but never good alcohol.

"So, May, are you feeling ok now?" I asked.

"Absolutely. Feels like real Scouting for Couches. Friendship and fun," she said smiling at me then turning to gaze across the moonlit rooftops of Paris.

"Yea, this is really nice. So glad I chose you as my couch host, Victor," slurred Loviise. The toffee skin of her cheeks was blushed. Whispers from the wind had blown groomed brown curls unkempt.

She'd had enough to drink. "Some more?" I asked.

"Well my glass is empty," she replied with a cheeky grin.

"May, I think you don't like wine much, right?" I said nodding at her glass.

"I don't like the taste. Too bitter. Sorry." Don't apologise. More for me later.

"It's fine, really. So, is Xian quite a crowded city? I just have this image of every Chinese city being so full. You know because China has how many people now?"

Letting out a weak whistle, she said, "Oh, I think 1.4 billion. Crazy right?"

"Yea. Holy crap. How many in Estonia, Loviise?"

She was holding her glass in both hands, slurping at the blood-coloured liquid like an alky vampire. "I think"—she hiccupped then laughed— "I think about million? Maybe little more?"

"A million? That's a Chinese wedding party" I said smiling at May. We all laughed. "Although people don't realise that India has almost as many people these days," I injected.

"Really?" said May in surprise.

"Yea, I got told that a few times when I was studying in Kerala. That's in west India. Beautiful place."

"Oh, what you study?"

"Nothing fancy, just reflexology. It's massage of the feet and a little of the legs."

Then May surprised me. A smirk spread on her sweet features. And not derisive or sceptical. She was bashful. "You trained in the massage?"

"Yes, I am." Kind of.

"My legs so sore from walking. I wonder if—"

"I'm not a massage guru or anything; just to warn you," I said with pretence at modesty. I could feel anticipation building in my stomach.

"You massage my legs? Please?" she begged. This was fucking fantastic.

"Yea sure if you really want. I suppose, being honest, I worry you might think I'm as bad as that dirty old guy you ran away from. You know if I give you a massage."

"Oh no, Victor. I don't think that. Never!" Good. Because I'm much worse.

"Well then if you're sure. Loviise, would you like a foot or leg massage?" Fuck it, luck is there to be pushed.

She was flicking through some bullshit social media app. The light from the screen reflecting off her pretty face. "That's sweet but I'll"—she hiccupped— "catch up on this and enjoy the stars. Is it ok to have more?"

"Sure"—I refilled her glass— "and help yourself to the bottle. There are also some beers in the fridge."

It was straightforward. May changed into a t-shirt and boycut bikini bottoms, and I laid towels on the guest room bed. I rubbed her smooth legs from the ankles to the thigh tops. I savoured the soft touch. It was wonderful. The calves were beautiful under my palms, but her thighs? The delicate, milky flesh was glorious.

I went fully erect for the first leg of the journey—so to speak— then deflated to a semi. The hard-on would have been obvious had she been looking, but her eyes were closed; the mind focused on pleasurable sensations. I made a note for the next time to have baggy clothing on my lower half in case the same matter should rise again.

"Feels so good," she murmured in a sleepy tone. "Smells so good."

Double yes. The massage gel was fragranced with ylang-ylang, lemon and geranium. A dessert for the nose. It slid deliciously over her slender pins.

"Where you get it? I want to buy."

"Well," I said in a gentle voice, "you can get anything on the internet these days. I got it from a wonderful online store that sells massage supplies."

I hadn't. It was from a nearby pharmacy, Lubex two-in-one massage and sexual lubricant. I'd noticed it when buying my monthly supply of extra strong vitamins for those who drink and do insufficient exercise.

I'd peeled off the sticky cellophane labels to leave it as a plain rigid plastic tube. The Lubex logo was certain to have put guests off having it rubbed onto their bodies. I must have gone through litres of the stuff while hosting.

Anyway, when the massage ended May was looking content and relaxed. She gave a big thank you hug and said she was ready for bed. I handed her a warm wet hand towel to wipe off the residue and bid goodnight.

I would have cut off a pinkie to join her under the sheets.

Returning to the balcony, I saw Loviise had guzzled all the wine, even May's glassful; and dragged the central armchair to act as a leg rest. With arms crossed and head sagging, she was drooling onto my DYKEA blanket.

I tried rocking her shoulder back and forth, whispering. Nothing. I then spoke in a stronger tone, shaking her with vigour. Only a sleepy groan. The girl was shitfaced.

Swinging her limp arm over my shoulder; I heaved to the guest bedroom's door. Thank god she wasn't a fatty like me.

Knocking while trying to keep balance with Loviise, I said,

"May, can I come in? Loviise's had a little too much to drink."

The answer came from the bathroom. "I take a shower. The massage gel so sticky." I heard the spurt of water.

"Ok, I'll just help her on the bed then."

"Ok, I will be there after shower," she replied, her voice muffled by the din of spray.

I lugged Loviise round to what I presumed was her half. As I was lowering, I lost my balance and she flopped onto the mattress face first. No reaction whatsoever. She'd drank quite a lot of strong wine for such a petit young woman. I hoped she wouldn't throw up. I manoeuvred her head as close to the edge as possible and went to the kitchen for a plastic basin.

Once this was all done, I noticed her thin cotton sweater had ridden waist high. The bare skin of her lower back was exposed. Those yoga pant-clad buttocks were on full display. Even amid extreme intoxication, Estonian bum cheeks were proud and healthy. The shape was tantalising.

Could I peek? Nobody would know. And she did drink about a hundred euros in wine. A little flash wasn't too much to ask as repayment, was it?

Looking across at May's bedside; I was reminded I'd forgotten to take the Lubex gel. The tube was still sitting there; perched upright. I wondered. It was a two-in-one product, wasn't it? The massage aspect had been successful. Would its lubricant properties be as effective?

"Loviise? Loviise? LOVIISE?" Nothing.

Sin is thrill. Adrenaline giving me a stomach slap, hands fidgety—despite the wine—I pulled back the rim of her yoga pants half a centimetre, to see the lining of her underwear. She had a frilly pink thong on. The tiny label flopped. Size S, of course. Perfect bitch.

I hooked my fingers under both layers of clothing and tugged. Her bare ass looked like a toffee apple. Fucking delicious.

Spreading the cheeks apart; I examined both holes. Clean and hairless. Her puckered asshole looked virgin and unexplored. I'd start there then move to the front bubble gum.

I reached for the Lubex, took off the cap and coated my left index finger. Couldn't wait to enjoy the taught sphincter of her squidgy stink gripping my digit. I nestled the tip among the tiny folds of brown skin and began gently pressing.

But it was not to be. The door started opening behind me. I pulled Loviise's undies and pants back in half a millisecond.

"Is she ok?" asked May, walking into the room.

I pointed to the basin with a look of sombre concern. "I've been worried about her puking; trying to keep her head so anything goes downwards. There's a risk of choking most people don't realise until it's too late."

May patted my back with her tiny hand. "You're very good couch host."

"It's nothing, really. Can you help with her clothes? It wouldn't be right for me to do it. I'll leave. Call me if there's an emergency."

Pulling the sleeves of her white and pink striped pyjama top, she said with a smile, "You are gentleman, Victor. True gentleman."

More fool you, asshole. "Thanks, May. You're too kind."

Anyway, Loviise didn't puke and was surprisingly unscathed the next day. She apologised for drinking all the wine and being a burden. It was fair enough. I'd tried to finger her rectum and vagina. Nobody's perfect.

They stayed one more night and we spent it having dinner in one of my favourite brasseries on the Champs Elysees. I bid them safe travels. Both posted excellent references on my profile, emphasizing my generous and gentlemanly nature. What a hoot. I was loving SC!

Positive reviews about skilled hands snowballed. As they did, many female guests were simply writing about massage and not mentioning feet. This enabled me to progress to a more encompassing level of therapy. Opportunities for handling flesh escalated exponentially.

I began to explore the world without leaving my apartment.

YOGYAKARTA

"The greatest wealth is to live content with little." – Plato

The name of Icarus is well-known, but most people don't know the details about his fate. It's usually remembered he didn't listen to a warning—from his father, Daedalus—about flying too close to the sun, and perished because of it. He was wearing a pair of prosthetic wings held together with wax, and the solar rays melted them, sending him crashing to the earth. I personally understand the moral there as being a warning against reckless ambition. The storyteller was cautioning us to recognise our limits and stay within them. I've never had lofty goals, so the risks from trying to overreach in life haven't been a major concern.

However, heat wasn't the only danger Icarus was told to be mindful of. Yes, there was flying high, but he also had to avoid flying too low. This was because, as he and his father escaped captivity their flight path took them over the sea. Icarus was told not to swoop close to the waves in case splashes soaked the feathers on his wings, making them unable to keep him airborne. This part of the myth could be telling us not to do things beneath ourselves. They may keep us there forever. Or, it might be saying not to expect too little from life, as, if we do, that's all it will ever give us.

Those concepts make sense, especially since moving from Bali —which had too many drunken westerners like me—to this new place. It's a city called Yogyakarta. And it's not what I expected. Yogyakarta is a special regency within Indonesia; ruled semi-autonomously by its own sultan. I thought the area would feel unique in some ways. It doesn't. I was also misled by photographs of the city and its tourist attractions into thinking the architecture would be quaint and pleasing. I had visions of traditional Javanese houses and temples, constructed with ornate wood and stone masonry. Nope. The buildings look the same as any Indonesian city; slapdash, ill thought out, and devoid of charm. I was also assured Yogyakarta didn't have bad traffic. It does. Not as awful as Jakarta's, but that says little. The worst thing though, is the apartment I chose to rent. It's not in line with what I'm accustomed to. My wings are starting to feel a tad wet.

I'm a spoiled person. I disagree with Plato's view on wealth. I can't be happy with only a few pennies. I like to be more than comfortable. Luxury feels right. And, to be clear, I'm not a snob. I don't despise the poor. I just don't want to be one of them. Life is woeful enough without having to do vacuum cleaning and scrub faeces from the toilet bowl. Trying to piss it off can be a fun challenge, but that's at least still an optional leisure activity.

My attitudes aren't those of my parents either. They were a pair of miserable bastards. My dad's idea of splurging was a takeaway Indian curry—for himself only—accompanied by supermarket brand whisky. As for my mum, the best things in life were free, Bible meetings and intimate talks with invisible Jesus.

No, I can't blame them for my behaviour. It's been a gradual process over the years, in correlation with the rise of salary. I'm not used to having to do menial tasks like cleaning, washing the dishes or changing the bed. I hate wasting time on those things, which is why my time in Yogyakarta hasn't been fun.

After considerable levels of expense in the cities I've stayed in during my travels, I thought I'd try more budget-conscious accommodation for a month. I'm not short of money, but the rate at which I've been spending it has been rapid. What I dread is running out of the stuff before I've had a chance to die in shameless luxury. Once my story is completed, I have romantic visions of demise. I want to end this miserable existence in a five-star hotel suite, sipping fine whisky or Cognac, with a belly full of beef and bearnaise sauce, overlooking somewhere scenic. Rio de Janeiro or the Swiss Alps would be good. I also want precipitation, depending on the location and season. To the sound of rainfall or the sight of heavy snow wouldn't be the worst way to exit the stage. Someone else can deal with my shit-soiled corpse.

I wouldn't want to snuff it in the apartment I rented here. It's student dormitory accommodation. Cramped and dark; there's no housekeeping, no room or laundry service, and its bug infested. The pool needs a good clean, and people use it for free. The staff never seem to enquire about people's room numbers. Mind you, if I were being paid a hundred dollars a month, I wouldn't give a shit either.

Even worse, the road next to the building seems to be busy twenty-four hours a day with rasping motorbike exhausts and honking horns. As if that weren't bad enough, the crappy bar which sits at the bottom of the building, directly under my room, has live music events; the horrendous thrash metal blasted at full volume. I've made effective use of my ear protectors, but I would rather have had an AK-47.

Two things of note have happened in Yogyakarta so far. The first was I saw Mt Merapi, the nearby volcano, erupting. Sounds exciting, right? It wasn't. The peak was smothered in clouds, a minor event. I was the only person in the crowded pool area who noticed it, due to the tell-tale sign of lightning flashes centred around the volcanic activity. The locals were too busy taking selfies with the sunset. Idiots.

The other thing I saw, which was more like a passing oddity than anything interesting, occurred a few days into my stay in this city; also around the pool area. I went one afternoon, hoping nobody else would be swimming there, and was surprised to find it so. There was, however, a group of five Indonesian people sitting around one of the tables at the poolside, drinking beer. Three men and two women, all dressed formally. The basic café sells a couple of kinds of the local piss water, and they'd had a few bottles each. This would be no big deal in Bali, but in conservative Yogyakarta seeing early daytime drinking was unusual. I thought no more of it, as I'm hardly one to be shocked by alcohol consumption.

I swam for around forty minutes, doing my usual mixture of strokes at leisure. I had finished my session, and was leaning back in a corner, waist deep getting a little sun, when I noticed the people were in a circle, praying. I knew the café's food was awful, but this seemed more than a request for protection from E Coli.

They'd captured my attention. I watched with mild curiosity. The men took off their ties and shoes, and meandered round to the poolside while chatting and beaming. Then one of the guys took hold of the pool ladder and started descending. At first, I thought he'd had one pilsner too many. I mean, it's common to see Muslim females swimming with all their clothes on, and occasionally the men will wear a t-shirt in the pool, but I'd never seen anyone enter in near-complete formal attire before.

Once the two other men got in though, it became clear it was a baptism. The two ladies remained in the café area, filming the momentous occasion on their phones. Another prayer was said, and then the believer was dunked under. He arose, washed by the blood of the lamb, to start his life anew, freed from the damnation of inherited sin.

While all this was taking place, I had walked through the water and stood as close as was polite, to get a better view of the spectacle, whilst giving a reassuring smile. By the time the new disciple had emerged from being dipped, and congratulatory hugs were given between those spiritual brothers, bound by their union with their saviour Jesus Christ, I felt a wonderful sensation of relief. Bliss. What exactly is it that's so relaxing about peeing in a pool?

I never saw the point myself. The only person in my family to be dunked was mum. It happened before I was born. The effects were felt long after though.

Anyway, as I write, that dorm is sitting empty. Two nights ago, during a particularly grating performance by one of the bar's live acts, I snapped and left. It was either that or join their concert with my own instrument: a claw hammer.

Escaping stress is simpler and involves no flashing sirens. I moved into an opulent five-star hotel nearby, which is owned by the Sultan of Yogyakarta. This place has got everything you would expect. I'm lying on Egyptian cotton sheets and goose down pillows of a massive king-sized bed, sipping scandalously priced Reamy XO.

I feel like I'm back where I belong. My wings are drying, and I'm soaring above the dark sea's smothering depths. For now.

PARIS VII – CATALINA

"The human soul needs actual beauty
more than bread". – D.H. Lawrence

The next SC account isn't the darkest chapter of my hosting, but it could be the most bizarre. It was this experience which reinforced my belief, without doubt, that it's not important who you are. Its who people believe you to be.

By this point, I was around two and a half years into my SC venture. Though only half had been spent in Paris hosting, because of my rotational work schedule. I'd collected quite a few positive references on my profile. These were public opinions about me. And, according to the evaluations of my guests, I was the kindest guy on earth. The high quality and cleanliness of the apartment was often mentioned, and sometimes any free meals given or fun activities we did together, but the focus—surprisingly—was always on the host. I must have had around 80 references. I'd also been accepting couch requests from occasional male guests and couples, usually for one night or sometimes two. I liked my profile to have some diversity. It lent credence to my respectable image. I also enjoyed the guys' company, to be honest.

SC had become the focal point in my life. It was like nothing else. Despite having the odd crappy guest at times, the thrill of wondering who might walk through my door next kept me addicted.

So, as mentioned earlier in my story, I was working half the year in West Africa. Surrounded by barbed wire fences and huge concrete blast walls; these places looked and felt like prisons.

I was living an austere lifestyle there. My movements were restricted, and I wasn't allowed to exit any camp without an armed escort. When I did go into the field to complete tasks, the terrains were inhospitable. Desert or parched savannah awaited me, and always under scorching sun. Compounding my misery was company policy on intoxicating substances, and random but regular urine tests. I sizzled in sobriety. These places were devoid of joy. I needed the anticipation of fun times in Paris to survive tough times and climes.

SC was a lifesaver. Entertainment, *real* entertainment, isn't easy to find. Of course, there are plenty of movies, tv series and songs which are enjoyable, but they are passive pleasures. You listen or watch, and someone with talent takes the reins. You're not involved in the experience. Taking in a show at the theatre feels more immersive, due to the fact the performers are doing it live, but it's not far from tv. You also have video games, which are fun for occupying one's mind and passing the time, but the storyline and actions you can choose from have been determined by the developers. You play them within pre-set boundaries. That's not freedom. Then there are books—which some say are a window into another world—but for me they're words on paper. Looking at ink only interests me when it's on the surface of a woman's body.

Legal falls short.

So, if you're like me, and you aren't content with those things which placate and enthral the masses, you must look elsewhere for thrills. This is to counteract the dreariness of life. I managed to find something close to that; considering I usually wallow in the numbness of depression. And with SC it was ironic the truest form of entertainment was one founded on lies. Real-life drama and intrigue were there to be experienced daily, and the show revolved around me. I was the star.

And my sham was progressing. The reflexology I'd studied—in my imagination—evolved into a full range of courses covering treatment of the whole body. Glowing references on my profile reinforced respectable image, and I was able to get more hands on with female guests. It was surprising how relaxed things could get.

And though I enjoyed it a lot, the efforts involved in getting to these pleasant moments took a huge amount of patience. It required me to sit through the tediousness of identical conversations and even the most beloved of city landmarks will grow tiresome if you visit them ad nauseam.

So yes, despite it being entertaining, SC also had its challenging moments. Of course, humans being the way we are, sometimes personalities clash, or culture and lifestyle difference make getting along impossible. I'd only had a handful of problematic scouts but wanted to avoid hosting them. There was nothing more deflating than meeting a guest only to realise within three minutes you didn't want them in your home. Even worse if you'd agreed to a stay of three nights plus. On those occasions, SC was a real chore, and, with my strong aversion to boredom, these types of people would make me question why I was continuing to take part in it all.

As part of efforts to weed out uninteresting visitors, I began to vet. The SC messaging service is basic, and not suitable for the type of flowing conversation necessary to measure character. Instead, I decided to use social media or messenger apps. There was the advantage of being able to do video and audio calls. I wanted to circumvent coping with others' stress-inducing behaviour; like committed contrarians or anyone who whinged about saving the environment.

I surprised myself at times by refusing couch requests from very pretty girls. I would do this if they seemed suspicious of men, aggressive, defensive, or perceptive. It wasn't worth the risk of raised blood pressure. Unfortunately, the vetting process was imperfect, and you can't always get an exact idea of who a person is until it's too late. Similarly, it's impossible to tell if they'll be so disagreeable you develop an uncontrollable urge to murder.

✳ ✳ ✳

Anyway, the person I was talking to on this occasion was a twenty-two-year-old woman from Argentina. Her name was Catalina. She was coming to the end of her exchange year in the Netherlands and wanted to see Paris before returning to South America. I was halfway through a four-week work rotation and we'd arranged an online chat prior to confirming her stay. It wasn't uncommon for me to talk to future SC guests during my evenings in Africa. I arranged as many as I could while there, so when I got back to my Parisian abode there were plenty potential shenanigans to be had.

We tried four times for a video call, but the internet was poor. I got flashes of her face on the camera. Profile pictures hadn't lied. We settled on audio, so the weak connection could cope. My ears would enjoy a meal of feminine tones.

"Hi Catalina, can you hear me?" I asked, hoping it wouldn't be a back and forth of the same question twenty times.

"Hola! Yes, I hear you. How are you?" Her voice was melodical, the accent strong and sexy.

"I'm ok thanks, Catalina. It's like an oven here, but the air-con is keeping me alive. How are things where you are? You said on Scouting for Couches you're in Rotterdam, right?"

"Yes, yes, Rotterdam. Is not so hot here. Raining today. Is 21 degrees."

"21? And rain? That sounds nice. It's 44 here."

"Mira vos! 44? You're in the desert? In Africa?"

"Yes, the Sahara. Western Sahara."

"Oh, where's that?"

"Well, in the west of the Sahara. It's between Morocco and Mauritania."

"Oh, two nice countries. I want to visit both."

"Yeah? I'm not so sure about Mauritania. Not a lot to do there."

"Really? I hear it's so beautiful," she replied.

She either had a weakness for fly-infested hellholes or had confused it with Mauritius, which is a paradise island off the opposite coast. "That's Mauritius you're thinking of. And yes, I've heard it's nice. Mauritania is extremely poor, strict Islamic, and it's all desert. I don't think you'd like it much there."

"Oh ok, I see. The name sound the same. I'm always getting confused so many times. Sorry! So, what time is there? Here is 8:10pm."

"Same here."

"Same? No difference? You sure? But you are far away!"

Both places were found within the same band of longitude, so, despite being far apart in distance, the time zone remained equal between them. "Yes, positive. If you're five minutes late to the office here, you get your ear chewed off. I have to keep my watch, laptop and phone exact."

"Wah, same time zone. Ok is interesting." No, it wasn't. Look at a map. "Western Sahara is a country? I never heard of it before."

"It depends on who you ask, I suppose. It's claimed by Morocco, but there's also a group called the Polisario Front which controls some of the territory and asserts independence. You could say the region is in political limbo." This was going to take a few explanations.

"Ah limbo. Ok, same in Spanish. So, is not clear who owns it?"

Spot on! Maybe she wasn't as ditzy as she seemed. "Yea, more or less." I thought I'd insert a little humour. "But speaking of limbo, I'm very good at that kind of dance, you know?"

"Ah, limbo dancing, yes. You're good?"

"Oh yes, in those competitions I always set the bar high."

"Oh, that's great! Ok, in Paris we will see. You versus me, ok?"

Fuck. Were all my jokes going to fall on unwitting ears? She was still pleasant though. And good-looking, which covers a multitude of idiocies. "Erm, sure. So, on the Scouting for Couches site you asked to stay four nights. You still want that?" Sometimes guests would only put in rough date ranges or alter their plans after they'd requested to stay.

"Yes, four nights please. Will you have time for me? To go out to some places?"

"Sure, as long I can drink some wine along the way. I can't wait to have a few glasses." Gallons.

"Oh, you can't drink there. Is illegal?"

"Well, the region isn't dry, it's just the company prefers it that way."

"The region isn't dry? The Sahara is very dry, no? What do you mean 'dry'?"

It's the language barrier, Victor, have some patience. "'Dry' in this case means no alcohol. My company doesn't allow it when we're on shift. It's for safety reasons. So, I do tend to enjoy it when I'm back in France. We rarely even go out of the camps when we're here. We have a lot of armed soldiers who guard us. You never know who might want to make some easy ransom money. Can I ask what it was you liked about my profile on Scouting for Couches?"

"Oh ok, dry, I see. Yes, let's drink wine together. It will be nice. And I chose you because your profile shows like you are such an interesting person, working around the world, you like history, culture and you have visited many countries. And even give guests the free massage. But we will see about that. I will rather meet you first."

Damn, I would gladly treat her lithe physique. Time to do a bit of light-hearted reassurance. "Yes, I've massaged a lot of female guests, although it tells me I must be gay, because I never get excited by it. I'm always very professional."

Laughing, she said, "Oh, yes? Yes, that makes sense! Of course, so you can touch the beautiful girls and no problem. Then I will definitely have a massage from you."

Oh, yes please. This girl was dim, and her English wasn't the best, but who cared if I could give her an oiling, or more? I'd been unsure about whether to cancel her stay due to her irritating language failings, but she'd sealed the deal.

She giggled, "So, you must be happy with all those men in uniform, eh?"

Catalina was getting cheeky, but I liked it. "Actually, this camp is quite low security compared to the ones in Nigeria. There you're surrounded by huge black men. They've got big ones. Rifles, I mean."

She got the joke first time. I got the impression her mind was more attuned to naughty humour. "Oh, Victor, we will have fun together. I can't wait."

Neither could I. "By the way, what do you study in Rotterdam?" Not geography, I hoped.

"Oh, communication."

Communication? Fuck me. "Oh, great. And how are you getting on with it?"

"Well, I'm currently how you say? 'Top of the class'."

"Oh, ok. You're a smart communicator then." The smartest thing to come out of that girl's mouth was her professor's cock.

We agreed on her coming to La Maison de Victor for four nights and said see you.

* * *

Two weeks later, having had a quick nosey around Casablanca in Morocco, I was back in my beloved Parisian haven hosting Catalina.

First impressions were tantalising. She was a beautiful woman at around five feet six with wide hips and a round bottom, but slender waisted. Thank you to the inventor of skinny jeans. I estimated her breasts to be a D or DD. Everything was in lip-smacking proportion. She also had sparkling cinnamon eyes, and toffee skin. All Sans make up. Nature's craftsmanship, unspoiled. I caught delightful nose tickles of marshmallow and cherry as she gave me a hug hello.

What made her looks above average though, was the hair. It was jet black, with thick shining curls reaching to the middle of her back. She kept it swept to one side, and it hung there as a testament to her femininity. It really did look magnificent. A feast for the eyes and soul. St. Paul—who had hated Jesus at first, but then became his drone after an incident involving a donkey and a large stick—was a horrendous buzzkill in his views on fucking and drinking, but I'll admit his opinion about long hair being a glory to women was spot on.

Catalina's visit was surprising. Oddities of truth trump fiction.

PARIS VIII - SCRAPING THE BOTTOM

> "I do myself a greater injury in lying than I do of him I tell a lie." – Michel de Montaigne

Catalina and I were enjoying a day of decadence in Paris. After lunch in my favourite brasserie, I'd had to unfasten my belt a notch. Many women joke about having a second stomach for dessert; I might have one. I mean an actual biological anomaly causing the macaroons I shove into my face to be deposited in a compartment separate from the main digestive process. Blessed?

With happy bellies, we strolled to the Eiffel. She latched as we ambled, and bare forearms pressed. What enchantments from soft skin. I hadn't expected touching to be such a relaxed issue. It was like we were moving towards holiday romance. God, was it possible? We talked and laughed with inexplicable ease. An invigorating day: the sunshine felt like it was soaking my bones. I was as content as Victor E Fyric could be.

On the Avenue de New York, with the landmark coming closer into view, I insisted we stop for glasses of Stella Artois. To stave off dehydration in the summer weather of course. This helped ensure both my blood alcohol level and mood remained buoyant until we got fired into the champers in the Eiffel bar. Catalina—despite her slender figure—seemed to be matching my drinks. I mean for two I had, she finished one.

We reached the base of the tower. It took some time, thanks to my rambling style. Using legs and mouth. Before entering the lift, we had to go through security screening. The staff were surly. One of the fellows was rude to Catalina. I confess though, I can't remember what about. Alcohol has made some details hazy. It couldn't have been stinging, as we both laughed it off within a few minutes. I recall feeling a lack of malice towards him though. I'd also be frustrated if I had to spend my days looking at tourists beaming happiness. It must suck being a private security guard. Even more so at the Eiffel Tower.

First, you have the French soldiers patrolling, with badged berets tilted to one side, assault rifles cradled, sidearms holstered across chests, as they keep vigil in their body armour and camouflage. Then, you have the regular police doing their rounds. They aren't quite as elite looking, but at least they carry state-of-the-art weaponry, and have powers of arrest. In contrast, the guys and gals watching as you pass the metal detectors are redundant. They may as well be bleeping wedges of camembert through checkouts of a supermarket, for all the respect their positions get.

No matter what I'll face soon, I'm grateful I was never stuck in that type of life. What existence is it to do joyless tasks in perpetual monotony? Worse than death. The way I chose wasn't easy. In fact, it has damned me. But at least I've lived free.

So yea, we went up to the Eiffel Champagne Bar. I knew it was basic—a small kiosk—but I thought we could kill an hour. Catalina would be mesmerised by aerial views of the most beloved city in Western civilisation. I would have some champagne.

Being summer in Paris, the observation deck around the bar was beyond popular. I had to queue for twenty minutes to get drinks, and the bartender wouldn't even sell me a whole bottle, citing safety. Give me a break. What did he know about hazards and risks? I wrote the book on it, buddy.

Three plastic flutes of overpriced bubbly had to be settled for. There isn't any seating there, so whenever she stopped to admire, I leaned against the railing, and the steel grille which crisscrossed from floor to roof. I was far from shitfaced, but the support from the structure helped take some of the burden off my aching feet. I wasn't used to walking so much in one day. Thankfully, alcohol is one of the world's most effective painkillers. And causers.

Catalina was really enjoying the panorama. Fantastic. Problem was, she'd mistaken me for a professional guide. I knew the Louvre, the Eiffel, and the Arc de Triomphe. Oh, and the Champs Elysees. I was aware of their existence. Not much else. I hadn't taken any interest in finding facts, historical or otherwise, about my adopted home. I risked coming across as a fool.

"What is this building over there?" she asked, looking through one of the mounted telescopes and pointing to a prominent golden dome and spire. "Do you want to look in it, to see what I mean?"

"Oh no. No need. I'd know *that* place anywhere," I replied.

"What is it? Looks very important."

"Important? Important?" I scoffed, with eyebrows raised. Chuckling I said, "Yes you might say it's important." I nodded at the remaining champagne flute in my hand. "Can you just give me a few minutes? I'm absolutely bursting."

I returned ten minutes later. She was still waiting at the same spot. "So sorry for that urgency, Catalina. I'd been holding it in so I could enjoy this amazing view with you. And sorry for taking so long. There was a queue. I'm so glad it moved quickly. Phew."

"Oh, is ok. Are you ok now?" she said, handing me back my glass.

"I am, but if I'd had to wait one minute longer for the urinal, the people below would have experienced a Parisian microclimate."

To my surprise, she got it first time. "Oh, Victor," she laughed. "What am I gonna do with you?"

"Whatever you like, I'm all yours today, my dear," I said.

She pinched my cheek. "Ok, no more champagne, por favor. We don't want you peeing off the side, eh?"

"Well, ok. That's sensible." Balls. "Now, what were we talking about before my emergency? Ah yes, you wanted to know about that building over there."

"Oh yes, do you know much about it?"

"Do I? You're a cheeky one, aren't you? I've been living in Paris for a while now, you know. I feel a duty to learn the history of where I live. That huge complex over there is Les Invalides."

"Invalides? Like sick? How you say...disabled?"

"Yes, that's right. And do you know why it's called that?"

"No, but I'm sure you will tell me, the Paris historian," she said, wrinkling her nose.

"Well, it was built by Louis XIV, also known as the Sun King, in 1676. It was a hospital for wounded soldiers and a retirement home for veterans. You know that was still the case even early into the 20th century?"

"Oh, how interesting."

"But what makes it important now, apart from the Army Museum, which is one of the best in the world by the way, is that someone very famous is buried in that golden-domed building."

"Oh, who?"

"Have a guess. Someone known for their military abilities."

"French?"

"No, Taiwanese. Of course, French," I sniggered.

"Taiw...Don't be cheeky, bulado. Hmmm...Is it William the Conqueror?"

"*Good* guess." Shit guess. "But it's actually Napoleon Bonaparte".

"Oh, of course. I don't believe I said William the Conqueror. You must think I am so stupid," she laughed.

Yep. "Nope."

As we continued further round the walkway, I gave her some interesting facts about the Eiffel Tower too. Including Hitler having ordered it to be destroyed during the last stages of the war, but the German general in charge of the city had refused to do so.

"Really? I didn't know! Wah, you love to learn, eh?"

"Hmm I don't know if I always enjoy learning, but I enjoy knowing. As Aristotle said, 'The roots of education are bitter, but the fruit is sweet'."

"I'm so glad I have you as my Couches host, dear Victor."

"You're so kind. Thanks, Catalina." I placed my hand over the top of my trouser pocket; double checking I hadn't left my phone in the toilet. My mobile data was needing topped up.

"It's a very lovely up here, isn't it?" she said, taking in a deep breath and running her eyes across the horizon.

"Yes, it's quite special".

I resolved never to visit the bar again. It didn't feel luxury enough. If it weren't for Catalina being with me, I would have taken one look at all the tourists and returned to the street. It had nowhere to sit, only one choice of wine, plastic glasses—cone-shaped with no bottom, so you can't sit them—and dozens of people getting in your way. I suppose if your bar is at the top of the most famous tower in the world you can get away with shit.

After another ten minutes, she had drunk her fill of the view. If only I could say the same about the bubbly. There were still two hours until our planned night out, so we took a taxi back to my apartment to change clothes and refresh. At least in my solace palace I'd be able to have a seat and a more regular flow of alcohol while I waited on the evening's festivities.

I didn't want to get shitfaced though. At least not so early on. The highlight of the day was going to be a 3-course champagne dinner at the Moulin Rouge. I'd thought it prudent to book the tickets well in advance, even before I'd finished my work rotation. At 175 euros per person, she had protested I was spoiling her. Damn right I was. Did she use SC because she was a millionaire? Just enjoy it, bitch.

* * *

There we were in front of the iconic red neon windmill. Even if the show was disappointing, I didn't care. Cognac had me glowing on the inside and fuzzy on the outside. And the evening was an easy one. There was nothing to do but drink, eat, watch, repeat. Despite Catalina's earlier concerns about me spending too much on her, she was beaming as we anticipated a night of Parisian spectacle.

It was pure fiesta. A combination of fantastic food, glitzy showmanship on stage, and easy company from Catalina made the experience one of revitalisation. My mind was hazy, and speech slurred by the time the final curtain fell. She had only nursed one glass of champagne while I'd had two bottles, preceded by three large aniseed aperitifs, and an Irish coffee after dessert.

One thing to be aware of about the shows at the Moulin Rouge is that, although there are dancers of both genders, the girls strut their stuff topless. For the lower body, thongs are the apparel in favour. Their toned ass cheeks are all present and correct throughout the act.

So why didn't I find it sexy? Tough one to answer. I suppose there are a few reasons why I wasn't sitting for the whole show with the crotch of my chinos in a teepee. Firstly, they're dancing and singing in these fantastic examples of choreography that make the nudity an afterthought. It's not intended to be an erotic show, just a tad risqué. Even I, a committed pervert, was distracted by the razzmatazz of it all. And another thing, if the organizers were serious about trying to sexually excite the audience, they'd have at least some girls with fuller figures jiggling their bits. As it is, there's a uniform look to the performers. They all have similar shapes, heights, and breast sizes. A cup; B at most. I suppose if you're whirling, high kicking and prancing about the stage topless, it's not practical to have a pair of giant dirty pillows doing their own thing. And finally, there's nothing forbidden. Anyone with money can come and see the show. Even little kids are allowed in. It's all consensual. More than anything else, that's what removes the excitement for me.

No such issues for Catalina who had a blast. And she wasn't even drunk. After we'd got back from the Eiffel, while I was glugging hard liquor and massacring zombie hordes, she took a nap for an hour and a half to recover from day drinking. I should have done the same. There are a lot of instances in my life where I could have benefitted from following the sensible examples of those around me. It's a pity I seem hardwired to do the wrong thing. Is that a viable court defence?

Anyway, the party was finito. I was slumped in the taxi beside her. It had been a full day and night of consumption. The world was fogged, my speech was slowing to a mumble. I could feel myself sinking towards unconsciousness.

I felt a warm kiss on my forehead and a hand stroking my hair. "Thank you so much. That was one of the best night of my life."

"Welcome," I murmured. Her words were entering my ears, but my ability to process the information held within them was fading.

"I won't forget your how you say...? Generosity! I try and do something nice for you before I leave Paris."

"Welcome."

"Those dancers were amazing."

"Yea. First class."

"Would have been good to see more of the guys though, no?" she asked.

Whatever. Time to sleep. "Shame."

Then I passed out.

❋ ❋ ❋

Waking several hours later, I was certain I'd had an altercation with an enraged hippo. I was in boxer shorts but didn't remember undressing myself. My memory was blank about a lot of things though. I spent the entire day and night under the covers sleeping and groaning. She went sightseeing by herself. Apart from her popping into my room a few times to check I was still alive; we didn't chat much.

The next morning, Catalina was in pyjamas and a good mood. Having recovered from my self-inflicted alcoflu, I'd got up early and been to the café around the corner for a takeaway. We were sipping iced coffee and munching on huge ham and cheese croissants. Both of us had our sunglasses on as we relaxed in the rattan armchairs of my balcony. Pulling the neck of my t-shirt out at the chest and wafting the air back and forth, I could already feel my underarms starting to soak. I had another slurp and licked my lips. It would be a glorious day for us to get naked at Bois de Vincennes.

"So, you had an enjoyable time yesterday then? Sorry for not going with you. I could barely get out of bed to pee," I said, before taking a large bite.

"Oh, that's ok. The weather was like today, so it was perfect for exploring on foot. Are you ok now?" she asked.

I patted the top of my head. "More or less. Yesterday, I felt like someone had inserted a whole aubergine up my nose. Today though, it's barely a Brussels sprout. I think I'll lay off the drinks in any case."

"Is a good idea. You can't have so many days like that if you want to healthy," she chided me, "but what a time we had eh? The lunch, the Eiffel Tower and of course the Moulin Rouge. Muchas gracias for all of it. You are the most amazing host."

"Oh, my pleasure. What was your favourite part of the day?" I asked.

"You know, at first I thought it was the Eiffel Tower, and that was fantastic, but then the Moulin Rouge at night, mira vos!" she exclaimed.

"It was quite something, wasn't it? I think my favourite part had to be the human sacrifice part. That pool of snakes was a surprise, and I didn't think she'd actually jump in it."

"And naked, too! Well, except for that little bikini panty."

"Yes. It's funny, because, although it wasn't terrible seeing all that nudity, I didn't enjoy it as much as I thought I would have."

She smiled but looked puzzled. Laughing, she said, "Why would you enjoy it? It was the girls. I was waiting for the men to take their outfits off. Weren't you?"

Although not sure what she was talking about, I wasn't about to commit to a straight yes or no. "Well, I…"

She leaned forward. Confusion was in her eyes. "But…you're gay?" She was confirming, but doubt was sprinkled on top of the tone.

Stop. Hold on a moment. My internal search engine went into action. A dozen thoughts flashed through my mind in a millisecond. Why would she think I was homosexual? Ping! 1 result found. Our first conversation, via audio call. Had she…? Ah! Wow. She'd misunderstood my jesting around massage and the camps' big boys in boots. Either the language barrier, or her being a bit scatter-brained, or, more likely, a combination of both, had resulted in this bizarre failure to communicate.

I'd been oblivious. Thinking about it though, it explained a lot about why she was so relaxed. It wasn't because this young hottie felt at ease with mature men or had a thing for guys twice her age. All the hugging, the touching, the cheek pinching, and the lack of awkwardness over my compliments on her appearance, hadn't been because I'd had a chance. Quite the opposite. She hadn't placed me on the potential rapist spectrum, because of my perceived love of man sausage.

Shit. Then it dawned on me her agreeing to practice nudism together in Bois de Vincennes was based on this same incorrect conclusion. Catalina wasn't ashamed or scared to frolic in front of me in the buff, because she assumed, I wouldn't be interested in what was on display. Crap. I had been looking forward with a great deal of anticipation. We were due to set off after breakfast.

This was daft though. All these crossed wires were so unnecessary. I would clarify things.

I put the straw back in my mouth and took a long suck of my iced coffee. Then, giggling, I said, "I think there's been a misunderstanding"—I paused and smiled— "Of course, I'm gay, silly. Duh." I reached across and rubbed her slender forearm. The extra dark tint of my glasses was emboldening. "What I meant was, I love the unclothed form of both genders, because it represents liberation for me. I just felt the nakedness wasn't necessary for the show to be enjoyable, that's all. Obviously, I would never *enjoy* the girls' bodies in *that* way." Damn, where had that come from? Nice lying.

Her smile stretched again and so did she. Leaning back in the chair, she mumbled through bread, "But you didn't want to see some nice asses and cocks? I did."

Of course, you did, you dirty little senorita. "Well, ok, asses yes. I think we both would have liked to see that. But cocks? They would be flopping about like loose fire hoses. As tasty as they are, they're not suited to that kind of dancing. Same as girls with big boobs." In for a penny in for a pound, Victor. "Do you think it would be comfortable for you, having those melons loose while trying to do a pirouette?" I nodded at her chest, then made a spinning notion with my finger.

The adorable little bimbo took hold of her breasts in both hands, squeezed them, then laughed. "Ok, good point. But I hope we see some big dicks in the forest today."

This Latina was really into her chorizo. "Well, I'll be keeping my sunglasses on if you know what I mean," I said, tapping one of the lenses.

She grinned. "I know what you mean, bulado."

"Exactly." So I could look away from male genitalia, unnoticed.

✽ ✽ ✽

Having finished breakfast, with all preparation done, we jumped in a taxi. With an area of 1000 hectares, Paris' Bois de Vincennes is massive. The Espace Naturiste de Paris is a small section of it. We trekked through the main part of the park and arrived at the front entrance to the nudist zone. A sign listing the rules of behaviour was posted, both to warn and exhort. The gist of them being don't complain if you see nudity and don't bother naked people. I intended to do neither.

The site was a bit disappointing. It was only poorly tended gardens, wooded areas and tracks joining them together. No facilities. Not even toilets. Fortunately, we'd filled one of Catalina's backpacks with things to eat, drink, or use for the day. I focused on breathing and wiped the sweat from my brow as we walked around one of the fields, trying to find a suitable area. I wasn't sure which sun deity had heard my earlier plea to ward off the rain, but he or she was taking pleasure in slow cooking my sinful ass.

We had plenty spots to choose from. The handful of people who were there had all claimed shaded spaces under or near trees. There were several large bushes as well. Speaking in botanical terms. We settled on a quiet corner beside an oak, which gave us shelter, but also meant we could have an area for sunbathing close to it. I had to be careful, as too much direct exposure would result in a frazzling for my skin. She'd go from toffee to mochaccino, no doubt.

I surveyed the ground in the vicinity. It was semi-parched. My visions had been of landscaped green lawns. You know fresh cut grass smell? It wasn't there. I sighed inside. I'd gone gay for *this*. A little part of me had died. Turning around, I was presented with Catalina standing stark naked. Then again, a large part of me was still alive.

Eve. The mother of mankind. Vitality and fertility in abundance. Jesus, I needed a cognac. As I undressed, trying not to fumble with the buttons, I consumed radiance. Unrestrained by clothing, her enormous breasts were magnificent. Sagging, due to the lack of support, they were shaped like giant grapes. At the bottom of her svelte abdomen sat a triangle of light black stubble, in the middle of which was a tight-looking slit. Her thighs and calves were those of a nimble warrior princess, displaying the perfect combination of athleticism and femininity. They ended in her beautiful feet, the toes of which were manicured and painted light pink. And of course, the crown of her beauty was her shining hair, black as black gold, swept to the side, draped over one shoulder. A Woman. I wanted to devour her. If lust were people, I would have been China.

And this was my first time seeing her in this state. My trusty deodorant camera's lens had a malfunction, and I hadn't got around to re-ordering. But I was glad this Christmas present hadn't been opened early. HD quality can't compare to what's in front of you. Hoping she wouldn't sense the turmoil in my voice, I asked, "So, how do you feel, being like this in public?"

She threw her arms up, jumped in the air, and, as her tits bounced upon landing, said, "Feel free! How do you feel?"

Like a fat horny fuck pretending to be gay. "Me too!"

She broke out the sun lotion and started coating her front. Giving a greasy shine. I hadn't thought she could look any better. I was wrong. Face, get used to these sunglasses.

She handed me the bottle and turned around. "Can you do my back please?" she asked.

Hell, yes. Her caramel ass was like a juicy, giant peach.

"And can you put some on my butt? I don't think I covered it all properly."

Can I? "Yea, sure. No problem." Toes tingled as I masked my rapid breathing and rubbed lotion into divine skin, making sure no area was neglected. Talk about firm. She could have cracked walnuts between those cheeks. Then she did the same for me. Her hands were silk, running across the whole back of my body. Oh, delights. I was the happiest fake faggot in France.

We laid a large blanket in the sun and relaxed with a cooler bag full of sodas and mineral water. As the park got busier, and people started to mill around across the field au naturelle, her sleazy side knew no bounds. She was sharing thoughts on male bodies that should have been making her cringe. But not with her gay pal. And most patrons were guys, but I didn't care. This was fucking brilliant.

I'd even bought one of those stupid ping-pong paddle and ball sets people always use—for some inexplicable reason—on beaches. I didn't care about showing off my sporting prowess. I only wanted to see her boobs and bum jiggle. And they did.

Time passed, and although her body was hot, the temperature was scorching. My skin was starting to turn pink, and I knew I had to retreat to the shade or suffer later. I sat under the tree, sunglasses still on of course, while, a few metres from me, she lay bronzing her perfect physique. At her request, I topped up lotion on the body parts she couldn't reach. That is what friends do.

We'd spent less than three hours in the park, but the heat was such we decided to return to my apartment to enjoy air-conditioning, a hearty lunch, and a long nap. Catalina had seen how flushed my face was and worried I had taken in too much sun. True, but tantalisation had also contributed its fair share to the redness.

* * *

In the evening, we were both feeling lazy, the strong sunshine having drained us, so we decided on a food delivery and watching TV. Before we sat, I uncorked a bottle of ever potent Chateauneuf du Pape, and countered her tutting with a reminder it was her last night in Europe. She would fly back to Buenos Aires the next afternoon, so we should drink to celebrate her time on the continent.

Vino did flow, and I laid on the central couch which was across from the TV. She sat in one corner of it, lifted my bare feet, put them on her lap, and started rubbing them as I sipped at my wine and flicked between channels. Those hands were warm velvet as they caressed my soles and toes.

This was heavenly. But I wished my mum were alive. Would have been so wonderful. To see her reaction to my sodomite status. C'est la vie.

Anyway, Catalina sank a couple of large glasses, and I opened a second bottle. Into the fourth glass, and her cheeks grew crimson. The wine was staining her lips. We'd watched a couple of wildlife documentaries and then I switched over to a US news network.

As we took in the headlines, she slurred, "Do you like...BBC?"

"Well, I'm not that picky, as they all seem the same to me, but yea, sure. Why? You don't like this channel?" I leaned over and took another sip.

She erupted into hysterics. "You're so funny!" I wasn't entirely sure what the joke was. "Can I ask, are you top? Or bottom?" Oh shit. Ok, this sounded like gay terms. And I didn't know the right answers.

Fuck it, what did it matter what I was? She was leaving the next day. "Oh, uh, bottom, mainly," I bluffed.

"I see. When you last have a boyfriend? I think is been a long time, no?" The question ended in two hiccups, the second of which was stifled by her hand. She gulped again. The glass almost slid off the coffee table as she placed it with a thump.

Correct. Never, in fact. "Yea, well, you know, I'm not exactly in shape for the scene, am I?" I lifted my t-shirt to expose the flab underneath. Christ, I hoped they still called it that in homosexual circles. "I've been on that dating app, erm, what's it called again?" I tapped my forehead and feigned an internal search.

"Kindler? Or you mean Poundr?"

I'd used the first one before; unsuccessfully. "Ah yes, Poundr. I've been on there a few times, but not much interest. And the ones I do match with aren't really what I like. But that's ok, that's life." Said the martyr, with his 80-euro vintage red and young beauty rubbing his feet.

"Que lastima." She looked at me with kind, albeit wine-glazed, eyes. She tugged at my pyjama bottoms. "Ok, take off this, and underwear. I'm gonna do something nice for you."

What the fuck? Was she going to give me a massage? Did she mean take off everything? I tried to sound nonchalant. "You mean, just these? Or everything?"

"Only these. I will back in one minute," she replied as she swayed towards the guest room. Holy shit. She wasn't drunk enough to give her gay pal a mercy hand job, was she? Or even a blowjob? Did women do that for their queer friends? If they did, wasn't it against the whole concept? These were all questions I could continue to mull over whilst taking my pants off.

I lay there musing. This had been a bizarre day, but it was all going in my favour, so why not roll with it?

She leaned her upper body through the guest room doorway. "Close your eyes." Holding on to the door frame, her hand slipped. She caught herself in time, but it was clear her alcohol limit had been far exceeded.

Done deal. "Ok, I'm ready." I could hear her teetering across to me and felt the leather of the sofa compress. It seemed like she was kneeling between my legs. My cock and balls were hanging in front of her. Oh boy, Catalina was the most awesome guest ever.

She placed a silky hand on my exposed hip. "I hope is clean. You need to go have a quick wash?"

I'd had a shower after returning from the Bois de Vincennes, so no lying was needed. "Yea, all ok down there. Everything good to go." I was trying to hurry her along. The anticipation was building to unbearable levels.

"Ok good. Turn over then."

"What?"

"Turn over. I can't do from the front."

I opened my eyes. Holy hell! She was grasping a giant black dildo with a pink condom rolled over it. It looked about 25cm and thick as a... massive cock! Oh Jesus, I realised what the term bottom meant. For God's sake, Victor, you idiot, the clue was in the name. Fuck. What was I going to say to get out of this? Was I on my ass period? Was I in fact a neo-Nazi gay, and couldn't accept black sex toys? Was I allergic to latex? Could I confess I wasn't queer?

"This is my little friend. I bought it in Amsterdam. Is good, no?" She rubbed her finger around the tip of the monstrosity.

No, it wasn't good. And little? You could parry a samurai sword. I saw, upon looking more closely, its veiny surface was glistening with a thick coating of bum gum. She tapped the side of my hip and insisted I turn over.

"Everyone have needs. Is ok. My gift to you." So sweet. It might have been more appealing if it weren't the prelude to being skewered alive.

You'd think I'd have been able to refuse, right? It sounds so stupid, but I would have felt rude. This situation was happening because of a lie I'd been telling her all day. She thought the greased dildo offer was a huge favour, as thank you for spoiling her in Paris. I didn't know what to say in refusal, so I found my-self turning on to my stomach. Before I did, I reached over to the coffee table and gulped my remaining wine. This was for medicinal purposes.

I don't want to go further into details. Suffice to say, I'd sunk to new lows in my quest for gratification.

I'd reached my bottom.

LIGNOCAINE FOR THE BRAIN

"Alcohol is the anaesthesia by which we endure the operation of life." – George Bernard Shaw

I've never been one to cope with the horrible reality which is our existence. I require frequent breaks from it. I tried my first glass of beer at university—black Irish stout—and discovered I liked myself and the world around me better when I was wrapped in the cotton wool of intoxicants.

This is one of the few things I learned from my dad: Alcohol is a companion. Albeit a backstabbing one. As for my mum, she didn't partake after finding Jesus. Not booze anyway. Literary laudanum, however, was guzzled to excess.

Now, beer is a soft drink. I've been shackled to strong wine and liquor for decades. Problem is, there's a price to pay, and the debt I've been building is getting closer and to the time of final demand.

I can feel myself disintegrating. It's slow but steady. My muscles twitch a fair bit now. Although it's not like they do it all at the same time. It's unpredictable which of them will start on any given day. At times I feel a puppet of sorts. I'm moving, but it's not me doing it. It's not scary right now, but it will only get worse.

As well as that, my skin itches whenever I go more than a few days without a drink. My fingers and toes go numb and tingly, as do my hands and feet. I've lost all feeling in the bottom two fingers on my left hand after bingeing in Podgorica.

My stomach is also taking a punishing and is upset most mornings. Sometimes it lasts all day, even if I haven't drunk much the night before. My paunch is getting bigger too, along with my body in general. The weight gain has been consistent over the past couple of years, mostly due to alcohol and late-night inebriated junk food sessions. I can't see myself being slim ever again, except after a spell in the coffin of course.

Hangovers can range anywhere from mild dizziness and lethargy, all the way to borderline psychosis. I've spent some of my most hellish moments coiled in bed, in a cold sweat, wondering if I would live to see Helios ride once more.

And it's not only the aftereffects of excess, but the bad decisions made while drunk. So many rock-bottom lows of wretchedness, strife and regret can be attributed to my excessive alcohol consumption.

Despite all these ill effects, I can't stop drinking. Even as I write this, I'm sedating myself with a bottle of Dulschinnie single malt whisky I ordered from room service. This was at a cost which exceeds most locals' monthly income. The general manager of this hotel is Scottish, so he makes sure the main bar is well-stocked with a range of malts you won't find elsewhere in the city.

My crystal tumbler is swirling with toxic nectar. One of countless brunettes which have made tainted love to me; she smells like cinnamon and vanilla blended with faint dry pear. I'm putting my nostrils deep into the glass; the vapours sting them in a satisfying way. Every drop is a tiny bullet of self-enslavement, impacting in my belly with a glowing warmth and delayed exit wound. Death by a thousand sups.

And SC didn't help these inclinations. In fact, my final week of hosting in Paris accelerated them. I used to have months off between boozing sessions when I was employed in Africa. Half the year in total, due to camp sobriety policies. You might have called me a part-time alcoholic. Not since I quit my job and fled France.

I also started to become dependent on benzodiazepines

around that time. If I can't get hold of scripts, I need the bottle. And vice versa. Going without both at the same time would be life threatening. The shock to my central nervous system would be too much. I've painted myself into a corner; when do I leap for the emergency exit?

Anyway, enough depressing thoughts for one evening. I'm not in the ground yet, so I'm carrying on with my story. I'm still in Yogyakarta. The city is growing on me. Probably because I've barely left the grounds of this luxury hotel since I moved in. The only outing I've had was to one of the small clinics in a street nearby. I paid around thirty dollars for a quick chat with a disinterested doctor and walked away with prescriptions of diazepam and alprazolam totalling sixty pills. By their company policy, the most given on any one script is ten, but there's nothing to stop you asking for multiple ones. Money never gets told to shut up around here.

Aside from that little expedition, I haven't left my room in three days. I've spent about seven hundred dollars on room service. I'm keeping benzo consumption to a maximum of two per day. Any more and I tend to black out for hours and wake covered in spilled whisky. I can't abide waste.

Oh well, time for a top up.

DILI

"The sea is everything." – Jules Verne

Ok, so it's not *everything*, but I must confess to liking it. And I'm talking about the sea. In this case it's the Banda. I'm listening to its waves crash against the shore, as I type updates to my epic saga. Or bullshit palaver if we're being honest. I've flown to Dili, the capital of East Timor, which is otherwise known as Timor-Leste. I had to leave Indonesia, due to my one-year business visa —the one I got in Kuala Lumpur—allowing a maximum of sixty days for each individual period of stay. Once the limit's been reached, you must exit and re-enter to renew it for a fresh duration. I could have flown out and returned at once, but I thought I'd spend a long weekend somewhere different. My 5-star haven will still be waiting for me back in Yogyakarta—the room's paid for the next four weeks—but in the meantime I'm slumming it in one of the world's newest and most obscure countries.

So here I am, on the eastern side of Timor Island. I'm sitting under a hole-ridden and shabby mosquito net, which is secured to the canopy of an ostentatious four-poster bed. Faux-golden carvings of painted wood adorn the frame, and the colossal headboard looks like it belongs in Windsor Castle rather than the ramshackle one-bedroom bungalow it furnishes. This is up-scale Timorese.

I'm not moaning though. It's ok here. The air conditioner is keeping the room cool, the Wi-Fi speed is acceptable, and they've got a half-decent choice of Portuguese dry red wines in their little restaurant and bar. The fare served is overpriced, but the quality of the vino is solid. I'm currently sipping on a velvety Jaen. It's accompanying a filling meal of feijoada pork and bean stew. I swallowed a diazepam along with the first couple of pourings, so feeling chilled right now. The warm fuzziness of intoxication is spreading throughout my body, enveloping me in its reassuring embrace. The bartender gave me a wine glass, but I find a coffee mug is much easier to balance steadily on the surface of this bouncy mattress. Who cares about the vessel you use if you get the pleasure, right?

This trip didn't start off in a content way though. Due to lack of options, I took a flight on a so-called budget airline—In Indonesia, no frills and dry as a 99-year-old titty—the cost of which was so inflated I could have flown to Western Europe for a little over the same price. The money being asked is laughable.

However, it wasn't the expensive ticket which I found upsetting. I hadn't taken a flight in a couple of months. While boarding the plane to Dili, it became clear uninterrupted decadence had taken its toll on my already ample frame size. The ergonomics of economy class were designed with slender Asian builds in mind.

In other words, my ass could barely fit in the seat. Worsening this embarrassing situation, was the fact the safety belt didn't fit around my bloated waist. I had to suck in my gut for the clip to snap together and no more. It was horrible. During take-off and landing, when wearing the seatbelt was mandatory, I developed pins and needles in my lower body. It was almost total numbness by the time we landed in Dili airport.

And, although garrotting myself via the abdomen wasn't much fun, I felt I had no choice. It was either that or suffer the humiliation of being one of those pathetic blimps who need to request an extension part to make their belt fit. It's a public declaration to the cabin crew you are a pitiable lump. I opted for the risk of thrombosis instead.

The taxi I took from the airport was an old banger. Despite the air conditioning being on full blast, it did little more than supply a strong flow of warm air. By the time I reached this coastal resort on the outskirts of Dili, my t-shirt was drenched in sweat, as was my whole face and hair. Fortunately, check in was quick and I was shown to my bungalow within less than ten minutes of arrival. Once inside, I stripped off all my wet things and headed straight to the bathroom to take a cold shower.

And in there, hiding on a shelf next to the towel rack, something caused me to shudder in fear. Weighing scales. I've always hated those things. They're the bearers of unwelcome news. After the incident on the plane though, it was time to do a damage report. I needed to know. How far had I demeaned myself?

I was aghast when the needle declared its judgment. Christ in a sidecar! Had I gained that much? The shock hit me hard. I was in the fat fuck class of society, with no quibbles. What a degradation.

Something gave way inside. I started to experience rare stinging sensations behind my eyeballs as they released liquid. And, with my face and lips contorting, I launched into a fit of sobbing. Wailing, in fact.

My knees buckled and I collapsed to the cold tiling of the floor in a heap of blubber and misery. Leaning against the wall for support, with my head in my hands, I howled and spluttered expletives at being trapped in a revolting prison. How the fuck had I come to this wretched situation? I thought I'd never be able to stop crying.

Funny though, isn't it? How when you shed a lot of tears, afterwards you usually feel much better. Nothing's changed at all about your situation, but there's a sense of relief. Even if it's temporary, it has a calming effect. Turmoil has been building inside me for a while. About forty years. And I've been through a lot recently; trying to cope with it by ignoring, dismissing, or laughing off the presence of demon hordes conniving inside. Intense release of sorrow was cathartic. I've gained some solace, even if it only lasts for this weekend in East Timor. I'll take what I can get.

Since that mini-breakdown, I've resolved once I'm back in Yogyakarta I'm going to cut all empty carbs. It's Protein and greens from now on. No more wine or beer either. I'm going to try to swim more there too. The pool bar will only be utilised after at least fifteen lengths have been completed. And even then, I'll only allow myself whisky or cognac. The odd cocktail on special occasions.

You might ask, if I'm frittering away my health, with an inevitable early death on the cards anyway, why would I be bothered about losing weight? It's a fair question. The answer is because I don't want to spend my remaining time on earth as an obese blob; treated as an object of pity and derision. Semi-fat bastardry is expected in middle age, so I'll aim for that. It's ok to have a belly, but one airplane seatbelts can wrap around.

＊ ＊ ＊

So, let's talk about Timor-Leste. What is there to say? I've been here for two nights, so my observations may not be the most rigorous. To be honest though, with East Timor's history of gangs and violence, I was expecting something exciting to happen. I know it's only been a brief time, but so far this island is the most boring place on my travels. I'm glad I didn't decide to book for longer.

There doesn't seem to be much here. I had a wander around the town yesterday. I was hoping to get a flavour of the country and see any noteworthy sights. I didn't last long, due to the insufferable humidity and lack of air conditioning in the bars, cafés, and restaurants where I'd normally seek refuge and refuelling in a tropical climate. My body is pissing sweat.

Everything looks like Indonesia. The traffic—including myriads of rasping scooters and motorbikes—the locals who are friendly but conservative, and the general air of poverty can all be found in Yogyakarta.

However, a couple of things which do distinguish Timor-Leste from its neighbour are decaying Portuguese architecture, which is beautiful in a bleak sort of way, and churches instead of mosques. And the Timorese population is 100% Christian.

They even have a Rio-style statue of Christ here. I saw it from the airplane before we landed. I couldn't be bothered to take a trip there. I'm not going to climb 600 sweaty steps to look at a dead opium peddler. My mum would have endured the climb to pay respects to her idol. Leaving me alone at the bottom if necessary. But I didn't inherit her passion for religion. Despite the vehemence of pressure.

What else? Dili isn't the lamppost capital of the world. Walking drunk on the roads at night seems an effective way to solve all your problems. But fuck going out as roadkill.

In any case, I'm content spending my time in this rustic little resort. Its shabby chic pleases. The main plus is it's next to the sea. As mentioned earlier, my bungalow is so close I can hear the waves crashing against the beach. I find it soothing. During the day time, I can wander ten seconds on the cobbled path, and either slip into the swimming pool or sit under a poolside cabana in a rattan armchair and look over the dark blue depths, enjoying the hypnotic sights and sounds of old briny. A few metres beyond the recreational area, the grounds extend to the edge of a rocky face with a steep gradient. It drops about six or seven metres to the shore. There aren't any steps to get to the water, and there's a double railing in place with mesh wire between to discourage guests from either falling or traversing there.

Earlier on today, after noon, I sat with a bottle of wine under one of the cabanas. The encompassing shade didn't stop sweat coating my forehead as I analysed the sparkling surface of the blue expanse. I enjoy how the waves slowly build from afar. Like an aquatic pulse. Then, upon approaching the shore, their tops start to curl in on themselves and quickly cascade, exploding into a mass of saline froth as they hit the shore. Just as pleasurable to see is the water retreating into a marbled plateau of aquamarine, teal, and periwinkle hues, before returning to its source to crash again later. It's pretty. Almost feels therapeutic. Or is it the wine?

However, it's not colours, rhythms or sounds drawing my attention. Its giant reptiles. Leviathan, to be precise. Crocodiles can be seen in the waters off Dili, and even on the beaches. I've yet to spot one, but I'll keep trying. It's interesting listening to the staff talking about them. The animals are talked about with profound respect because legend says Timor was long ago formed from the body of one of these fearsome creatures. They're regarded as sacred. Of course, like most of these ancient legends, it's utter bullshit. Yet it still fascinates me. And, looking on the internet at maps, the island does resemble the form of a crocodile. You could say it makes sense, in a Biblical sort of way.

* * *

A conversation the day before had sparked this ignition of interest in the island's most revered apex marine predator. While I was sitting at the bar, waiting on my food being cooked, I started a conversation with the bartender. He was a young lad called Rogerio. His English was broken, but decent enough for a chat.

"Do you like living in Timor?" I asked.

"Yes, sir, if you live in Timor, no need to go another place," he said, smiling.

Ten bucks says you've never been anywhere else to compare it to. "And why is that?"

"Because, have the sea. Can see the sea every day."

Well, he did have a point there. The water was therapeutic.

"And do you swim in the sea often?"

"Yes, with my friend. We swim at Jesus Backside Beach".

"Jesus' what...?"

"Jesus Backside," he replied. I hadn't misheard him.

"Why's it called that?"

"Because, have Jesus. It called Cristo Rei. Very famous here." I could see him grasping for the correct vocabulary to make his explanation simple. "I don't know how to say in English. Look like Jesus. Big like a tower."

"Ah, of course. The statue up on the hill is Cristo Rei. It's quite far from here, right? The word is *a statute*." I said, sitting straight and still, making the gesture to confirm the meaning of the word in visuals.

"Yes, sir, a statue. Yes, it little far. Have a big, big statue of Jesus," he said.

"And the beach is at the back of that, right?"

"Yes, sir, correct."

"Ok, now I understand. And how often do you swim up Jesus' backside?"

"Every weekend, if not working."

"Well, I'm sure he's used to people doing that kind of thing by now, especially on Sundays," I said. The bartender's smile was oblivious. "And is the water warm?"

"Little. Not too warm. The water is good though. But have to be careful too," he said with his smile broadening.

"Careful? Why's that?"

"Sometimes crocodiles. Come swimming or even come on the beach."

"Crocodiles? For real?"

"Yes, but don't worry. They are good. Special crocodile. They only eat bad people."

I raised my eyebrows. "Are you sure? Do you know any people that have been eaten?"

His smile disappeared. "Yes, my cousin. He was swim at that beach down there," he replied, pointing over my shoulder to the cliff area past the swimming pool.

Now I was more than poking fun. I was interested. "That beach right there? Your cousin was eaten by a croc? No joke?"

"Yes, sir. His wife she see it happen. Crocodile take him and did went under the water. Nobody see him again", he said with his tone becoming more serious.

"I'm very sorry to hear that."

"Thank you, sir".

"Call me Victor, please".

"Ok, Mr Victor." Sigh.

"And, if it's ok, can I ask...Do you believe your cousin was bad? If the crocodiles only eat bad people?"

"For me, he is good, I like him. He is very funny man. But nobody know, right?" He pressed the fingertips of his left hand against the centre of his chest. "Maybe the crocodile did see something we don't see?"

Of course, it did. It saw a source of calories. Apex predators know a meal when it floats by. Your cousin wasn't bad. Or at least no worse than the rest of us. He was simply a collection of juicy internal organs and bone marrow in blood sauce, all wrapped in a delightful coating of paper-thin skin. Like a horrible dim sum for dragons.

"Yes, I suppose. If they have magical powers, then yes. So, if I meet one of them in the water, and they swim past me without attacking, it means I can't be a bad man?" I asked him.

"Yes, Mr Victor. Sure", he said with confidence.

I'm not stupid. I know it's a load of baloney. But still, the romanticism of it does appeal to me. Not an old man seated at a bench declaring you innocent or guilty, but the wisdom of dinosaurs. And who's seen more of human behaviour than them? I love the idea. Perhaps I'll finish off three or four bottles of wine, stand knee deep pissing in the foam and see if judgement ends in jaws? If nothing happens, is it some kind of admonishment? Does it mean I'm not evil, after all? Then again, I don't fancy the prospect of being processed into reptilian faeces. Perhaps I'll stick to guzzling booze and watching skin flicks on my laptop.

Even that feels a bit humdrum though. I wish something eventful would happen. Anything. The big green snappers don't seem to be making an appearance and I find myself enveloped in frustration. A hilarious accident would suffice. For example, there are tall palms trees all around the resort, which line the footpaths and public areas. Coconuts of diverse sizes and shapes grow in the eaves of their floppy branches. The biggest of these drupes—yes, I had to look it up too—are soccer ball-sized, with a thick, fleshy skin. They feel like they weigh around 1.5 kg. I know this because three have fallen onto my roof so far, creating a large thud before they roll off it onto the grass verge. I've also seen one the size of a mango drop as I sat on my bungalow veranda. It hit the cobbled path with quite a smack. I can see potential for slapstick.

But involving who? I can think of a candidate. There's a young blonde who walks around the resort in her skimpy bikini. The only women I see are frumpy local staff covered from chin to shin. This girl stands in contrast. She wears a perfume like pina colada, which is appealing for an alcoholic leche. She looks hot. I despise the presence of her untouchable beauty but feel compelled to look at it anyway. Her body is svelte. The legs and feet are slender, with toenails painted white. She has a slim waist, but no abdominal muscles show. The flesh looks soft. Heavenly to massage, no doubt. Almost no tits, but such a lovely rear end. There's a small birthmark on her left cheek—ass, not face—which adds character.

I'm not sure where's she's from, but I've heard her on the phone. Eastern European language, but it's not Russian. I wonder what she's doing here. It doesn't look like I'll get the answer. I've said hi to her twice by the poolside. But, with the Ray-Bans dark black and the face expressionless, despite her face towards me, there's no reply. Not even a smile.

That cannot be excused by linguistic barrier. You don't need English skills to communicate polite hand or facial gestures. Honestly, what's wrong with people? Is it too much to ask for some common courtesy? I wish that bitch harm. No, I wish her dead. It would be absolutely perfect if one of those big ol' nuts could drop from the tallest trees, right on to her arrogant skull. I wouldn't even have to see the accident, if I could enjoy the aftermath of her bikini-clad corpse laying splayed on the ground. Let Shinigami, Thanatos or Mors send her death by coconut!

In fact, fuck fruiting, it's not harsh enough. Even better would be if she were stupid enough to swim at the beach below. One of the island's sacred reptiles could make a meal of her. Beauty and the beast; Timorese style. I'd love to see the flailing, screaming, and splashing. Ferocious snap on toned young limbs. Crunch of bone, tearing of flesh, and dark crimson water. A death roll to Davy Jones's Locker.

Of course, that won't happen. I'll keep hoping though. But does that mean I have a rotten soul? That question shouldn't be bothering me. This is the way life is, isn't it? We all fuck each other over, don't we?

Anyway, I've ditched the return leg of my budget ticket. I managed to find a business class seat with Indonesia's top airline instead. I hope their dimensions will be more forgiving towards fat bastards. It can't be any worse than the flight in here.

I've just heard a bump on the bungalow roof. There goes another wasted coconut.

PARIS IX – BUSYBODY

"One crime has to be concealed by another."
– Seneca the Younger

Yogyakarta got old. I'm in Macau now. The gambler's paradise, as it's known. Of course, there's no such thing. Go to casinos often enough and misery is guaranteed. But I'm not worrying about the long-term, so I thought I'd come and risk a few grand. Any winnings will go straight to my favourite charity.

I'm staying in the penthouse of an apartment building with a clear view of the territory's glitzy skyline. At least it would if not for the storm raging. Has been for hours. Inside this opulent living room though, only tranquillity. The torrential rain is calming. Forked flashes and rumbling booms comfort me. The universe is making it clear to us mortals that, despite our delusions of grandeur, we're no better than ants scrabbling around on the surface of a decaying apple. Our lives mean nothing. So, neither must our actions, right?

Yet I still have dreams about what happened. Not nightmares. I don't wake screaming or in distress. The images play like a movie with an unsettling storyline. I'm there, in my Paris apartment, hosting my final guest. The ending never changes.

This isn't the sort of thing you can talk over, except for with a defence lawyer or a police psychologist. I've never shared the details with anyone, but you're here to listen now. So, is it finally time to have a crack at catharsis? Yes, fuck it. I'm ready to reveal what sent me on this journey. It's going to be a long recollection, so I hope you're sitting comfortably with suitable refreshment. My glass of Swedish vodka is in hand, with plenty more in the freezer. I stocked up on diazepam before leaving Yogyakarta, so a couple of those have been added to the mix. I'm fuzzy round the edges but be assured these memories are prickly piranha teeth.

✳ ✳ ✳

Let me take you back to Paris a few months ago. It was late autumn, on the brink of winter. I'd deactivated my SC account after the unfortunate experience with Catalina. It had made me feel foolish, but, even worse, confused about where my life was heading. And my ass hurt.

It's not easy to discard a lifestyle though, so I thought I'd have one more venture into the world of Scouting for Couches. I reactivated my profile, and, soon after, received a last-minute couch request from a 23-year-old Italian girl called Beatrice. She had been doing a tour of Europe by rail, and, of course, wanted a few free nights in the French capital as part of it. Since I was loafing around the apartment with nothing better to do, I accepted. She had asked for three nights, but I agreed to only one. I'd cited commitments, but the truth was she had no references and a scant profile. I liked her eyes though. And anyway, she was arriving evening and leaving the next morning, so if we didn't get on then I'd soon be rid of her. Inviting her was a minor risk. I'd been drinking since lunchtime, feeling lonely and trying to occupy my mind by massacring enemy soldiers on PSBOX. Some company would perk me up. And maybe she'd want a body massage. I hoped so. I hadn't touched soft skin for a while.

Within five minutes of us meeting, I did wonder if we would get along. There was something uncomfortable about her vibe. She was taller than me, even in flat shoes, but, as much as I'm not keen on that, it wasn't her height which made me uneasy. In her profile pictures on the SC website she'd been smiling and given the impression of having an easy-going manner. In person, she looked and sounded stern. It was unnerving. She was hyper-confident, and it showed in her speech. I suspected she was used to looking down on men from more than a physical standpoint. Her English was impeccable though. She had the Italian accent of course, but it didn't affect her ability to form flawless sentences and choose from seemed an extensive vocabulary. Would have been fantastic if she'd used it for pleasant communication instead of snide remarks.

So then why did I decide to treat her to an expensive meal? Firstly, I wanted to go somewhere fancy, and didn't want to do it by myself. I had been eating at home far too often as it was, getting bored and frustrated. Secondly, I thought being shown extreme generosity might have softened Beatrice. It's not unheard of for gestures of goodwill to have a positive impact, especially if they're of quality. And lastly, spending limited time with disagreeable individuals can be good. It helps you re-evaluate your own level of loathsomeness.

I hadn't reckoned on the abrasion between us being so extreme.

She was pescatarian, so I took her to a seafood restaurant in one of the city's plushest 5-star hotels. Seated at the table in the luxury surroundings, I tried to make the conversation about food. We would talk about the meal all night. Safe subject, right?

"I've never been here before, but the reviews online are exceptionally good. I hope you enjoy it," I said with an insincere smile.

She yawned and replied, "Yes, I hope so. I haven't eaten all day. Can we order some wine?"

Charming. But booze would melt the icicle in her ass. "Of course, I think something like chardonnay would go well with the seafood. Is that ok?"

She gave a strong exhale, still looking at the menu. Speaking distantly, face still focused on the menu, she raised her open palm towards me and said, "Actually, I prefer Italian pinot grigio. May I see the wine list?"

May I? Well aren't we so fucking polite. "Sure, here you are."

She was acting like a countess addressing a sub-standard sommelier. You wouldn't have thought there had been an agreement, albeit silent, I was paying for the entire night, taxis included. All aside from the fact I was giving her a free room to stay in, in one of the world's most expensive cities. What a cunt.

I'd been perusing the choice of wine while she was engrossed in the menu. It was extensive, but, being in Paris, as you can imagine, most options were French labels. I mean, it's a staple food in France, a product of national pride. Why would you look further afield? I'd only seen one Italian pinot grigio choice, at 85 euros a bottle. The chardonnay I'd wanted was 105 euros, so she would have saved me money with her choice, but I still sent a little prayer to Dionysus, asking for help.

She didn't confirm with me the wine or the price were acceptable. Looking from the list, but not at me, she raised her arm to catch the attention of the waiter. And then, because his field of vision hadn't crossed over our table, she clicked her fingers. Four times. The waiter, a young lad, came over in his swish bow tie and black waistcoat. She broke into proficient French. I was impressed. This bitch had skills.

Tapping her finger on the page, she asked, "May I have one bottle of this, please?" That 'I' jarred. Was she having dinner alone here?

"I'm so sorry, mademoiselle, this is no longer available. I do apologise for that," replied the garcon. What a pity.

She tutted only once, but I saw the boy's eyes react. "Then one of—"

"Ah, sorry, Beatrice, if you don't mind, I think I know what'll do the job nicely. Monsieur, please bring *us* a bottle of the Chardonnay Chateau La Monde 1994, if you will? Thank you, my man." You had your chance, bitch.

"Excellent choice, monsieur," said the waiter with a wry smile, "one of our most popular wines. A superb vintage."

"Fantastic, I think we'll need a little more time to choose. If you could bring the wine in the meantime though, thanks a lot."

I could see the disgruntlement. She wasn't trying to hide

it. Drinking expensive wine for free, but it wasn't what she'd chosen. I was irritated, but also chuckling inside at how entitled she was. Had she sprung from the defunct House of Savoy? Or maybe she was a descendent of II Duce?

In fact, it struck me Beatrice, with her tall, athletic stature, dark blonde hair pulled back tight into a bun, lightly-tanned skin, sharp facial features and beautiful blue eyes, wouldn't have looked out of place as a Bitch of Buchenwald-type concentration camp guard. I pictured her whipping the startled new arrivals as they tumbled from train cars, shouting, "Schnell! Schnell!" and utilising her jackboots to kick victims towards gas chambers. At the very least, I could see her goose stepping in one of Mussolini's parades. Yes, if that Italian nubile had lived in the World War Two era, she would have made an exemplary fascist.

Anyway, we had our starters. For main course, she opted for the lobster, which was the most expensive dish on the menu. As we ate, the conversation, at her direction, citing information on my SC profile, turned to the oil and gas industry. She was forthright in scorning my form of employment, citing the damage to the environment and the ruthlessness of the companies involved. I'd been drinking since lunch anyway, so I was numb to her disdain. It was also a silent source of amusement how she wolfed and guzzled the fare corporate evil was paying for.

She made valid points about the rape of mother earth. But that was how I made my money, so what's to be done? I suppose, if I were being a prick, I could have insisted she make the return journey to my place on foot instead of in a petrol-powered taxi. I didn't. It would have been the first negative reference on my SC profile, and I was aiming to keep a clean sheet.

After being lectured and patronised for two hours, she'd helped me feel better about myself. I asked for the bill and it was 325 euros. As expected, she didn't make any gesture to contribute, and neither were any thanks offered. Worthy as the lesson was; I'd had my fill of the food and her.

Back in my apartment, I switched on the PSBOX again, and

poured myself a glass of single malt. I bid her goodnight as I made a show of putting in my earphones and then plugging them into the controller. I was done with hosting for the evening.

She disappeared into the guest room. Thank fuck. But reappeared in front of me about 60 seconds later. Fuck. I paused the game.

"It's so cold in there. I don't know how your guests put up with it," she whined.

I noticed she was still wearing her grey slim-fit woollen coat. It was double-breasted style, with four sets of buttons. There was no way she'd had time to take it off and put it back on. And still, she found it freezing?

I was bored. "Well, you do know you can switch the air conditioner to heat mode, don't you?" I asked in a soft voice, somehow knowing she'd take offence at my question. I was right.

"Of course, I know. It's not working. Come and look." Yessum, Miss Daisy, I is a comin'.

After inspection, it seemed the problem was the batteries in the remote control. I didn't have any spares, not even in other appliances. Fuck it, I was going to be playing Stalingrad Sniper until late anyway.

"Why don't you just take my room? I'll sleep on the couch. The cleaner changed the sheets this morning, so it's all clean." Not true. Dilara was due to visit the next day. The Italian princess could spend the night nestled amongst my dried semen stains. I didn't care. If she complained about anything else, then negative reference or not, I was kicking that bitch out.

So, after asking for the Wi-Fi details, off she went into my room, locking the door behind her. I continued to game and sip whisky. Bliss.

About half an hour later, she appeared back into the living room, not only fully dressed in coat, but wheeling her suitcase too. Was she leaving? It was early morning now. Was the bed really *that* crusty? She placed her luggage beside the door, then perched on the couch to my right. I paused my game again and this time placed the earphones and controller on the coffee table. I was drunk, but still lucid and well in control of my faculties. I leaned back into the sofa, whisky in hand, waiting for her next joyous uttering.

"How's the game going, Victor?" she asked, looking at the screen in obvious false interest. Strange. It was the first time she'd used my name.

"Yea, not bad. What's wrong? Are you off? My room isn't cold is it?" It had to be the sheets. I hoped she wouldn't berate me on my excessive masturbation. She was the sort of person with the audacity to do so.

"No, it's not cold, but...I studied journalism you see, Victor." Ok, unexpected. Plus, she had now referred to me twice as Victor.

"Ok so...? I'm not quite with you, Beatrice."

She extended a loose fist. I held my hand open. She dropped a small black object into the centre of my palm. It was the memory card from the hidden camera. Oh fuck.

A smug smile spread across her face as alarm did the same on mine. "And, I'm ashamed to say, the journalist in me is nosey." She paused, as we both looked at the conversation piece. "Are you with me now?"

I was in the shit. I'd left the spy deodorant on my bedside table. The broken device was open with all parts on display. I'd been meaning to go and discard the casing a couple of blocks away, while keeping the memory card, but distractions had blended with alcohol. I'd been on Stalingrad Sniper for a while, then invited in a couple of cute Jehovah's Witness girls for a cup of tea, and after that I'd got the last-minute couch request from Beatrice on SC, so had gone to get a few groceries. She'd arrived around 8:30pm, and we'd gone straight to dinner. I hadn't even changed my clothes. It had sat there by my bed. With her taking my room for the night, it would have been impossible for her not to spot it.

Over the time I'd been hosting, I'd recorded countless women. And it wasn't only nudity. Aside from Kimiko's wanking, I'd also captured guest couples performing sex acts, and many girls shaving their pussies or pissing in the shower. Most files had been transferred to my laptop, as the amount of storage on the card wasn't high. If I forgot to erase the memory card, it wasn't a problem, as it overwrote itself every 14-15 guests, depending on the length of their washing session. But, since the camera was broken, and it was sitting in a locked drawer anyway, I had become lazy and watched the last dozen by plugging the whole gadget into the USB port. I hadn't moved the videos to my computer. Big mistake.

I'd try and bullshit to the safe zone. I played dumb. "What's that?" I asked, trying to appear confused. My question ended with a nervous swallow.

She looked into my eyes. The only time she'd done it since we'd met. Reading the guilt, she broke into derisive laughter. "Don't embarrass yourself. We both know you're a sad pervert. How many did you spy on? I only counted thirteen, but I'm guessing there were a lot more, weren't there? How long have you been hosting for? You've got a lot of references, don't you? Most of them from beautiful girls. How many files are stored on your laptop?"

That sneer. It made me dizzy. I'd seen an identical one from my father on high school prom night. My tuxedo had been too tight, and I'd had no date. He'd found it hysterical as I waddled to the door alone. Everyone else had managed to find someone. Not me.

This bitch was digging into old wounds with a rusty spoon. Feigned ignorance wasn't going to work. I tried the indignation path. Keeping the semblance of calm, while my head was near to exploding, and making my speech more rigid, I said, "I'm sorry Beatrice, but I don't know what you're talking about. I took you for an awfully expensive meal tonight, and you've been nothing but ungrateful. And now you're accusing me of sex crimes? What the fuck? What the fuck have I done to you, except be extremely generous?"

She laughed again, mocking my attempts to wriggle free of the situation. "Fine, fine. You're innocent. The problem is, we both know your face is in those recordings, switching the camera on and off. I saw you clearly. Anyway, I suppose the authorities will decide. I called the police hotline and they gave me an email address. I sent them the file, along with all your details of course. They said a couple of officers would be round tomorrow, to talk to you."

I could feel my cheeks flaming burgundy. Nausea and shaking made an uninvited appearance. I didn't cope well with this level of stress. I needed it to stop.

She cackled, "I wish you could see your face. It looks so serious! Relax, I didn't really send anything to the police. At least not yet. But I did email a copy of those videos to my friend, along with your name, address, email, phone number, and screenshots of your SC profile. I've asked her to hold on to it all, for now. So, you can keep that, it doesn't matter," she said nodding with her head at the memory card.

Fucking bitch. I didn't appreciate her attempt at humour. And I knew where this was going.

She continued. "It's ok. I understand. You wanted to see all those young bodies. The ones you couldn't have. God knows what else you've been doing though, eh? You certainly like massaging a lot, don't you? Did you make up some imaginary certificate? Anyway, its fine. You're lonely; you're not good-looking; you can't get the girls you want. I understand you. You had your reasons. Now, if you were to give *me* a reason to forget all this...?"

Voices may trail off, but eyes never stop speaking. Her beautiful blue irises were adamant.

"How many reasons do you need?" I asked, feeling calmer. If it was just a one-off payment scenario, I had quite a lot to spare.

"Well, let's see, tonight between dinner and taxis you must have paid about 400, right? Were you hoping to impress me? You had no chance from the start. I only like handsome men in good shape. Look at that belly, disgusting," she said, giggling. "You didn't blink in spending that much, did you? So, I think...10,000 reasons would be a bargain, wouldn't it? To avoid

all the embarrassment, police involvement, legal fees, court at-
tendances, and, of course, prison time. Also, think of the stain
this type of thing leaves on men. Even if you don't go to jail, do
you really want to be labelled by the media as a sex offender?
And of course, when I send it to their safety team, you'll be
banned from Scouting for Couches for life. Wouldn't that be a
shame? What about of all those nice references you've got, saying how gentle and kind you are. I think you need that, don't
you? For your self-esteem? And you also need SC for socialising,
right? Would be a pity to lose that. You can carry on as before if
you give me all the reasons I need. I won't even make you wipe
your laptop. Keep your dirty little movies, you pathetic loner."

The floor was blanketed with eggs. From all my chickens come
home to roost. I would be outed. I wondered what the punish-
ments were for voyeuristic sex offences in France. I didn't want
to know. Plus, other things I'd done might be prosecutable, like
practicing massage therapy without a licence. Then, being a for-
eigner under criminal investigation, there was the whole issue
around not declaring residency or paying taxes, despite spending substantial amounts of time in the country. That would be
the most serious of all. I'd be looking at a huge financial penalty.
Considering the French authorities' attitude towards taxes, it
could amount to a six-figure sum. If I could pay a small fraction
to Beatrice, and forget about it all, then I would.

"How would I give you these 10,000 reasons?"

"You have online banking, don't you? You can transfer it right
now. Problem solved. Just give me whatever cash you've got
too, and I'll take a taxi to a hotel."

"You seem well trained in shakedowns, Beatrice. Did you do an
internship with the Cosa Nostra?"

She cackled, "No, but I did a black belt in karate. And you're a
fat drunk. So be careful I don't kick your ass as well as take your
money. I'm giving you a good deal, so watch your mouth. Is it
yes or no?"

"Yes. But I don't want any bank transfers on record. I have
8,500 in my safe. I can give you that if you promise to delete the

files, and that we never contact each other again."

She stared at me for a couple of seconds, grinning. Fucking crocodile smile. "Ok," she said, "go and get it then."

I went through into my room and unlocked the wardrobe. The safe was on the right while the left side held a collection of protective equipment I'd misappropriated over years in the industry. Safety gloves, respirators, high visibility vests, ear plugs, and so on. I punched in the code and removed a stack of 20, 50, and 100-euro denominations. Walking back through to the living room; I placed it in front of her.

"Oh wonderful." She stared at the pile of money and chuckled. "Just consider this an unofficial fine, for your perversity. And, I was thinking, I saw an ATM in the next street. How much is the daily limit on your cards?"

"500 euros. I just use the one card." I had 3, all with the same withdrawal limits.

"You've only got one card? Really?" she scoffed.

"Well, I have a credit card, but I don't use it for withdrawals. The cash advance fees are harsh."

"So is the punishment for watching naked people without their consent. Now go and take out the maximum from both. I need a little more. You can get 1,000, can't you? And that's a real Croleix you've got on, right?"

I looked at my wrist. "Yea, but it's an old one. It's not worth much." Several thousand euros.

"Then if it's not worth much, you won't mind giving it to me."

"My dad gave it to me. It's got sentimental value." All he'd ever given me was his disappointment and bruises.

"And I'm sure he'd be ashamed of your criminal behaviour. I promise it'll go to a loving home. Now hurry up and go to the ATM. I want to leave soon." She hunched over the coffee table and began counting the money.

"Ok if that's what you want," I sighed.

I walked back into my bedroom. A hint of her perfume was lingering. It smelled like mouldy lemons. Or my nose was out of joint. I looked inside the wardrobe again. My cards were stored in the still open safe. I removed my wallet, took off my watch, and placed both inside. I closed the thick metal door and re-entered the passcode. It was now locked.

I need a little more. This cunt had an appetite. And her presumptuousness; the bullying, as if I were a helpless child, couldn't go unanswered. My system was full of alcohol, but I felt able-bodied. I wasn't as incapable as she'd assessed.

I checked the pile of industrial gear. Lying on top of a box of ear plugs was a pair of chemical safety gauntlets. Like dishwashing gloves but far longer and thicker. I found myself putting them on. They reached to the middle of my bicep. Testing the dexterity of my fingers within the rubber coating, I could feel it was adequate. There was also no problem forming a solid fist.

Hanging out the back of the TV, with most of it coiled on the desk below, was an HDMI cable. I kept it plugged there in case of occasional bedroom PSBOX sessions. I slid it from the socket. The whole thing was about 1.5 metres. I wrapped the excess length around my gloved knuckles, drawing what was left tight between my hands. My entire system was agitated and twitchy, heart exploring new rhythms. I took a deep breath and crept into the living room.

Torso curled over, focused on my cash; Beatrice's golden bun was bobbing as the moolah was divided into piles. I crept further, until I was only a few centimetres away.

I couldn't hold the noise from my breathing. The crush of stress on my nerves was too overwhelming. This was no video game.

She turned around, gasping. I dropped one end of the cable I was holding and smacked her in the eye. The force knocking her into the corner of the couch, she yelped and placed a hand over the injury. Her mouth was wide open. She'd seen me as an easy target but regret must have been flooding.

The other hand thrust into the right pocket of her coat, fumbling. I dropped the whole cable on the floor and pounced. A pepper spray appeared in her grasp, and we started wrestling. I knew if I took a blast, I'd have no chance of finishing what I'd started. I was trying to pry it from her clutch. As we tussled, her legs flailed into the coffee table. Money flapped and fluttered.

I shifted forward and was pushing with strength and weight. Her finger was creeping closer to the activation button of the cannister, but I was twisting her wrist. She was squealing, but had all energy directed elsewhere, so no scream. My face was being bombarded with girlish slaps. This bitch didn't know karate.

With my heavy frame exerting maximum pressure, the spray was turned towards her. Forcing the nozzle into her mouth, I put my finger on top of hers and pressed the button. The gas hissed and her eyes bulged.

Gagging, she was drowning in a lake of spice. It was fucking strong stuff. Even the tiny amount of haze escaping from her lips made my eyes water and lungs itch. It tasted like metallic cloves; the smell was curry made with rotten meat.

There was now no resistance. She was clawing at her throat; face contorted with fear. I pulled the saliva-covered spray out; it released a huge puff of peppery malice as it slipped from my sweaty grasp onto the floor. I collapsed against the couch's arm.

Panting, I tried to get my breath back through spasms of coughing. I felt sick but was doing a hell of a lot better than Beatrice. Exhausted, but I stayed below panic level. Eyes watering, but I could see.

She was choking. Her eyes streamed, and there were large strings of drool flowing off her tongue as she wretched. All the noises and fluids were unnerving, but I was also fascinated by how much distress she was in.

I focused on slowing my breathing, while I coughed and sneezed. Once I'd regained a bit of composure, I took hold of the pepper spray. Those gorgeous blue eyes were ravaged, with the liquid coating her supple cheeks. Terror replaced smugness.

"Extra spicy stuff, eh? You don't look so good, dear. Shall I call you an ambulance?" I puffed.

She nodded her head with vigour; hands staying at her throat.

"Ok, now are you sure you want me to call you an ambulance?"

More rapid bobbing ensued.

"Ok then,"—I paused— "you're an ambulance." I yanked her head back, emptying the remaining contents of the cannister into her eyes.

There was an inaudible wailing. I bet she wished she'd just put up with the cold guest room.

I grabbed a sofa pillow. Teal at first, then changed to green. She couldn't see me approaching as her eyes were screwed tight. I launched on top.

I could hear muffled squeals as manicured nails clawed at my hands and arms in vain. The thick gauntlets protected me. Her energy depleting, she tried to scratch my eyes and neck too, but I reared my head back and kept my hands firm in place.

Noises died. As did movement. I held my position until even the twitches petered. Then, with arms aching, I removed the pillow. She was a corpse.

Damn, strong chemical. I was still coughing and sneezing. I opened all the balcony doors and windows in the apartment and went to the bathroom to douse my eyes and nose. What kind of fucking bitch went around with weapons in her pocket?

And she hadn't known karate. Upon seeing me in HDMI mode, there was no ninja response. When my fist flew, she didn't try to block or retaliate. Instead, she'd reached for the spray. And those slaps had been laughable. Some women knew how to fight, but she sure as hell didn't. Was sending my info to her friend also bullshit? There was no way to know for sure. Her phone and laptop were there, but I had zero hack skills.

I took off the gauntlets and threw them in the kitchen sink. Then, I sat next to the open window, delighting in pure air, and poured myself an exceptionally large drink of 30-year-old Scottish single malt. Super pricey. I found it difficult to enjoy though. The glass kept knocking against my teeth, and the spirit sploshing about as I struggled to keep it steady, despite holding it in both hands. I was trying to return my breathing back to normal, but the waves of adrenaline were interfering. I looked at my watch. 1:46am. It wasn't an unusual time for me to be up having a nightcap or three, but Mr Sandman was keeping away. It's hard to nod off when your entire system is feverish with anxiety.

Sleep wouldn't be a problem for my would-be blackmailer. She was in the painless embrace of Sh'eol. Lucky her.

After gathering the money and putting it in the safe, I topped up my drink and perched on the coffee table, sipping while I looked at the mortal remains lying on the couch. I looked into those eyes again. They were bloodshot, but still had their beautiful centres. Red and blue combination sparkled under the lights. Exotic star sapphires from Mars.

But they were the only part showing signs of blood. Surprised me. I supposed I'd seen too many movies. I was expecting the red stuff to be pouring from her facial cavities. The life is extinguished, but the essence stays inside. It didn't make sense.

I cracked the memory card between my fingers, wrapped it in wet tissues and flushed it. The easy part. There was still the issue of what to do with the corpse.

I lay it flat on the couch. I smelled urine and faeces and didn't want them soiling the rug. The leather sofa would be easily cleaned with disinfectant. It could be said Beatrice had shat and pissed herself. Putting it so made it sound like she had merely suffered an embarrassing accident. But that wasn't the case. She was now nothing, except a potential photo exhibit at my murder trial. No longer a person, it was a prettily packaged bag of blood and visceral, already starting to spoil and stink.

I sat on the balcony, admiring the magnificent array of shining stars. What a beautiful night. The whisky was helping to slow my breathing, and I could hold my glass steady, but I was the most terrified I'd ever been in my life. Even the malice of my father's fists had been relegated to second place.

The crisp air was refreshing in comparison to the toxicity of the living room. I still found my throat irritated, but at least my eyes were free of sting. I sneezed a couple more times before my sinuses returned to normal. I sipped again. What was I going to do?

Dilara would arrive at 11:30am. I could let her deal with the carcass. Tidying away dead bodies was normal in Albania, right? I guessed they even had dedicated wheelie bins. I laughed but stifled it with the back of my hand. You could never be sure who might hear. I would have to cancel her visit for this week but would need to wait until at least 8:30am and call her landline. Of the remaining three people on earth without a mobile, she was one. I hoped I could get in touch with her before she arrived at the door.

I finished my whisky and looked over at the long piece of shit lying prostrate on my furniture. It wasn't going to fit in her suitcase. There were two realistic options for removing the corpse. Carry it in a bag or walk it. After that, I had no idea. Dump it somewhere as far from my home as possible. I suspected I was fucked either way.

There was no bag I had which was big enough. It would have to be a walking solution. I decided to knock back a couple more whiskies and think of the best way to go about it.

The balcony beckoned; bottle clasped. I found it hard not to refill the glass each time it became empty. I didn't want to be sober as I strolled the streets of Paris with a corpse on my arm. Besides, those hours of precious freedom had to be savoured. They could well have been my last.

* * *

I dozed. When my eyes opened, the sky was a lighter hue. 5am. Fuck. I had to make my home cadaver-free before people started milling about.

It would be the classic drunk corpse routine. Hilarious in movies, except in this case with the attached barb of life in prison being at stake.

I needed to create the impression of someone who had gone wild with the booze. I went to the kitchen and opened rotgut supermarket vodka which I'd bought for Dilara. But it didn't have a powerful odour. I looked at what else was on offer for the dead customer. Sri Lankan black rum. Yikes. An SC guest had given the bottle as a gift a couple of years previously. The top's seal was broken but it was full. Unscrewing the top, I smelled the spirit and remembered why. It had aromas of molasses and cirrhosis. This would work.

I opened the mouth of the corpse and poured in the nasty rum. It spilled and covered the lapels of the woollen coat. Perfect. I poured some into my hand and rubbed it into dead, blonde hair, and all over the lifeless face and hands. If we happened to bump into anyone, I wanted them to smell the stench of alcohol. Young people these days, eh? There was a park nearby, and I could follow a route through side streets. I'd dump this piece of shit on a bench and hope Satan was feeling sympathetic.

The whiff of nasty excretions continued from the lower section. I went to the bathroom and got the Ganel Antioch, spraying it all over the back of the body. It didn't help much, but was all I had. Christ, what a reek.

Time to get it the fuck out of my place. After I made sure of my housekey, wallet and phone in my jacket, I lifted the corpse from the couch and put one arm over my shoulder. It was a difficult load. The long pins were an issue. Even worse, rigor mortis had set in, so they were inflexible. The arms weren't as bad, but I still had to give a violent tug to the one I was using to drag, so it would fit around me. The crack was like kindling.

I closed the door and started negotiating the narrow stairwell. The width wasn't great for two people at once, but I had to try. Those legs were stiff as boards, with the one nearest to the iron railing smacking the stabilising poles as I struggled with each step. I cringed as metallic clangs sang, disturbing the early morning silence. If anyone opened their front door as I passed, there was a fair chance they would deduce this was a corpse, not an enthusiast of economic beverages.

By the time I'd struggled with it to the ground floor, my muscles ached, especially in my lower back. And this was a nasal nightmare. Odours of cheap rum, shit and piss were blending and filling my nostrils, and I'd just cleared the pepper spray from them. Fuck the park, I'd dump it in the alleyway across the street. With a bit of luck, a homeless man might disregard its soiled nature, and make a plaything of it. Anything which would throw the police off guard and buy me some escape time was most welcome. In any case, it looked like a 1-way ticket was in my immediate future.

I took a minute to catch my breath. As I began to nudge the communal door open, a familiar voice rasped from the rear. "Monsieur Fyric, what on earth is going on?"

I looked back into the landing and saw Madame Fontaine's withered bonce peeking behind her open front door. The old bag was an early riser. One of many elderly people who got up at dawn, so they could have an extra-long day of sitting around doing nothing.

A vision flashed through my eyes.

"Oh Madame Fontaine! Thank God! There's been a horrible accident," I said, barging into the apartment. "She must lie down at once. I'm so sorry for the intrusion."

"What happened? This is most irregular, Monsieur Fyric!" As I heaved the body onto the grubby old couch and laid it flat, a waft of foulness rose. Madame Fontaine grimaced, and said, "What is that smell? Oh my."

"As I said, she's had a horrible accident."

"Then why did you bring her here? I don't want that filth on my furniture." We could agree. "You must call her an ambulance."

"I already have."

The old woman stooped over the corpse, peering at the lifeless face.

"Look, Madame Fontaine, the truth is she's dead. It was no accident, and I'm the one who did it."

She turned and looked at me with disbelief, which turned to terror as she confirmed the statement from my eyes. "My God!"

I nodded. "Today, I am." Grabbing her frail neck, I fired three uppercuts into those fragile ribs. She collapsed with a wheeze. Moving her into the armchair, I took a nicotine-stained cushion and held it over her mummified face. After a couple of minutes of pressing the pillow, it was done. The emotions weren't as potent as before. Fontaine was a walking skeleton anyway. It was euthanasia.

I left the front door closed but unlocked, went to my own apartment, and brought my former guest's suitcase, along with everything else could hold DNA evidence. Including the clothes I'd been wearing. RIP to my favourite sneakers.

My forehead was a ruptured hydrant by the time I returned into the pensioner's ashtray. I put the safety chain on but didn't use the locks. I needed a rapid exit.

Now, you don't work in the oil and gas industry for decades without knowing how to control the hazards and risks you meet doing your job. The materials you deal with are often flammable or explosive, and the biggest threat is they will be exposed to sources of ignition. If that happens, you have the creation of pitiless forces. I'd gained a certificate in fire safety management, which taught me a considerable amount about how to avoid that disaster. Of course, in learning how blazing infernos are prevented, I'd also found out how they're started.

I assessed the living room. It was loaded with combustibles, and the floor covered in thick carpeting. Any fire in here would have plenty of fuel and be able to spread unhindered. I opened the booze cabinet and looked at all the bottles.

This was going to be tragic.

PARIS X - UN INSPECTEUR VISITE

"There's no such thing as paranoia. Your worst fears can come true at any moment." –
Hunter S Thompson

"Do you think she had any enemies?" asked Inspector Juliette Petit. Stretching the last syllable, she seemed to focus on the response from my eyes, not my mouth. Feeling my throat turn dry, I wanted to swallow hard, but resisted the urge. Trying to get the answer out of the way, I didn't speak with as much care as I should have.

"She was a sweet old lady," I sighed.

"Sweet?" She stopped and made a note. "So, you would describe her as being pleasant?"

As a jar of horse farts. "Yes."

"So, you can't think of anybody who might have been a danger to her?"

"Philip Norris?" I blurted. Shit. A lunch of diazepam and cognac made that joke, not me.

Her stare sharpened; the vision narrowing on me. "Philip Norris? Do you know this Mr Norris? Who is he?" She readied her notebook and pen.

With a sheepish grin, I said, "It's a tobacco company. Because she, eh, smoked a lot."

The inspector pushed her thick black spectacles back in place onto the ridge of her bulbous nose. With red nostrils flared, she inhaled deeply before saying, "Monsieur Fyric, this is not a laughing matter. Two people are dead. Their bodies are burned beyond recognition, and we are trying to establish exactly what happened. Can you please be more serious?"

"Yes, inspector, I'm so sorry. I sometimes make these stupid, just stupid, jokes to cope with tragic situations. I even did the same after my own father's death. It's a nervous tic I have." I pursed my lips, grimaced, and shook my head. "I need to work harder on it. Again, I really do apologise, Inspector."

Humour was going to get me nowhere with this bitch.

It was two days after a fire which had ravaged the apartment of the now deceased Madame Fontaine. The police were conducting door to door visits. The cop who had rung my bell and introduced herself with a flash of ID was an inspector Juliette Petit. And oh my, was she something. As soon as I laid eyes on her, I experienced a semi-erection. Unfortunate, as I'd had a full erection before opening the door.

My porn session interrupted; she had asked if I had time to answer a few questions about the incident. And what could I say? Go fuck yourself, fatty?

"Of course, inspector, please do come in," I had said, extending an arm of invitation into the living room.

"Thank you," she replied, looking around. "This is a beautiful apartment. May I sit down?"

"Of course, may I get you a cup of coffee or tea? Some water?"

"Oh no thank you, I'm fine." She sat on one of the couches. In the exact spot.

"So, may I take down some of your personal details, Mr...?"

Fuck. Questions. Should I lie? It didn't seem like she was going to ask for proof of my answers, but if she did, it would be a big problem. I wasn't a suspect under investigation, so lying might make unnecessary complications. Then again, what if evidence against me emerged later? I would aim for the truth but be flexible in my interpretation of it should the need arise. "Fyric. Victor Fyric."

"I see. Mr Fyric. And this is spelled F-I-R-E-C?"

"Ah no, inspector. It's F-Y-R-I-C."

"Oh, I apologise. And do you have any middle names?"

"Yes, Elijah. That's E-L-I-J-A-H. Do you need the spelling of my first name too?"

"No, that's fine. We have this name in France. Thank you. And you rent, or rather, rented, this apartment from the deceased?"

"Yes, that's correct, inspector." Make her job easy, give her a sense of power and status. She's the inspector, not some fat cow I wouldn't pleasure with another man's pecker.

"And your French is very good, but may I ask where you're from?"

"I'm from Arkansas in the USA, and thank you very much, inspector. I don't always feel confident speaking in French, but your compliment is encouraging."

"You're welcome. And may I ask what you do here in Paris?"

"Oh, actually I don't live in Paris. I work in Africa and live in Arkansas. I just take about three months holiday here, at varying times of the year. I work four-week shifts, off and on, continuously."

"Oh, that sounds like an interesting lifestyle. This is in the oil industry? Or something else?"

"Yes, I work in oil, inspector."

"It seems you have a very good job." I saw her glance at my Croleix, and then at my designer moccasins.

You should try it some time, you fucking flatfoot. "Well, maybe. It pays the bills, at least," I said, with a modest smile.

"Ok, well I know it may be uncomfortable for you, and I do apologise, but I'd like to ask some questions about the night of the fire. Would that be ok?"

"Of course, inspector. Please take as much time as you need. I'm at your disposal." Asked and answered. Asked and answered. Asked and answered. Get your fat ass out the door.

"Before the fire occurred, was there anything you saw or heard that night, which might have been out of the ordinary?"

Quite a lot, luvvie. "Well, to be honest, no? I sat on my balcony in the evening for a while, to enjoy a drink and look at the stars, but I didn't see or hear anything unusual at all. It's just an incredibly quiet building. I hardly see any of the neighbours, and I didn't even talk to Madame Fontaine often. We had a few nice chats, but that was about it."

It was then the Inspector Petit asked about enemies, and I cracked the unwise joke.

"Would you mind if had a glass of cognac?" I asked. Even though it was my apartment, I knew the best way to deal with police was to make them feel important and powerful. Ass kissing was the order of the day. This chunky cow could cause me problems in leaving France if I didn't watch my words. The stupid quip about Philip Norris was a mistake and would not be repeated.

"It's your home, Monsieur Fyric. There's no law against drinking, as long as you don't intend to drive afterwards." She spoke in a stern manner, but the annoyance from my inappropriate comment seemed to be fading. She heard much worse while doing her duties, and I had been apologetic.

Her appearance was of a gourmand. Or, fat fuck to put it in slang terms. Hospitality would be of benefit here. The gesture of it would be enough. I returned from the kitchen holding a bottle of cognac. "I would offer you one, inspector, but I'm guessing you can't accept while on duty?"

She sat forward and peered at the label in the centre of the ornate, circular bottle. "Reamy XO. You like the good stuff. It's not cheap."

"It certainly isn't. That's why it's only half empty," I replied, smiling. I hadn't paid a cent.

Looking at her watch, she pondered, "Hmm normally I wouldn't. This will be my last call of the day—"

"Ah, but of course you have to drive back to the police station, I imagine, inspector. I'd forgotten about that, sorry."

"No, I'll be driven home by one of the gendarme downstairs who are interviewing your neighbours, so that's not an issue." She sat further forward, took the bottom of the bottle in both hands, and eyed the dark amber liquid resting inside it. "I don't think there's any harm in a small taste. I am a fan of cognac."

And everything else, from the look of you. "Fantastic. Thank you, inspector, for saving me from drinking alone." For the fifth time today.

Shit. Hadn't thought she would accept. Was she allowed to? Tutting internally, I polished two cognac glasses and placed them on the coffee table. I started pouring hers and was waiting on a hand being raised in protest as the volume increased, but nothing was said. It finished a treble, at least. I gave myself equal measure.

She held the glass in her palm with the stem between her fingers, swirled it, and placed her scarlet schnoz over the top, breathing in the fine vapours. "Do you always buy such expensive liquor?"

"Well, my dad always said, 'If you're going to drink, drink the good stuff'." The poison he guzzled nightly was two steps from supermarket perfume.

"I agree with your dad, within reason. I've seen this type of Reamy in the liquor store before, but I can't justify paying that price."

"Well, I hope you enjoy, inspector. And, I feel I should make up for my insensitive comment earlier. I'd like to make a personal toast to Madame Fontaine. I'm sure she's up there, looking down on us right now." From the smoking section. "To Madame Fontaine, and also to whoever that other unfortunate woman was." I raised my glass and tipped.

The inspector continued holding hers. She bit her lower lip, then smiled. "How can you be so sure the other victim was a woman?"

Oh, fuck. The way she asked inferred either they hadn't proven it, or it hadn't been released to the public. I leaned into the leather of the couch and did my amateur sleuth impression. "Well, I'm not a professional detective like you, inspector, but Madame Fontaine seemed quite a conservative and reserved lady to me. She was unmarried, and was, let's say, of a certain age, putting it politely? It seems much more likely she would be alone with a woman, not a man, doesn't it? I may be wrong, of course."

"That's logical," she said taking a large sip. Pausing, she stared at the ceiling in a moment of savouring. Or was she mulling over the shallowness of my so-called logic? More graced the gullet. "You were right. The other victim was female. And this is excellent quality." She gave a smile in appreciation and started to unbutton her coat. "May I hang this up? Cognac quickly warms the insides, doesn't it?"

"Of course, inspector, feel free to use the hooks by the door." Jesus. I had expected her to refuse the alcohol, and now she was going to fish for a top up. Was every minute this police officer spent in my company increasing the chances of me saying something incriminating? Had I already given off too much suspicion? Or was it all in my head?

She took off her jacket, and, on her bloated waist, nestled in its holster, was an automatic pistol. A subtle message, perhaps? I'm drinking alone with you, but I have a lethal weapon at my side. It was either a Panther 45 or Fraker 9mm. With the leather obscuring, it was hard to be sure. Nice-looking gun. I would have cut off two of my fingers for it. Well, two of hers anyway. The metal cock on her hip had the power to take life. The one in my undies only the ability to make screaming little shits. I knew which was more profound.

Once she was seated again, the questioning resumed.

"I know you didn't talk with her very often, but did Madame Fontaine ever mention having relatives? Or close friends?" she asked, taking another sip. It was delicious, and so was the irony.

I searched my brain for her viewing benefit. "She may have. I mean, perhaps? Please bear in mind, inspector, the first conversation we had was around three years ago. It's not always the kind of thing you note as important is it? I mean, most people mention family, at least in passing, at some point, don't they?" I said.

She rubbed her upper lip as she listened. There was the faintest of moustaches. Disgusting. "Yes, that's true. Did she ever have any visitors?"

Eyeballs to the sky and then back to the copper. "She might have. I did see people at her door a few times. But they could have been anybody: family; salespeople; Jehovah's Witnesses. I wouldn't like to say for certain, but it's definitely possible."

"I see." She smiled again. Was it sincere? I didn't like the way her cheeks wrinkled.

"May I ask, if it's not too nosey, how did the fire start?" I wanted to see how competent the authorities had been in their investigation.

"It's not nosey. Everyone living in this building was caused a great deal of distress. You deserve to know the cause."

"Thank you, inspector." Her drink was all but finished. Perhaps I was taking the wrong view of this police presence? If she was going to start giving details of what they knew and didn't know, then maybe her having a long chat with a loosened tongue wasn't a dreadful thing. "May I give you a top up, inspector?"

She looked at the glass, and with a small lick of her lips, said, "Perhaps just one more then."

I brought the cognac from the kitchen, and again poured a large measure. There was no comment on the amount, only a thank you. Nice to meet you, fellow alcoholic.

Swirling it, she refocused on answering my question. "Yes, so, it seems, from what the fire department have told us, that it started in the living room, most likely because of a dropped cigarette. It appears that Madame Fontaine and her companion may have been drinking heavily, although that is not entirely clear at this point. What we know for sure is that one of her storage cupboards around the origin of the fire held flammable liquid. The investigator I spoke to said it was a lot of bottled spirits, which caused the fire to rage even more quickly. Things were further complicated by lack of access for the arriving fire engines. As you know, the street leading to the building is narrow. The delay in reaching the apartment with hoses meant the inferno went unchecked for some time. Both bodies were virtually incinerated. We were only able to confirm Madame Fontaine's identity by consulting her dentist."

Unbelievable. She had a dentist. Anyway, detective porkchop had been given correct info by her colleagues. Although the ladies hadn't been drinking so much—especially after I'd killed them—but a bottle of 75% alcohol absinthe had been placed next to each body, with a glassful beside it. I'd calculated Fontaine's entire living room would be engulfed in flames and reach over 1000C within three to four minutes, considering all her furnishings were a combination of wood and textiles. I also knew the investigators would suspect arson if the fire had started in multiple places, or if an accelerant, in this case the liquor, had been poured all over the room. A couple of well-placed bottles and open cabinet doors were as effective. I'd lit the cigarette, puffed on it a few times, tapped the ash to expose the red-hot tip, and placed it on the grimy polyester cushion wedged between corpus crusty and the arm of the chair. As it began to smoulder, I blew on it gently until a flame appeared. Once the pillow was ablaze and the furniture underneath it started to catch fire too, I got the hell out of there, making sure to close the door as quietly as possible.

Then I went to my apartment, thankful of not seeing anyone. My front door was rated to withstand radiant heat and flame for 30 minutes, and with the building being stone, I didn't anticipate any risk of structural collapse or spread of fire through the communal area, which had nothing for the fire to feed from. The apartments were also gas-free, so even though there would be a certain amount of thermal conduction through the walls and metal water piping, I estimated the risk of outbreak on other floors as low, and near zero for my own one, being right at the top.

Smoke, however, was a different story. It would be a guaranteed hazard. I fished an ESCBA from the bottom of the pile in my wardrobe and put it in my bedside drawer. What's that you say? It's a smaller version of the breathing apparatus firefighters use, with a full mask respirator connected to an oxygen tank. It's usable for ten minutes in case of needing a quick escape. I'd kept it close to hand, alongside a high-powered torch, but had confidence the brave firefighters of Paris would arrive in time. I hoped to be saved in a similar fashion to the other occupants, which would mean being rescued in night clothes, coughing, and distressed for all to see. And that's what had happened.

"It's all so terrible," I said, staring into my glass and pretending wistful contemplation. "All I remember is being woken by the fireman hammering on my door, and him helping me through the smoke. I was still half asleep. I couldn't breathe very well when I got outside. So scary how thick the smoke becomes. I was actually in the hospital yesterday, getting an X-ray on my lungs, just to be sure." And milking the situation to get a hefty prescription of diazepam.

"It's very frightening how much devastation can be caused. And from the smallest of mist—" Her attention seemed drawn to the floor. She peered at the edge of the rug underneath her feet, which of course caused me to do the same. Bending, she lifted it at the corner, then sat upright again holding a crumpled 100 euro note. It must have been pushed under there during the fracas with Beatrice, when the piles of money flew off the table. I hadn't taken any time to do a count. I'd collected it, having a quick look under the couches and behind the pillows, assuming it was all there.

Stretching it flat to confirm what it was, she looked surprised, saying, "You must have a very good job indeed if you can afford to have 100 euros lying around on the floor."

"Oh, you found it! I've been looking for that for ages. I don't know how on earth it got under there. Isn't that funny?" I had no idea what to say, but it wasn't illegal to drop money in your own apartment. I was overpaid and clumsy? She smiled again.

Her nose was wrinkling. Something was giving off a pong. She held the note closer to her nostrils. "What a strange smell. It's familiar though. Where have I smelled that before?" She was scanning her memory banks. I had more than an inkling of what it was and needed to throw her off the scent.

"Have you ever had your home treated with pest control liquid? There have been one or two cockroaches in here, so Madame Fontaine very kindly agreed for the professionals to visit a couple of weeks ago. I was told to leave for the afternoon, to let the chemicals clear from the air. I came back at night and the place was still stinking. I had to open the balcony and all the windows. It seems they were a little overzealous with the spraying. The paper must have soaked it up."

She continued to sniff the note, pressing her nose against it. "Yes, I suppose that must be it then. Here you go. That's almost another bottle of Reamy there; you should be more careful." As she handed it to me, there was a story told by the mouth and eyes. They appeared to be in conflict.

"Thank you so much, inspector."

"You're welcome. Do you have a copy of some official ID I could see? And if you'll be leaving the country again soon, we'll need some way to get in touch in case of any more questions. You and the other building occupants are witnesses to the event, and we haven't ruled out foul play for now."

"Foul play? I thought it was an accident?" Shit.

"That is the most probable cause, but we can't dismiss other possibilities just yet. Especially until we have identified the other victim and established why she was there. Now if I can take your ID and contact details, I'll be on my way." She itched her right eye then did the same across both nostrils.

"Yes, sure. I'll get it now." Was she on to me? The way she'd looked at the 100 euros made me wonder.

The inspector took a scan of my passport info page with her phone, and questions focused on my contact details, both in Arkansas and my company in Africa. I gave her mostly truth, as I was a witness, not a suspect, and, so far, it seemed all the immediate evidence had turned to ash. My next rotation was due in four days, but I would leave a little early and relax in Casablanca first. I felt on edge. Was there something the inspector was suspicious about? Was she playing me? Or was I being paranoid?

What niggled was the communications I'd had with Beatrice via the SC website, where member messages could only be archived not deleted. Even if the whole email to a friend story was bullshit—which I still wasn't sure of—she wasn't a vagrant. People in Italy would be searching for her. If the police were to identify the body, they could make the connection to SC and I'd be fucked.

Inspector Petit finished the cognac, stood, put on her coat, and thanked me for my hospitality. She would be in touch if there were any more questions. While showing her out I wished her a good evening.

As she opened her mouth to give the same in reply, she stalled. With eyes flickering, nose twitching, and crepe hole agape, she let rip with a colossal ACHOO! Apologising, she finished what she had intended to say.

I watched her overweight figure navigate the narrow stone staircase. As she reached the first landing below, she looked at me one last time. The smiles had disappeared. Her stare remained fixed on me until I closed the door.

I heard her sneeze again.

Powerful gut instinct ricocheted around my stomach. A nauseating ache throughout my body in fact; telling me the police would find out. It might take them some time, but they would. I didn't know if I was being rational, but I had to leave. It was time to say adieu to Paris.

With a lot of money saved in my offshore accounts, I had no intention of wasting any of my remaining freedom doing 12-hour days in a desert hellhole. Not for a salary I didn't need. I emailed Human Resources in my company, giving my resignation and the excuse of having a mental health crisis. The lie and the truth were near parallel.

Podgorica sounded obscure and quiet, so I booked a ticket there. And this journey began.

I wasn't going to sit around for my worst fears to prove themselves true or false.

ENCORE UNE FOIS

"Anger is a short madness." – Horace

One murder does not a serial killer make.

Problem is, I've already committed two. And now I may well have added more on top. The FBI coined the term and their definition says after the second killing you're in that category. Seems a bit low, doesn't it? Didn't it use to be three? Or even four? I'm a victim of them altering the goalposts. I don't like the thought of being labelled. According to them, I'm a monster. I mean ok, I'm far from perfect, but don't compare me to Ted Bundy or Jeffrey Dahmer. Those guys were crazy. They searched for people to satisfy their debauched cravings. I shouldn't be lumped in with nutjobs.

Five murders should make a serial killer. Seems fair, doesn't it?

I had to leave Macau. I'd planned for a week, but, after 3 nights there, I'm now typing this from a first-class suite onboard Emirati Airways, with a destination of Muscat. And yes, I know that's an unusual place to go. Totally random, in fact. Thing is, I didn't have hours to peruse the flight choices. You try navigating a travel app with shaking hands covered in blood. Murcia in Spain popped into my muddled mind, but jittery fat fingers mashed the Omani capital into the pop-up suggestions first. The departure time was best and it's far away from Macau, so I booked.

However, we'll first be stopping at Emirati Airways' hub; Dubai. And, as I mull, it seems a better choice. The city has millions of expats from all over the world. Might be a good place to get lost in. Even disappear off the face of the earth. I'm still thinking of what to do.

And while I consider it, I'm enjoying this pampering. The leather chair is enclosed in its own self-contained mini suite, with a desk area in front of the large TV screen, and a pop-up bar stationed next to the arm rest. Naturally, there are vast amounts of leg room.

The best bit has been the service though. The stewardess is incredible. She looks like a tall Marilyn Monroe. Enormous tits, even though she's tried to hide them, a nice round ass in a tight skirt, silky blonde hair, green eyes and pale skin, all topped off with a sexy shade of red lipstick covering those blowjob lips. She smells like vanilla bonbons. Probably tastes like them too. It should be compulsory for stunning women to do their jobs naked. And why not? Wouldn't that make me and the Arab guy happy? Why can't life be more fun? It's all blood, tears and misery, is it not?

I think the alcohol's worsening my melancholy. I've been hitting the sauce hard since I got on the plane. My laptop screen's a bit blurry, but I'm ok for now. I had a couple of steaks not so long ago, and they'll have provided ballast. I'll save my benzos for the Middle East, as prescriptions might be hard to come by.

So why have I left Macau early? It wasn't because lady luck ignored me at the tables. Quite the opposite. Both blackjack and roulette gave massive returns. Of course, I lost a few hands and spins, as tends to happen when you gamble, but the reason I'm sitting here with 5,000 USD—in Hong Kong dollars, the currency used in Macau casinos—in my wallet and another 20,000 USD stashed in my cabin luggage, is because, against all expectations, my most reckless stakes proved to be winning ones.

✳ ✳ ✳

My first night there, neither the storm nor my drinking eased until the early hours. The litre of vodka was dispatched down hatch with diazepam. I must have taken at least ten pills. I slept for most of the following day, and was lucky to wake, considering the chemical strain. I'm not sure I wanted to. On the third night I lazed around the apartment, lying on the couch, and, then, at around midnight, I decided it was time to order a taxi over to the Grand Macau Casino. It wasn't a difficult walk, but the weather was drizzly, and I didn't want to be sitting at the tables in damp clothes.

I managed to fit into some formal trousers and put on a black and white striped shirt which had previously been snug around my torso and man boobs. Reducing carbs was working. I completed the outfit with a pair of black loafers and decided to put on my Croleix instead of the Deitling, because it co-ordinated better with what I was wearing. Checking in the mirror; I was still fat but looked sharper than in months. My double chin was less prominent too. Making sure I had plenty cash on me, off I went for a splurge in one of the biggest casinos in the world.

After walking through the metal detector, supervised by a suited employee and two swaggering police officers cradling pump-action shotguns, I entered their bustling floor area. It was vast, covered in plush carpeting, and stretched off into multiple directions, leading to sections each dominated by specific types of game. I could smell air freshener mixed with broken dreams. I took a wander among the hapless gamblers. Wherever people risk their money, tension won't be far away. You could feel the greed, frustration and disappointment emanating throughout the concourse. A wide spectrum of emotion could be seen, ranging from yelps and table slaps of elation, all the way to muted bulging eyes of desperation.

And the Grand Macau supplied myriad ways to experience these feelings. They had card games like blackjack, Texas holdem, pontoon, baccarat, and of course poker. Then there were countless craps and roulette tables, obscure Chinese games, and hundreds of slot machines and electronic gaming stations. The patrons were Asian, with a mere smattering of whiteys like me.

I had no ridiculous visions of winning big. I didn't need to. In fact, I'd already written off the 4000 USD cash in my wallet. I wanted to enjoy the nearest thing to a thrill one can have within the law.

I decided on roulette first. Picking a table at random, I had to nudge through to be able to get the attention of the dealer. The betting grid in the centre was littered with chips. I cashed in 1000 USD and asked for medium value ones.

A few numbers spoke to me, and, as a result, I was 250 bucks down within 15 minutes. The spins of the wheel had long breaks in between, as people kept elbowing their way to the rim of the table and handing over large wads of cash to the dealer. It all had to be counted and exchanged for chips. That was ok though, as I had all night to fritter away my money.

I'm not going to bore you with every bet I made at roulette. All you need to know is, I had lost 800 of my first 1000 within 20 minutes. The last 200 of it I decided to place on the only green number in the game; zero. Seemed as good a choice as any. Everything amounts to that in the end, doesn't it?

And wouldn't you know? Green said hello. The return was the equivalent of 7000 USD. I took half of that and placed it on the colour black. Up it came. 10,500 USD within two spins. I wasn't sure what was more fun: watching chips be slid or seeing quiet envy in faces. Both were enjoyable.

Pockets full of plastic wealth, I decided on a drink break in one of the lounge bars on the edge of the main gaming hall. Champagne seemed appropriate, so I eased onto one of the leather couches in a corner booth area and ordered a bottle of some of their better stuff. It was 975 USD, but life is too short to consider the cost.

As I waited, I noticed the clientele included a considerable number of prostitutes. Beautiful ones, I must say. At least, the slim-fitting cocktail dresses, push up bras, high heels, make up and perfume made them appear so. They were either sitting round in groups chatting, or solo at the bar nursing glasses of wine. When the waiter presented my fancy bubbly for approval and popped its cork, it drew some attention.

One of them approached me as I was reclining and sipping

France's finest. With hair jet black, make up flawless, cleavage shameless, and red dress scandalous, she asked in functional English, "You lonely, mister?" Her voice was low. My impression was these girls were tolerated but not celebrated.

"Always", I replied. "Even when I'm surrounded by people, I feel alone. How about you?"

"Oh, you lonely. You want me stay with you?"

How boring. I supposed she didn't get much English practice from her Chinese customer base. You only needed basic language skills for the arrangement I wanted though. Using the index finger of my champagne glass hand, I made a sweeping motion in front of the seated groups of escorts. "Do you have a good friend in here?" I said with a wink.

She broke into a knowing smile. "Yes, have friend. Very beautiful girl. That her there, in green dress."

I laid eyes on another pro. Grinning like her rent depended on it; she waved, and I did the same straight back. "Very pretty girl."

"Yes, she very beautiful. You want go with us together? Only 4000 one hour. 2000 me and 2000 her."

She meant Hong Kong dollars. The price she had quoted was about 250 USD per girl. I held a 5000 HKD casino chip. Her eyes focused as I turned it over in my fingers like a coin. "You want this?"

Her voice turned deeper. "Yes, I want. We make you happy. We suck your cock same time, mister."

"Nah, too easy. Where's the entertainment?"

"Sorry, mister, I not understand."

"You want this chip, right?"

"Yes, mister, I want."

I enclosed my fist around it and made a small jabbing motion. I also tapped the bridge of my nose. "Then go and punch your friend here as hard as you can. No warning. Just do it. If you hit her hard enough, I'll give you this 5000."

"What?"

"She has a pretty nose. I want to see how much it bleeds." I made a gesture back and forth from my nostrils, to illustrate blood flow. "Punch her as hard as you can. If blood gushes, I'll give you this 5000. Split the money with her if you want."

The girl scowled. "You crazy. Stupid gweilo."

"This is a lot of money. If you don't want it, then fuck off or I'll call security."

She walked back to her friend, they exchanged words, and then projected venom through their pupils. I raised my glass to them and smiled. The girl in the red dress flipped me the middle finger. Laughing, I turned my back to them. If you're not open to offers, then why put yourself on the market?

I took my time over the fizz. Several the working girls found clients and exited the bar, while new ones entered to sit and take their places. I wondered what they looked like when all the aesthetic enhancements were removed. Disappointing, no doubt.

Once the bottle was empty, I paid my tab, watched the waiter's joy as I tipped him 1000 HKD, and headed back into the gaming hall for more action. This time though, I had a hankering for some cards. I took a stroll round the blackjack section. My preference was to play only against the dealer. Each table had 5 spots, but most were full. After ten minutes watching play, two seats opened beside each other, so I sat. The remaining places were already occupied by morose-looking Asian pensioners; two males and one female.

I thought I'd start off with a large bet. 10,000 HKD staked on my first hand. The cards were drawn, the dealer busted, and my money was doubled. Fuck it, I left the winnings in place and watched them ride again. I got blackjack, and the dealer had no way to match it, so my winnings were paid at 3:2. I had a sizeable pile building.

A young woman, about mid-twenties, came to sit in the remaining empty seat. Handing over 1500 HKD in cash, she didn't acknowledge anyone else as the dealer counted and exchanged it. Her shoulder-length, light brown hair was damp around the fringes, and the tight-fitting purple t-shirt she was wearing had speckled water stains across it's top. The weather hadn't deterred her from saving taxi money. Nice big tits for an Asian girl. Not gigantic, but a definite handful. Face was pretty even with minimal make up. No perfume either; that I could smell at least. Pretending to count my chips, I saw she had on plain blue jeans and white sneakers. Didn't look like hooker attire, but you could never be sure.

We met eyes, and I said a simple, "Good luck."

She looked at my pile and, in clear English, said with a faint smile, "I'll need a lot of it if I'm to catch up with you."

She sounded like a native speaker. Nothing at all like the floozies in the bar. From her accent I judged she might have been Asian-American. I found her voice quite sexy.

The cards continued to be drawn, and I lost three smaller bets in a row. The opposite was true for the girl. She got blackjack on her first game, then 21 from three cards, followed by 21 from four cards. For those reading this who don't play, I assure you that's lucky. And she'd been betting high, in relation to how much she had to risk. The result was her smiling and counting through a growing circular stack. She leaned over and whispered in my ear, "I think I've stolen your luck. I do apologise."

The warm breath sent tingles buzzing through my scalp. "No need. I don't have a monopoly on it," I replied, smiling.

The play continued for a dozen more hands. My pile reduced by a few thousand, but I didn't care. The atmosphere of shared tension, relief, frustration, anticipation, celebration, and disappointment was enjoyable. Better though, I'd struck up a whispering exchange with the lady beside me. Her mouth went close to my face, and I liked it. I looked into those light green eyes and made a compliment. Contact lenses, she'd confessed, but the colour was enchanting, nonetheless.

One of the pensioners, having depleted either funds or enthusiasm—probably the former—upped and left. The spot didn't remain empty for long. I felt a heavy tap on the shoulder a few minutes after granny had gone. Turning my head, I was met by a man in his early thirties, about 5'8 tall and almost as wide. No-necked, with bulging biceps and arms sleeved in tattoos, he motioned with his hand for me to make space. I moved my chair to give his stocky frame room to manoeuvre into the vacant seat. I was glad to increase the distance. When it came to cologne, he valued quantity over quality. Head shaved like a marine, cheeks puffy and pock-marked, he had the demeanour and sour expression of a thug.

With his presence, the vibe changed. He lost 1000 HKD at his first hand, and thumped his fist on the green felt surface when the dealer's winning cards were revealed. Even people at adjacent tables took notice when the thud landed. This was a strong-looking hombre, and I guessed it wasn't his first unlucky draw. A black suited security officer tried to exchange a quiet word with him over his shoulder, in a dialect I wasn't sure of, but this chap wasn't listening, waving him away while focused on the table. He staked 2000 HKD and tapped the table, looking at the dealer with fuming eyes. Glancing behind this thug, I saw there were now three security guys hovering nearby, arms crossed in front, looking agitated. The dealer, a young fellow who wouldn't have made a trustworthy chef, stared across at his colleagues in a silent plea for help, and must have received a nod to accept the bet.

This was too much amusement to ignore, so I gave all remaining cash in my wallet to be exchanged for table collateral. The inked bull snorted as the dealer started a meticulous count. He clenched and unclenched his fists, breathing deeply, grumbling things I couldn't understand. This guy needed to watch his blood pressure; especially with me trying hard to raise it. I was given 15000 HKD in chips. I added to what I had in my existing pile and slid it all into the betting area. It dwarfed his risk. I saw him stare in envy at my cluster. The two remaining pensioners, along with the girl next to me hadn't bet a thing. It was like they didn't want to be involved. This guy seemed known.

The dealer drew. Both my and the gorilla's cards were triumphant. Having made 2000 HKD profit, he chuckled and grunted. I then had a small fortune pushed across to me in a tray. He looked at what I'd won, and then started speaking to the girl as if I were invisible. With an oak branch arm laid across my table section, his bulky shoulder forced me to lean backwards so they could have a back and forth. What a prick.

She looked at my watch, put a silky hand on my forearm and said, "Do you want to grab a drink? Or maybe try our luck at a different kind of game?" Her eyes spoke urgency.

"Yea, sure. Why not both? I mean, this is a casino, not a Bible study group, right?"

I stared at the hoodlum's 4000 HKD with disdain, then tipped the surprised dealer the same amount. Jutting my elbow for shared departure, the young woman interlinked and off we went. I could feel daggers boring into my back.

We visited the cashier and I changed plastic for paper. It was much easier to have it all folded in my pockets than in a tray. Both legs of my trousers were bulging by the time the transaction was over.

"Where first then? Drink? Or more gaming?" I asked.

"I'd like a chilled beer. It feels so hot in here," she replied. Taking my hand in hers, she placed the back of it against her cheek. "See? I'm boiling. Must be the excitement from the cards." The temperature of her skin felt normal, and it was baby soft too.

We approached the watering hole I'd previously been in. It was teeming with boisterous gamblers and escorts feigning interest in what they had to slur. "This place is ok, although I think we'll have to shout."

She peered inside, scanning the bar's patrons. "The cream of skanks and jerks. Let's see if there's anywhere quieter upstairs?"

This woman had poetry inside her. "Sounds good. Lead on my dear."

We found an open-air place on the second floor. Busy, but with noise levels low enough for a relaxed conversation.

"Are you sure you only want a beer? I'm in a champagne mood tonight."

"I love champagne, but I honestly can't afford it."

I tutted. "I'm going to treat you, of course."

She tilted her head to the side. "Come on, you don't have to do that."

"I know I don't, but I want to drink champagne. What kind of an asshole am I going to look like, sitting here with a bottle of bubbly while you drink beer?"

"Well, if you insist. But it's so expensive." She looked at the wine list. "The cheapest one is 1200."

I smirked and said, "Do you think we're going to drink that mediocre piss with all this cash in my pockets?" I called over the waiter and ordered a bottle of what I'd had earlier.

"Wow, that's a fancy one. Are you sure you want to share it with me?"

"Life is unbelievably short. I'd like to drink fine champagne with a new friend."

She smiled "Well, that is very generous of you. Thanks. But I think I should tell you something..."

Oh shit. Was she about to ruin my good mood? "Ok..."

"My name. It's Jen." She laughed, as if reading my mind.

"I think you like to tease, Jen. And I'm Victor. It's nice to meet you."

"Congratulations on winning so much. I only have a few chips left. You stole your luck back from me at the table."

"It's not the money that's important. It's the thrill. Oh, and what did that blockhead say to you?"

She was hesitant and brushed the question off. "Not important, but I know those tattoos. He was a Triad. I'm guessing part of the Chung Clan. They're the main one in Macau. It's best not to mess with those guys. Why sit next to a man like that, when we have all these other places to choose from?"

"Triad? No shit? I thought they were only in Hong Kong?"

"Wherever there's money to be made, you'll find them." She raised her palms upwards and pointed to the bustle around us. "Welcome to Macau."

The bubbly arrived and we made small talk. She was 23, from a Chinese city on the border called Zhuhai. Her English ability wasn't because of dual nationality or international study, but from hundreds of television shows, movies, and songs she'd watched and listened to since her childhood. She was vague about her job. Financial adviser of some sort, specialising in risk management. Whatever, I was enjoying the tautness of her t-shirt across those ample breasts.

We finished the bottle, and then played craps and more roulette. Her luck fizzled as mine flamed. I gifted chips so she could place bets. The understanding being if she won then we'd split it. I didn't care about profits though. Sometimes it's nice to share a moment.

When it got to 5am her eyes examined my watch again, and she said, "Do you have any alcohol in your hotel room? This place is starting to hurt my ears."

Sounded like a plan. "I've got some vodka and beers. We could watch a movie and have a drink? I'm not sure what TV channels they've got, but there are some movies on my laptop."

"That sounds nice. Let's go."

Cashing out again, I had 200,000 HKD in total. It was a colossal profit. I'd come not giving a hoot about winning, but the Gods love their irony. It was a large amount of moolah, and she was staring as the cashier counted it on his side of the glass. I felt the need for one last clarification before we left. "Look, Jen, I'm sure you're a nice girl, so please don't be angry when I say I'm not interested in being a customer. I wouldn't normally say anything as you seem like a genuine person, but this place is full of professionals. I just wanted to be clear on that."

"It's ok, I understand. There are a lot of whores in here. And I'll clarify for you: I don't make money from sleeping with men. Also, you mentioned a drink and a movie. We didn't talk about something else. Don't go expecting anything, ok?" Her tone was assertive as she smiled and tousled my hair.

"Don't worry. I won't." Expectations were building.

❊ ❊ ❊

Stepping outside, the sky was free of clouds and starting to turn blue. The taxi to the apartment took only a few minutes. We entered the lobby and went past the reception desk. It was manned by a solitary security guard who was so proficient at his job he could do it with eyes closed. Lift access was supposed to be authorised by swiping your room card, but the reader wasn't working, so I pressed the button for the penthouse suite.

"I hope you don't have enemies," giggled Jen.

I opened the door and switched on the lights of the spacious open-plan residence, expecting her to be impressed. She wasn't. Odd. The place was fucking beautiful.

"Vodka or beer?" I asked.

"Why not both? This isn't a Bible study group, is it?" she quipped.

She sat on the suede brown couch, looking at the Macau skyline. I poured her a shot of chilled vodka and popped the top off a 33cl bottle of lager, placing them in front of her on the glass coffee table. She took the hard liquor and knocked it all back with a glug of beer. I gave a refill. This girl had had some practice with the sauce.

"Can I take off my shoes? My feet are aching, and this rug looks so soft."

Removal of clothing did not require permission. "Sure, just feel like you're at home."

She took off her sneakers and placed them under the table. Her bare feet were toffee brown, small, with the dainty toenails painted black. I wanted to get my hands on them. "If they're really sore, I could massage them for you?" The offer was clumsy, but at least acceptance would be a good sign of possibilities to come.

"Oh, that sounds nice. Do you have oil?"

Result. Although, I hadn't been expecting to give a massage. "No, but there's some moisturising lotion in the bathroom. It's mild stuff. I think that'll do the job."

"Sounds great." She knocked back the vodka in one and chased it with beer. "Can I have one more please? It's really nice from the freezer, isn't it?"

I gave her another. She was going through it quick. What the hell, I'd go for the gold. "And if you have sore legs, I can do those too. I mean if you feel comfortable."

"Well, if it's not too much trouble for you?"

I think I can dig deep for the energy. "It's ok, as long as it'll help you feel better."

"Great, shall I take my jeans off?"

I made a pretence at pondering. "Hmm, yes I think that's probably easiest." Ole, ole, ole, ole!

She tutted at herself. "Shit, do you mind if I message my brother quickly? He'll be wondering where I am. Is it ok to let him know the address of this place? I don't want him to worry."

"Of course, no problem. I'll go and get the lotion. Do you want to go ahead and take your jeans off?" Get 'em off, get 'em off, get 'em off.

She didn't answer. Glued to the messenger on her phone, she asked, "Are these the Guangdong Dragon Apartments? Or Guangdong Garden?" She glanced out of the window and saw a landmark confirming the answer.

I felt like I was with a minor under curfew, except a child wouldn't be familiar with different accommodation used by casino goers. While continuing to stare at her phone in one hand, she slipped her trainers back on. Her distant gaze wandered somewhere around my foot level. "This is awkward, Victor."

"What's awkward? I'm confused here. I thought we were having an enjoyable time?"

"Yes, that's the problem. Time. I was just talking to my brother. He says, because you've taken up my time, you owe him money..."

I laughed, "Good one! My kind of humour."

Mirth wasn't reflected in her face.

"You're serious?"

She nodded her head.

"Let me get this straight, ok, because I'm really confused. Your brother wants money because I've been spending time with you? That's quite an unusual business model he's got."

"Yes, he's so weird, right?"

"Yes, weird. That's what I'm thinking. Isn't that weird? I thought I'd met a nice, respectable woman and now I'm being asked for money because I spent time pouring her my champagne. Just what I was thinking; how weird."

I felt my temperature rising. I tried deep breathing, in the hopes of keeping my blood to a simmer rather than a boil. Agitating jolts pulsed through my body, from skull to toes, caused by the lightning which had struck yet again in my life. "I was pretty clear, wasn't I? About not wanting to be a customer. I thought I'd made that clear."

"Yes, and I said I don't sleep with men for money. I don't. It's just my brother; he thinks if people spend time with his sister, they should pay." Her eyes danced around, avoiding contact with mine.

I gave a deep sigh, walked over to the breakfast bar, and poured myself a shot of vodka. The glass spilled over. I necked it and continued to focus on my breathing.

"Your brother, eh? Are you really going to keep insulting my intelligence, Jen? Is your name even Jen? Fuck, who cares anyway. I can't trust a word you say now. Get out. You make me sick. It's people like you who fucked my life in the first place. I'm giving you one chance. Go. Now!"

She shook her head. "I can't leave without the money he wants. You should pay. It'll be a lot easier if you pay. You have a lot, and you said yourself it's not important" she said, nodding in the direction of my stuffed trouser pockets.

"Why don't I wake the security guard and have him call the police?" I had absolutely no intention of involving the law but scaring her off was worth a try. My stress levels were near to breaking point, and I could feel the tantrum building in me. It had to dissipate one way or another.

"Don't do that," she pleaded with theatrical concern. "Believe me, my brother doesn't care about police. And they'll take forever to come here. All they'll do is identify your body." Our bodies, my dear.

"And how much does your brother want?"

"20,000."

"20,000?" I exclaimed. "I could have fucked all the escorts in that bar for 20,000. You expect me to give you the same for a bit of whispering and chit chat?"

She continued the act of helpless mediator. "I know, I know it's a lot. He wouldn't normally ask for so much, but he made me say exactly how much you won. He knows you have a lot of cash. Sorry. Also, when you tipped the blackjack dealer 4000, you really pissed him off."

Oh, shit. "Hold on. He was one of the old guys at the table?"

"No, he's not old."

Oh, fuck. "You mean that fucking ape with the tattoos is your pimp?"

"He's not an ape; you just made him angry. You acted like money was nothing, so the tax is higher than usual."

"Tax? So now it's a tax? And if I don't pay this tax?"

"Please pay me what he wants, and I'll go. And he's not my pimp. I'm not a whore."

"Yea, whores actually provide a service. At least the girls in that bar are up front with men. You're a fucking honey trap. Fucking snake." My voice was shaking; my brow starting to bead with sweat.

Her eyelashes fluttered in rhythm with the insults, but she was focused on pay day. "Please. He said if I don't confirm you've paid within 15 minutes, he's coming over here. You don't want that. He's an extremely dangerous man. And he really is one of the Chung Triads. He might bring more people with him. I don't want to see you get hurt."

I took another deep breath, but it wasn't helping. "20,000, eh? And you go right now, yes?"

"Yes, I'll go, and you can forget about all this. Shall I tell him you'll pay?"

I fished a thick wad of 1000 HKD notes from my pocket. Thumbing through and stopping at 20, I kept them in my left and put the rest back.

My hand was trembling as I held the money. I said, "You can tell him—"

She started to type on her phone. "Ok, that's the best decision, Vi—"

"You didn't let me finish."

"What?"

"You can tell him to go fuck himself. I don't pay tax. That's one of my things. I don't pay it to governments; I'm not paying it to that fucking gorilla." I folded and replaced it.

She changed, as if flicked by a switch. "Fine then if that's what you want. You're going to be sorry though." She typed on her phone. "Ok, he's coming over. You could have just paid. Do you have health insurance?" Her inner bitch was revealing itself.

"Does he?"

She shook her head. "You don't know who you're dealing with, you idiot." The pot to the kettle did speak.

I pointed to the vodka. "Shall we have another drink while we wait? It'll help."

"Nothing's going to help you now."

"I meant with the pain."

"What pa—"

I strode across and dragged her off the couch by the hair. She shrieked as I lifted and slammed her beautiful face onto the glass coffee table with a mighty WHAM! There was a crunching sound. She staggered, groaning, then stumbled a couple of steps and fell to her knees. The glazed material was toughened, so it hadn't shattered, but there was now a large crack running from the edge to the centre. The white cashmere rug was sprinkled with red. Still buckled over and dazed, she spat blood and saliva into her palm. Iron and salt tainted the air.

She stared into the red mess pooled in her shaking hand. "Ma teef," she mumbled. Beginning to sob, she repeated, "You baschtard. Ma teef." Oh yeah, looked like the two big front ones?

I took a fistful of hair again, yanked it and looked in her bloody mouth. Yep, both gone. The ridiculousness was hard to bear. I started wheezing, trying to hold back the tears. Her silky brown locks firmly gripped in my left hand, I teetered, clutching my ribs with my right. I couldn't believe how stupid she looked. "From minx to meth hag in 10 seconds, eh?"

It was hilarious, but I wanted to teach her a more serious lesson. She was only needing to go to the dentist, but my mind was filling with visions of the morgue. I marched the cunt to the closest bathroom, kicked her feet from under her, lifted the toilet seat, put her arm in a half-nelson, and shoved her head into the bowl water. It smacked off the ceramic, and the liquid sploshed as she struggled. I counted to ten—which feels much longer if your nostrils and mouth are immersed in liquid —and plucked. Gasping, spluttering, chest heaving, she sucked in the precious air. Unable to break free from the hold I had, she pleaded.

"Please!"

"You know, Jen," I hissed in her ear, "some people don't see toilets as hazards."

"Please, Victor!" she gasped and coughed.

"Despite all the piss, shit and other nasty things that go down there, people don't always consider the risks involved in using a toilet. Bacteria like E. coli, for example. That bowl your head has just been in, could be crawling with the stuff. It can kill you; you know. If you don't use the right disinfectant, and plenty of it, those nasty germs can spread all over your bathroom. You swallowed some of that water, didn't you? Let's hope they clean it regularly."

Again. Gurgling and gasping. I could hear the muffled squeals in the water. I waited longer the second time before lifting her head. Even though she was barely conscious, I continued with her education. "You see, Jen, or whatever the fuck your name is, even something seemingly harmless that you use every day, like this toilet, can be a hazard if you interact with it in a way it wasn't intended to be. I mean, did you ever imagine you might drown in a fucking toilet? No, because you don't see them as dangerous, right? You sit on them and shit; never thinking what you're shitting on might one day fucking kill you."

Talking of shit, she looked like a hammered piece of it. I was done with Jen. I shoved her face into the bowl. The underwater noises were growing fainter. Here endeth the lesson.

We were interrupted by a hard thumping on the apartment door. I let go of the soggy bitch and her body collapsed onto the tiles. I wasn't sure if she was dead, but I had more important things to worry about.

Approaching the entrance, watching the wood shake, I looked through the glass peep hole. Fuck. Mr Chung was already here. He was alone. Not so good was the expression of fury on the front of his melon head.

While dealing with Jen, a mist had enveloped. I'd forgotten about the impending arrival of her supervisor. And now he'd intruded onto the premises, unchallenged. Frankly, building security had room for improvement. This hulk pounding and shouting to get in was going to send my stress levels into the stratosphere. The penthouse was the only apartment at the top, and the floor below it had the swimming pool, which was closed for maintenance. It was me and him.

Continuing to peer through the tiny circular window, I saw him stop using his fist and start to kick and shoulder barge the door. I had to move my eye further away to prevent the wood shuddering into it. The lock was sturdy but wouldn't hold much longer. I'd try verbal warnings before having to take on this bull mano eh mano.

"Hey! Fuck off, you Macanese prick!" My word smithery wasn't at its finest during confrontations like these.

I saw him pause. I think he was processing the English. Then he shouted, "Hey! Hey, what you say? Fuck you! I not Macanese! I Chinese!"

"Ok, fine, so I was half-right! Fuck off!"

"Hey, fuck you! I want money, gweilo!"

"Fuck off or I'll kill your little bitch!" He didn't want to risk seeing her hurt, did he?

"I not care! I fucking kill you!" Maybe not.

Fail. He continued cursing, but in his own language. The kicking and barging resumed, this time with more urgency.

This guy was a bruiser. I knew beating him in a fair fight wasn't going to happen. I needed a weapon to even the odds. The nearest choice was the vodka bottle. I tried a couple of swings. No good; I couldn't get a firm grip. I moved round the breakfast bar to the kitchen worktop. Knives. The classic weapon. There were six. Varied sizes and as sharp as you would expect. But they were all-metal including their handles. I tried a smaller one, being lighter and more versatile, and swiped and stabbed into the air. Not bad at all, but stress had caused my palms to drip and fingers to pucker. The liquid was relentless. How slippery they had become was made clear when grasping the smooth stainless steel to the hilt. How easily would the knife be knocked or pried from my hand and used against me?

The door juddered again. Not long now until that maniac was in there with me. I slid the blade into the back pocket of my trousers; keeping the handle exposed for easy grabbing. I would make use of the element of surprise, rather than entering the melee with him focused on it. Standing on the lever to open the bin, I dropped all the knives into it. I didn't need to know how sweaty his hands were.

My face coated in perspiration, I kept opening cupboards, looking for something heavy I could smack him with, or even throw before plunging the knife into his guts. I found a large frying pan with a long, thick rubber handle. I gave it a dance. Both the weight and grip were solid. It had a much longer reach than the kitchen knife and would be able to bludgeon from afar.

Under the pressure of an imminent bout of vicious combat with a 'roid raging Triad, my mind wasn't clear. The washing up liquid was though. There was a full bottle of it beside the sponges on the sink. The colour of water. Whatever happened to good old green or yellow? If you were washing the dishes and spilled some on the floor, you wouldn't even see it. That's what you call a slip hazard.

There was yet another forceful impact, causing the lock to

partially dislocate, wood splintering as it did so. I moved to the edge of the rug. With the frying pan in my right hand and sneaky stab weapon hidden, I held my breath for the inevitable.

This is where the special forces combat training would prove itself useful. If only I'd had some.

The door flew open, still on its hinges, but battering off the adjacent wall due to the force of the hit. Chung Chunk stood in the archway. The oversized pectorals expanding and contracting, the face covered in sweat, and veins bulging from his sinewy arms all told the story of a man who was desperate to meet me.

My chances of leaving the apartment unscathed were low, but at least he wasn't armed.

Fuming, eyes alight with bloodlust, he fished into his pocket and slid a pair of metal knuckle dusters over his left fist. Great. I tightened my grasp on the frying pan, and he slapped his hands together, ball and catcher style.

The friction in the atmosphere was palpable.

Although, unfortunately for my attacker, there was none to be found under his feet. Friction, I mean. Which became obvious when he charged at me across the smooth white tiles. I'd squirted washing up liquid onto them. He skidded, to beside me, and fell, smacking his elbow off the floor. My feet planted on firm rug; I swung a haymaker which battered off the side of his head. The clang of metal on bone sang throughout the apartment. Oh, the delicious melodies of a humble kitchen utensil!

A tough nut to crack though. Dazed, yes, but far from done. Full of malicious energy, he started picking himself up; struggling to gain a steady footing on the slippery surface. As he clambered to crouching height, I smacked him again with another frying fist. As I type this, my wrist still aches.

Anyway, he groaned and fell back onto his ass. Intending to give him one final wallop before driving the knife deep, I overstepped, slid on the liquid, and found myself on one knee. We were face to face.

He grabbed my hair and lashed out with his metal-covered fist, screaming as he did so. Even though it was a half-punch delivered from a sitting position, the pain from the knuckle duster connecting with my socket was sickening. I felt faint, and the vison in my injured eye went blurry. My immediate reaction was twofold. I rose my left palm to block the next strike and pivoted my right side to whack him with the pan once again. He collapsed on his back, and I crawled to the secured flooring. I stood looking over him as he made a feeble attempt to rise. Panting from the exertion and enveloped in sweat; I had enough left in my tank to give him one final resounding bash to his crown. Movement stopped. He was flat out. The eyelids fluttered; body twitched. Then nothing. His legs were open wide enough for me to kick him in the testicles, so, naturally, I indulged. It didn't register on his face. The frying pan appeared to have cooked his goose.

"You stupid fucking chink! You lost to soap! You fucking germ!" I shouted, between gasps. "You fucking chink bastard! Coming here to rob me! Fucking thief!" And yes, dear readers, I know what you're thinking. Isn't that so messed up? I'd committed grievous bodily harm with a heavy metal object, and all you can focus on is me using the word chink. Shame on you!

Racial tirades finished; it was time to cut short the career of this Triad casino grifter. At least, it would have been, had I not felt somebody fumbling at my lower back. I spun around to be met by Jen clutching the knife. She was wild-eyed and pale, which was understandable, considering she'd been on the verge of perishing in a toilet bowl.

Unsteady on her feet, with body shaking, hair darkened and straggly from the water, she started making defensive jabs in my direction. Her eyes darted back and forth between the open door and I as she stumbled towards it.

Backing away, I motioned with my eyes to the tattooed sack of shit on the ground. "Are you just going to leave your brother there? He needs a doctor. Maybe a priest."

She didn't even look as she shuffled around, answering, in a trembling voice, "I don't care."

My shirt soaked through; I raised my hands in a gesture of

surrender. Letting out a deep exhale, I said, "Then that makes two of us. I'm fucking exhausted. Hope you find a cheap dentist. Goodbye."

I took a further step back and lowered my arms. Turning her body sideways, but keeping eyes on me, she continued moving towards the door, with the knife presented as deterrent. I saw her step on a patch of dish goo, and her balance went. As she teetered over, I ran forward and threw a left jab. To my surprise, she recovered her footing and swiped with the blade. She caught me with a stinging slash across part of my knuckles, but the sudden shift of her body weight caused her to slip again. She fell over, with the landing impact sending the knife spinning across the tiles.

I pounced, took her head in both hands, and smashed the back against the floor. And again. And again. And again. By the time I'd finished, there was dark blood oozing from underneath her matted hair as those beautiful eyes turned vacant.

Climbing off, I assessed the carnage while bent over with my hands resting on my knees, recovering from the exertion. I was breathing in the scent of cheap dishwashing soap blended with the cloying reek of blood and sweat.

There wasn't a peep. If they weren't dead, then emergency medical attention was needed. In any case, their muscle-backed hustle was finished.

And so was my time in Macau. I made a clumsy but swift booking on my phone, used the first aid kit I'd bought in Kuala Lumpur to sort my hand, wiped myself with a towel and changed into a clean shirt. A couple of sprays of cheap deodorant were quick substitute for a shower.

The skin around my eye was tender but not pulsing. I didn't have time to apply ice to the bruise, as I had a flight to catch. I decided to only take my carry-on suitcase, making sure all essentials were in it.

Chewing on a diazepam and slamming a large measure of vodka, I closed the apartment door hoping neither of those two shitbirds would rouse and call for help. Then I made my way to the lobby to await an internet taxi. The security guard was still asleep and snoring with it. Suited me. I sidled past him and, after some tense waiting in the airport and on the plane before take-off, came to where I'm sitting now.

I keep asking myself why I didn't pay the money and laugh it off. It only amounted to a few champagne and steak dinners. Why did I opt for violence instead? Do I have a volatile temper? Or am I prone to bouts of insanity? I don't feel like I have mental problems, but then would I know it if I had?

Fuck it, my eyes are closing. Time to shut this thing and take a well-earned snooze. I hope the Triads don't have a branch in Dubai.

VICTOR, SH'EOL IS CALLING YOUR NAME

"I envy those who are dead and gone; they are
better off than those who are still alive." –
Solomon

Gabriel Ocampo wanted to kill someone. His supervisor, to be precise. The jerk had sprung a double shift on him at the last moment.

Anna, the other butler assigned to the Ambassador Suite, had called in sick. Despite having started at 7am, he'd been asked to work until midnight. It wouldn't have annoyed him so much, except for the fact it meant he'd miss his only chance of dinner and a movie with someone he found attractive. Daniela from Rio de Janeiro had been understanding when he'd cancelled, of course, but would already be looking for someone else to hang with. He tolerated his job, but not when it stopped him spending time with girls. Even more so when they were vivacious beauties with sparkling eyes and dazzling smiles. He sighed and pressed the button for the staff lift.

The doors opened on the 30th floor. He pushed the room service trolley across the corridor's luxuriant blue carpeting, towards the suite. At least he'd get some extra wages. Mind you, he thought while knocking, to pay for all the things placed in front of him, it might have taken six months of overtime. This guy knew how to treat himself and had been doing so for the past four weeks. The current order though, was far more decadent even than usual. And this was only lunch.

Gabriel heard a familiar voice, calling, "Just come in!" The hotel policy was either to be let in by the guest, or to have them grant permission to enter, via phone confirmation with the front desk. This was supposed to happen every time. In this case though, the norm had become something else. Opening the door with his staff card, he nudged the trolley through and into the reception area. There in the enormous living room, nestled into the corner of one of the central couches, was Mr Fyric.

As usual, Mr Fyric—or Victor as he insisted on being addressed—was staring into the screen of his laptop and making occasional taps on the keyboard. More unusual though, was he'd swapped his usual grubby sweatpants and t-shirt for the sharply pressed contours of what looked like a tailored suit. It was pale cream, complemented with a yellow shirt, golden silk tie and white pocket square. His suede loafers were dark orange, and the socks, peeking from under his trousers, were striped light green and blue. He looked dandy as hell. Perhaps somebody was coming over for lunch, hence the massive splurge? Gabriel doubted it. Victor had been in the suite for a month, and he'd only seen him go out twice. Even then, each trip was maybe a few hours. He didn't seem to have any visitors either. Who comes to Dubai to stay alone in their hotel all the time? An eccentric writer, it seemed.

Closing the computer, he placed it on the rectangular wooden coffee table. He squinted at Gabriel, then the room service trolley, and a thin smile spread across the stubbled roses of his cheeks.

Speaking in a weary voice, he said, "Fantastic, Gabriel, let the banquet commence." He grimaced as he rose from his seat; holding his abdomen in what looked like severe discomfort. Hobbling to the dining table, he eased onto the head chair. A film of sweat covered his brow, despite the suite's thorough air conditioning. The clothing may have been perfect, but Victor himself looked frayed around the edges. Faded, in fact.

"Are you ok, Victor?"

"Nothing that a solid meal and a few drinks won't soothe.

Just put it all here, please."

"Are you sure you're ok?"

His tone sharpened, but he was still forcing a smile. "Yes, I'm ok. Go ahead and do your thing; there's a good lad."

Gabriel reminded himself he was a butler, not a personal physician. He placed the meal items in front of Victor and lifted and put back the metal plate covers to reveal each dish in turn, describing them as he did so. "We have the double portion of grilled jumbo shrimp, with guacamole on the side as requested. Next, we have the fried halloumi, treble portion. Also, we have the sashimi platter, which includes both blue and yellowfin tuna, scallops, and a quadruple portion of salmon sake with extra wasabi. And, of course, we also have the chef's speciality, chateaubriand, medium rare, with separate potato gratin, roast vegetables, and sautéed onions with garlic. Here we have servings of peppercorn, bearnaise and mushroom sauces. The croissants are freshly baked, as you asked for, and we have some butter to go with them. And for drinks, in the bucket we have six cans of Rumpelstiltskin IPA, one bottle of Chateau Didier Bordeaux 2004, another of Reamy cognac XO, and finally the GlenDillich 30-year-old single malt. And here we have the Royo de Montevideo Delicisio Especial, with cigar cutter and matches. May I open the wine for you, Victor?"

He shuffled. "Yes, please. As quickly as you like. I haven't had a drink all day."

Gabriel glanced at his watch. It was 1pm.

"You're dressed very smartly today if I may say," he complimented, while cutting the outer foil from the top of the wine. "You look like you have a date."

"I do. Later. I'm not sure when though. For now, I'm celebrating the end of a story."

"Oh, you've finished your book. Congratulations."

"Thank you. That was me publishing it on Mississippi as you came in. It felt like a bit of an anti-climax, to be honest, after several months of obsessing. I think the front cover was the only interesting thing about it. Anyway, no going back now.

The die is cast."

Driving the screw into the cork, Gabriel replied, "Well, I think your reviewers will have to be the judge of how good it is. I'm sure it's a delightful story. What's the title?"

"Moderation: The Key to Success."

Gabriel paused, looking at the huge spread of food and liquor he'd laid on the table. "Oh..."

He chuckled, then, face contorting, his hand returned to his abdomen, bracing it. "Victor Tells Tales. Have a look for it on Mississippi if you get time. Victor Elijah Fyric."

"Yes, of course. I will." The cork was released with a light pop. "What's the story about?"

"I'll tell you later," he said, pointing with his eyes at the wine.

Holding the bottle by its base, Gabriel dripped a few splashes into the glass and stood waiting for Victor to confirm approval of the high-end vintage.

He tutted and looked at the tasting measure which had been poured, saying, "I don't want my balls tickled; I want them massaged."

"Erm, sorry?"

"Fill the sucker up. I'm thirsty." His impatience was notable.

"Sorry, of course." He poured until the large glass was more than half full, reading Victor's expression as he did so.

"Ok, that's fantastic. Thanks." He grabbed and glugged. No smelling or swirl; down the throat it went. The extortionate French red may as well have been fermented in a dirty bathtub for all the savouring. There was a sigh of relief. "Ah, that's better. Once again, please."

After re-filling the glass, Gabriel lifted the carving set and pointed to the concealed chateaubriand. "May I?"

"Definitely. I'm not to be trusted with knives."

He removed the silver cover. The thick log of prime fillet beef and its accompaniments were easily enough for two hungry people. He knew Victor was a big guy, but couldn't see him finishing it, let alone the other dishes on the table. Why had he ordered such a large amount? The food at the Dubai Palace & Towers cost a fortune and half of what was on the table would go to waste. Some people had too much money. He sliced through the seared outer layer to reveal the moist, pink flesh inside. The juices blended with the seasoning and butter it had been cooked in, and Victor leaned over to take in a noseful of the aroma. "That smells divine."

"It's the best beef in Dubai. The Sheikh even comes here for it sometimes."

He closed his eyes and took in the enticing vapours, saying, "Meat fit for a king."

"Shall I carve the whole fillet?"

"Why the hell not? Thicker pieces though. I want something to get my teeth into."

The carving and serving over, Gabriel asked if there was anything else. Mumbling through beef, he shook his head and pressed a tip into Gabriel's palm. Gesturing with an upward-pointing thumb, he slurped more wine from the glass and began to gorge on the spread.

Back in the corridor, he opened his hand to confirm the generous tip he'd been given. 1000 dirhams. Damn, two weeks' salary. Victor had been a good tipper since he first occupied the suite, with 50 here, 100 there, but this was something else. He decided to wire it back home first chance he got.

Descending in the lift, he couldn't help but worry about Victor's unhealthy appearance. Having been able to see his habits; he had concluded early on he was an alcoholic. The volumes of beer, wine and spirits consumed were frightening. One of the housekeepers had also told him she'd found empty packs of tranquiliser pills in the suite's waste baskets. Was he really mixing massive amounts of booze with those things? If so, what was he thinking? It was like he didn't care about himself at all. How could you have money and be so careless about your health? He decided to give curiosity a rest and take his lunch break.

* * *

Six hours later, and Gabriel had been sitting in the butler's section watching the rain falling for most of the afternoon. Seven years working in Dubai, and he could count on one hand the number of times he'd seen it this heavy. Still, at least he wouldn't have to travel far through the flooded streets once his shift was over. His company dorm took five minutes from the hotel by staff shuttle bus. It was a tiny room, with a bathroom and kitchen shared between four people. Such were the benefits given to those working in the Emirati service industry.

He'd messaged gorgeous Daniela a few times, but no reply. Someone with a flashy sports car was probably enjoying what he couldn't. It was the way of the world though, and nowhere clearer than in Dubai. The more figures on your bank balance, the nicer the ones curled next to you in bed. All he could do was look from afar and dream.

He exhaled through his pursed lips and continued to watch the sky pour tears. The rumbles became louder; brilliant forks flashed in black clouds. The heavens were as content as him.

The phone rang. It was from the Ambassador Suite. Gabriel was bombarded by loud singing:

"Blow me all day in my home. I'm tired and I want you on my bed. I have a little kink about a butler hoe, and now I want some head. What do you say, Anna? The usual fee?"

Victor sounded drunk. Again. But what was he talking about? "Victor? Can I help you?"

The line went silent for a moment, then his voice re-emerged, still slurring, but more restrained. "Gabriel? Where's Anna?"

"She called in sick around lunchtime. I'm working her shift tonight."

"Balls. I wanted one for the road."

"You mean a drink? I'm sorry, but I don't understand what you mean?"

He laughed. "That Russian cunt sucks. You watch yourself with her, ok?"

"Erm, sure. Can I get something for you? Some water? Coffee? Maybe some tea?"

"Fuck that. Bring me another Reamy."

"Single? Or double?" he asked in vain hope.

"Bottle. XO. Let yourself in. I'll be sitting on the terrace."

"Of course, sir. One bottle of Reamy XO. It'll be around 20 minutes."

"See you soon," he mumbled, hanging up.

On the terrace? There was a thunderstorm going on. It was bucketing. The suite's huge wrap around outdoor area had two full rattan furniture sets and parasols, but they were designed for sheltering from the desert sun, not torrential rain. It wasn't a night for sitting out.

And the rambling about Anna? Surely, he wasn't saying she had…? No, it was drunken nonsense. Poor Victor was intoxicated and lonely.

He decided to take a little longer over the cognac, in the hope by the time he brought it, his guest might have gotten tired of being wet, and gone to bed. He really did not need to be cracking open another bottle of liquor.

Forty minutes later, he opened the front door to the suite. There was only one solitary floor lamp on in the far corner, and it was struggling to spread enough light across the enormous open plan living and dining areas. Walking further in and looking at the shadowy objects on the long table, he could see lots of the food had remained uneaten. The chateaubriand was about half gone, but, of course, the wine bottle reflected only green. Over in the centre of the main area, a few crumpled beer cans lay scattered on the coffee table. A foul odour like rotten eggs hung in the air.

The terrace, and its impressive view of the skyscrapers on Sheikh Zayed Road, could be accessed through a glass door in the middle of the large patio windows which formed the outer wall of the suite. He peered, scanning the wooden-decked area and one of the furniture sets, which was gleaming wet as rain hammered off it. Nobody. The other door which led to the outside was via the sleeping quarters. Following the pathway of the suite round the corner, he walked past the giant kitchen and office areas, until he got to the internal door of the master bedroom. It was wide open, the bed empty, and, though the blinds were closed, he could see the furthest corner of the terrace was lit. He went across the room and looked through the glass panelling of the door.

There he was, reclining in one of the armchairs; the parasol taking a beating from the elements. His head was facing away from the wall of the suite, towards the skyline, which was shrouded in dark grey clouds. The billows of cigar smoke disappearing into the wind told Gabriel he was still awake. He placed the tray on the bedroom sideboard and decided to carry the bottle by its neck and base. It was against hotel procedure, as 'all beverages had to be served with elegance', but he wasn't going to risk it being blown onto the decking and smashed. Not with the manager's policy of recouping accidental breakages from staff salary. Victor wouldn't care how his fix was brought and Gabriel couldn't afford Reamy XO.

Opening the external door, he strode as fast as he could to underneath the large umbrella. From those few seconds of exposure his hair and face were dripping, and the shoulders of his black jacket were half-sodden. As he placed the order onto the glass-topped rattan table, he made a note of what was already there. The two liquor bottles from earlier, both empty, a long blister pack of pills, also looking like it was spent, a crystal tumbler with a smattering of liquor left in it, and an ashtray. However, it wasn't objects on the table causing concern. It was the carving knife. Wedged between the seat and the armrest on the side of the chair furthest away from Gabriel, it sat holstered under Victor's left forearm.

Victor turned, cigar in hand. His short brown hair was

wet with spray from the surrounding rainfall, and excess liquid streamed. Dampness polka-dotted the arms and shoulders of his suit.

A lightning strike shone its brilliant path as it rippled from the heavens. Thunder bellowed, now much louder without the insulation of the building. Victor rested the Royo, rubbed the water from his eyes, and said, "I shouldn't be here."

Gabriel wasn't expecting such a rational admission. "Then let's go inside, shall we?" he replied.

"I meant on planet earth. I was a mistake," he sniffled. His eyeballs had a reddish tinge. Was it rain he'd been wiping away?

"Oh..." The glimmer of the sharp-edged blade was distracting.

"It's ok. There's no comforting answer. Just the way it is. Pour a large one and sit. How 'bout you? You want one?"

"Well, truth be told, I don't really like straight liquor. It burns my throat. Maybe...you've had enough for one night? Maybe you should get some sleep?"

Victor gripped the ends of the chair arms, raised himself forward, pincered the cigar and puffed a few times. The reek of tobacco wafted before being dispersed by the wind. It smelled like peppery nastiness. What was the appeal of those things?

"There'll be plenty time for sleep. And you're a nice guy; I like you, but tonight, of all nights, you don't want to be mistaken for one of my parents. You get me?" He rubbed his palm around the end of the knife's wooden handle, stared at his feet, sniffling, and said simply, "Cunts."

Gabriel, former welterweight Yaw-Yan kickboxing champion of Cebu City, flexed his wiry upper body under his butler's uniform, and reminded himself of his capabilities. He was at least 20 cm shorter than Victor, and God knew how many kilos lighter, but there would still be no contest if violence started.

Seemed unlikely though. He wasn't being aggressive. Unhinged, yes, but sullen with it. Even aside from the fact he was personal butler to the occupant of the Ambassador Suite, he felt obligated to have patience with this guest who had shown such generosity to him over the past month.

Sitting in the chair beside Victor, he opened the cognac. "Good lad," said Victor, "This rain and wind is sobering me up, and fuck that. You take this stuff easier with cola?"

"Sure. I usually drink vodka like that when I have a night out. I'll be in deep trouble if I get caught smelling of alcohol though."

"So? Don't get caught. There's a bunch of cola in the fridge. You know where the glasses are."

Gabriel resolved he would sip one small cognac with cola and stay with Victor to make sure he didn't cause himself any harm. He wouldn't have to sit for long. With the condition he was in, he'd be heading to bed after one or two more shots at the most.

As they sat with their drinks, the weather showed no signs of easing. Spray spitting at his face and building in tiny spatters across his trousers. Why the hell did Victor insist on being outside, when he had one of the most luxurious hotel suites in Dubai at his disposal?

The blister pack was indeed empty. Deciphering the crinkled and torn foil, he saw the brand was Alprazo. Underneath sat the generic name: Alprazolam. A tranquiliser or not? How many had he taken?

A bolt of lightning dazzled as it struck the adjacent skyscraper on the roof. The accompanying thunder cracked like a shotgun. Nature's fireworks display. Best enjoyed from indoors.

"This decking's soaked. If that strikes here, it could kill. Move that chair closer and put your feet up on it." Victor's loafers remained planted on the floor.

He looked at the flapping parasol as its thin material was barraged by rain; the wind whistling round their ears. "We should go inside then. This is dangerous," he half-shouted.

"I told you. I've got a date," he said raising his voice. The double measure of cognac was swirled then dunked. "Another one, please."

Gabriel screamed inside and poured again. He pitied anyone who would drive through the raging elements to be met with Victor's addled musings. "A date? Is she coming here?"

"I didn't say it was with a woman."

"Oh ok"—he took a mouthful of his cognac-laced cola— "it's a guy?" asked Gabriel.

Mouth rupturing with grape alcohol and laughter, he stubbed the cigar, hammering it into the ashtray. Shards of charred tobacco leaf stuck to the tabletop. He spluttered, "Those things taste like shit! Why the fuck do I think they're a treat?"

He cleared his throat and spat into the wind, sending phlegm over the midriff-level steel barriers and into the grey abyss. Waves of rain were blanketing the terrace. A vertical line of superheated air flashed, desperate to reach earth. Deep grumbling followed soon after.

"Hear that? It's hungry!" He knocked the cognac back in one and unbuckled the beautiful Deitling timepiece from his wrist.

Standing, he stumbled towards the barrier and launched the watch into the haze with, Gabriel had to admit, an impressive throw for someone so drunk. But what the fuck? He'd seen his friends do some crazy shit after too much booze, but Victor was something else. Lucky for him, the weather meant nobody would be walking on the street below. Even more troublesome was what it must have cost. What a horrible waste.

Whole outfit a shade darker, he turned to walk back under the shelter. While in mid-stride, he collapsed to his knees, clutching his guts. Gabriel threw the chair from under him and leaped to where Victor was.

"This storm"—he panted, pressing his palm against his belly— "is time-consuming." His hair and face streamed with the driven rain.

"You're not well. Let me help you inside." The wet was getting in his eyes, he couldn't see.

"Sh'eol!" Victor gripped him by the shoulder, screaming against the whistle and roar of the storm.

"What?"

"Sh'eol! No heaven, no hell! Same for everyone!" He was hysterical. Eyes wild and skin gaunt; he fell onto his side and began coughing, convulsing, then vomiting. The banquet from earlier was spreading in semi-digested chunks across the slats of the wooden terrace; the sharp suit drenched with rainwater and puke.

Gabriel tried lifting him but there was too much bulk. "I'm going to get help. Just hold on, ok?"

"Gabriel"—he moved onto his hands and knees, retching—"come here."

"I need—"

"Take this." Shivering, Victor reached into his jacket and plucked a wad of 1000 dirham notes as thick as a Bible. It was more money than he'd seen in his life. Clutching it in his shaking hand, he pulled Gabriel's lapel to the side and drove the cash into the inside pocket, stuffing it with force as the large chunk of paper struggled to fit. He said, trembling, "Severance pay."

What the hell was he talking about? "I can't—"

"What are you? A fucking millionaire? Get help," he spat. Saliva coated his lower lip and trailed across his stubbly chin. His breathing was rapid, and eyes were glazing over.

Gabriel resolved to give it back when Victor's mind returned to him. Right now, though, medical attention was needed. He stood, soaked to the skin.

Victor floundered onto his backside, his tie flapping round his throat, the storm washing foamy vomit against his trousers. He gave a weak smile and cough, saying, "Adieu, Gabriel." An umbrella of light coated the sky as lightning yet again flashed nearby. The boom announced Thor was engulfed in tantrum.

As Gabriel turned his back to make haste towards the phone in the master bedroom, he heard Victor babble something like, "Wish it was the Alps." Deciding not to waste time deciphering shambolic ravings, he ran to the door, depressed its handle, and lunged through into the welcome shelter of the suite.

He dialled the front desk, watching water drip from his sleeve onto the black and white plastic buttons. The phone rang a few times before it was answered.

"Hello?" The gruff Australian accent confirmed identity.

"Glenn? I—"

"Ah, how's the patient?" That was the derogatory term Glenn Harding, his supervisor from Queensland, had for Victor, about his alcoholism, pills and never going out. Of course, the weasel was all yes sir, no sir on his rare flying visits to the Ambassador Suite.

"He isn't good at all. He's had far too much to drink. I think some pills too. He's thrown up; acting crazy. I think we should call an ambulance. Can you call an ambulance?"

"Ambulance? Are you sure? Look mate, hasn't he just had too much as usual? What about the doctor outcall service? He can afford it," said Glenn, sounding sceptical.

"You haven't seen him. Can you—" He looked through the window. Victor was back on his feet. Standing in the terrace's far corner, leaning with one hand against the metal barrier. On the wrong side. Nothing between him and the pavement. Except thirty floors. "Holy shit, he's—"

"What's going on, mate? What the fuck's going on?"

"Call the police."

"What? Why?"

"Because he's just jumped off the fucking balcony!"

"Wha—"

Gabriel hung up. Holy fuck. No longer caring about his drenched clothes, he walked to the section of barrier where he'd seen Victor disappear. There was a ledge of about three quarters of a metre, so he couldn't see. But he was well acquainted with the drop.

He'd jumped. There could only be one outcome. Jesus.

THE HAZARDS AND RISKS OF SCOUTING FOR COUCHES

"You cannot open a book without learning something." – Confucius

That was it. The last page. Gabriel had finished reading Victor's book. For the third time.

And he still wasn't sure how to feel. If it had been a random novel picked because of its appealing cover, he wouldn't have lasted more than the first chapter. Writing unremarkable, main character unlikeable, and story unbelievable; it would have made an awful work of fiction.

As true crime however, it was fascinating. A journey through the mind of someone infamous he'd interacted with on a personal level. Gabriel was among the privileged few who were able to do the delving. The readership was limited to him, agents from multiple law enforcement agencies, and anyone else who had stumbled upon it during its brief public display online.

This was because the day Victor had self-published it, the same one on which he'd committed suicide, the book had been deposited into the vast library of eBooks available on Mississippi.com. But the company had pulled it from their virtual shelves with haste, after, Gabriel assumed, they had been informed it was evidence in the investigation of serious crimes.

Of course, Gabriel had made sure to download a copy before it was censored. The first thing he did after an hour-long questioning from the police, was to go into the Mississippi app on his phone and look for any books authored by Victor Elijah Fyric. One search result had shown, but it wasn't called Victor Tells Tales.

The title was The Hazards and Risks of Scouting for Couches.

Which had made the situation even more bizarre. Scouting for Couches was Gabriel's passion. He socialised through it all the time. In fact, if it hadn't been for Anna calling in sick, he would have been with Daniella, a young Brazilian traveller he'd introduced himself to on the website. She'd posted a public trip scouting for a host, and, although he had no accommodation to offer, he'd managed to persuade her to meet for burgers and beer. It was a big deal for him.

Although disappointed over the change of plans at the time, the extra shift he'd done proved to be a far more worthwhile affair. There would be more opportunities to meet hot women. There wouldn't be further bonuses from Victor.

He remembered the adrenaline surge while he had counted crinkled 1000-dirham notes. 328 of them. Over 4.5 million in Philippine pesos. A fortune. Why hadn't he declared it to the Dubai police? They'd grilled him about every word and action from Victor. Gabriel had sat on a chair in the hotel's main conference room, damp and gobsmacked, with the large chunk of cash stretching his inner pocket to bursting point. And not said a thing.

It had been given as severance pay, had it not? Those were Victor's own words. And Gabriel had worked hard as the suite's dedicated butler, even until chaos came knocking. He'd earned it. That money was equivalent to twenty years of meticulous savings in his butler's job at the Dubai Palace and Towers. If he'd declared it during the police interview, some fat, corrupt cop covered in worthless brass would only have spent it on his spoiled wives. He knew how things worked in Dubai. No, the Fyric funds would be used for good instead.

Starting with a business class ticket home. After seven years in Dubai, serving the rich while he lived like a slave in his tiny staff dorm, a treat was long overdue. He wanted somebody to pander to his needs for a change. Considering he was leaving the country for good, it seemed like a proper send off.

Not that there had been any fanfare at the hotel about his departure. Probably because Gabriel had only requested holiday leave. He wanted the satisfaction of emailing dickhead Glenn his notice last minute, knowing the anger it would cause. That would be enjoyable.

As would life in general now, with the opportunity given to him from that fateful night. The money had been wired back in moderate amounts to his Manila account, from different cash offices, avoiding the financial radar, over the two months following Victor's death. It was going to buy him a nice 2-bed apartment in Cebu and a 50% stake in a jet ski rental venture with two of his uncles. No more Mr nobody. From now on, he was going to be his own boss. The opportunities were exciting. He said thank you, once again, to Victor.

Putting his laptop into its case, he slung the strap across his shoulder. This was farewell to the butler life. Such a cliché, but was he asleep? He grasped the handle of the bulging suitcase sitting upright by the door. The coolness of the plastic against his palm felt real enough. Mum's hugs would soon confirm if nothing else could. Home was calling his name and he couldn't wait. The glorified desert watering hole of Dubai had held his soul too long. It was time to live.

At the airport check in, they helped with this by bumping him to first class. The flight was overbooked. Hell yes!

And oh my, despite having worked in luxury hotel, he was impressed at what Emirati Airways provided to its elite travellers. Everyone had separate cabins. He was a king flying home in a suite. Smoothing his hands across the sumptuous white leather arms of the seat, he stretched. There was a vast amount of legroom unused. Zesty citrus scented the air; the metal and faux wood finishing gleamed. Fishing for his phone, which, like his ticket, had had an upgrade, he saved the momentous occasion in selfie form. The smile was all teeth. Not pursed lips like in the hotel. As he heard the champagne corks pop, he vowed not to sleep a wink during the whole 9-hour rock star experience.

Peering through the window at Dubai Airport, he felt pride. The way he'd achieved his goal wasn't as expected, but it had still materialised, nonetheless. Weren't you supposed to progress in life as you got older? Did rich people never get wealth from amoral opportunities?

"Mr Ocampo?"

He turned to be met with a blonde stewardess towering over him. Holy moly. He'd lived in Dubai for seven years, been driven to distraction by the beauty of women there, but this was the first time his mouth had dropped open. Cheek bones high, skin pale and contrasting with the bright red lips in a striking manner; oh Emerald-eyed child, why can't you be my heaven?

"Yes?" he replied, clearing his throat.

"Good afternoon, my name's Magdalena. I'll be looking after you for this flight. May I get you anything? Perhaps a glass of Don Ferrignon?"

Gabriel shifted in the armchair, flexing his muscles under the tight t-shirt he had on, saying, "Sure, a glass would be fine. Do you have wifi after take-off? Cause I have to stay in touch with my board for an especially important meeting."

Her long eyelashes fluttered for a second. "Of course, Mr Ocampo, once the plane is cruising, you'll have wifi for the whole flight."

"Thanks so much. The shareholders will be grateful," he smiled.

"Oh, you're welcome Mr Ocampo. I'll be right back with your drink."

Leaning, Gabriel watched her healthy behind jiggle within tight skirt confines. Board? Shareholders? Where the hell had that come from? It'd bubbled forth, like shit-tainted champagne. Fuck it, who cared? This was a celebration. The start of something new.

And it felt long overdue now. He realised how glad he was to be leaving such a toxic work environment. If it hadn't been for the police confiscating his passport until Victor's death was officially ruled a suicide, he would have soared into the sky far sooner.

Even Anna, someone he'd had an amicable work relationship with, despite her rejecting his offer of dinner more than once, had caused him emotional turbulence in the end. Because he owed Victor a hell of a lot. The man, even if he was a murderer, had given him a new life. How could he despise someone who'd changed his fortunes in such a positive way?

✽ ✽ ✽

Of course, two weeks after Victor's demise, sitting in a café across from the hotel, Gabriel hadn't said these things to her. When he'd suggested meeting, her keenness had taken him aback. The first time ever in two years working together they'd had a coffee.

"He was a monster," she had scowled, staring into the brown-freckled white foam of her large cappuccino. Taking a sip, she cradled the smooth oversized cup in her slender white fingers. The lights reflected from the varnish of her manicured nails as, still focused on the frothy milk of the drink, she asked, "Did he say anything? Anything about me?"

"No, he was out of his mind. Talking drunken bullshit. I didn't even—"

"He was a monster. I hope he burns in hell." Her voice didn't waver. It was cold, focused. "The guy was crazy. They're saying he was a serial killer. You haven't told anyone any lies he might have said about me, have you?"

"Of course not, the guy was a fucking psycho," he had tutted.

Her shoulders relaxed. "Thank you, Gabriel, you're a good friend." It was weird to hear his name spoken from those delicate glossed lips. She leaned forward and looked into his eyes.

The notes of her perfume sang about high quality. Subtle leather mixed with rose and cinnamon. "Can we make a promise never to talk about this again, with anyone? Please, Gabriel? Especially Glenn or anyone at the hotel."

"Of course, Anna, let's delete it and move on with our lives," he reassured.

She took hold of the sides of his head, smiled wide, and pecked him on the lips. "You're such a good friend, Gabriel." The smooch was soft, but something was lacking in the sweetness.

Around ten minutes of small talk followed before she appeared distant and disinterested in what Gabriel was saying. Looking at her dainty golden watch, she said, "I should really go. I was out last night. Feeling so sleepy. Enjoy your break. See you when you get back."

Gathering the small leather handbag and three boutique shopping bags she'd come laden with, she flashed a final beaming smile and clacked off in high heels.

Her cappuccino was only half drunk. He'd paid the bill.

* * *

That was the first time he'd ever been kissed by a white woman. He wasn't overflowing with confidence among their number. And that didn't stem from an out of shape body. The rigorous gym routine he did kept him in Olympic shape. No, the poor dating hand he'd been dealt was from a different shoe. Short, Asian and in a low-paid job meant the only thing shared with Caucasian hotties was the friend zone.

In Cebu, however, it would be a different story. It was an extremely popular resort, with lots of foreign tourists, so he made a promise to himself the apartment he was going to buy would be Couch Scouter friendly. He'd host and get to know girls of all races, not with a view to anything sinister, but to familiarise and relax himself in their company. To break the barriers which had stood for so long. He could give them free jet ski rentals.

Gabriel was going to become the best Scouting for Couches host in all the Philippines.

And, for certain, he wouldn't be mimicking any of Victor's old hosting habits. Respect was crucial.

The angel returned with a glass of champagne on a tray. "There you are Mr Ocampo." God, it was weird to be the VIP.

As she bent her waist offering the drink, he indulged. Those blouse buttons were under strain.

What amazing tits.

Afterword

Dear readers

Thank you so much for reading my first novel. I hope you enjoyed it. If you have time, please leave a review on Amazon. Your feedback is invaluable.

Best wishes

Caterina Alexandria Smirnova

Printed in Great Britain
by Amazon

74343994R00128